"The 87th Preci[...]
literary accomplish[...]
—Pete Hami[...]

"It's hard to think of anyone better
at what he does. In fact, it's impossible."
—Robert B. Parker

Praise for the 87th Precinct Novels from
America's Unparalleled,
Award-Winning Master of Crime Fiction

ED McBAIN

MONEY, MONEY, MONEY
Edgar Award nominee!

"Crisp and fresh . . . savagely brutal . . . [with] unexpected and amusing twists."
—*Los Angeles Times*

"McBain plays fair and square with the complications that arise from this clever setup. Over and over, he keeps telling us to keep an eye on the money, which slips through more hands than a third-grade bathroom pass."
—*The New York Times*

"Tight plotting, crackling police work, and bizarre people . . . a witty tale of counterfeit money that grows before the reader's eyes."
—*The Plain Dealer* (Cleveland)

"Captivating stuff."
—*St. Petersburg Times* (FL)

"An instant classic. . . . It's McBain at his best. And there's none better."

—*The Post and Courier* (Charleston, SC)

"McBain's *Money* is a sure bet. . . . [His] writing remains young, vigorous, sharp, and entertaining."

—*Publishers Weekly*

"The complications flow so effortlessly and the tone is so irresistibly ebullient that you can relax in the hands of a master. Merry Christmas."

—*Kirkus Reviews*

"Pure prose poetry. . . . It is writers such as McBain who bring the great American urban mythology to life."

—*The London Times*

THE LAST DANCE

"The fiftieth novel of the 87th Precinct is one of the best, a melancholy, acerbic paean to life—and death—in the fictional big city of Isola. . . . This is McBain in classic form, displaying the writing wisdom gained over more than forty years of 87th Precinct novels to deliver a cop story that's as strong and soulful as the urban heart of America he celebrates so well."

—*Publishers Weekly* (starred review)

"Having stripped down and refined his language over the years to the point where it now conceals as much as it reveals, McBain forces us to think twice about every character we meet in *The Last Dance,* even those we thought we already knew."

—*The New York Times Book Review*

Praise for
CANDYLAND
A Novel in Two Parts
by EVAN HUNTER & ED McBAIN

A *People* Magazine "Page-Turner of the Week"

"Hunter provides a compelling psychological portraiture. . . . McBain easily matches his achievement with an inspired police procedural, topped off with a completely unexpected and satisfying twist at the end."

—*People*

"A tour de force. . . ."

—*Kirkus Reviews*

"The plot is fabulous and the ending whapped me in the eyeballs."

—Larry King, *USA Today*

"A tribute to the skills of this great storyteller. . . . It is fun to read, despite the grim nature of its subjects. . . . *Candyland* exhibits a smoothness, a professionalism, a gritty energy and wit."

—*The New York Times*

"Superb. . . . A multifaceted, psychologically astute portrait of crime and punishment. . . . Each part of the novel works beautifully alone but also in tandem."

—*Publishers Weekly* (starred review)

"Under any name, this man is a master of his craft."

—*Library Journal*

BOOKS BY EVAN HUNTER

NOVELS

The Blackboard Jungle (1954) *Second Ending* (1956) *Strangers When We Meet* (1958) *A Matter of Conviction* (1959) *Mothers and Daughters* (1961) *Buddwing* (1964) *The Paper Dragon* (1966) *A Horse's Head* (1967) *Last Summer* (1968) *Sons* (1969) *Nobody Knew They Were There* (1971) *Every Little Crook and Nanny* (1972) *Come Winter* (1973) *Streets of Gold* (1974) *The Chisholms* (1976) *Love, Dad* (1981) *Far from the Sea* (1983) *Lizzie* (1985) *Criminal Conversation** (1994) *Privileged Conversation* (1996) *Candyland** (2001) *The Moment She Was Gone*** (2002)

SHORT STORY COLLECTIONS

Happy New Year, Herbie (1963) *The Easter Man* (1972)

CHILDREN'S BOOKS

Find the Feathered Serpent (1952) *The Remarkable Harry* (1959) *The Wonderful Button* (1961) *Me and Mr. Stenner* (1976)

SCREENPLAYS

Strangers When We Meet (1959) *The Birds* (1962) *Fuzz* (1972) *Walk Proud* (1979)

TELEPLAYS

The Chisholms (1979) *The Legend of Walks Far Woman* (1980) *Dream West* (1986)

*Available in paperback from Pocket Books
**Available in hardcover from Simon & Schuster

ALSO BY ED MCBAIN

THE 87TH PRECINCT NOVELS

Cop Hater* • The Mugger • The Pusher* (1956) The Con Man • Killer's Choice (1957) Killer's Payoff* • Killer's Wedge • Lady Killer (1958) 'Til Death • King's Ransom (1959) Give the Boys a Great Big Hand • The Heckler* • See Them Die (1960) Lady, Lady, I Did It! (1961) The Empty Hours • Like Love (1962) Ten Plus One (1963) Ax (1964) He Who Hesitates • Doll (1965) Eighty Million Eyes (1966) Fuzz (1968) Shotgun (1969) Jigsaw (1970) Hail, Hail, the Gang's All Here (1971) Sadie When She Died • Let's Hear It for the Deaf Man (1972) Hail to the Chief (1973) Bread (1974) Blood Relatives (1975) So Long As You Both Shall Live (1976) Long Time, No See (1977) Calypso (1979) Ghosts (1980) Heat (1981) Ice (1983) Lightning (1984) Eight Black Horses (1985) Poison • Tricks (1987) Lullaby* (1989) Vespers* (1990) Widows* (1991) Kiss (1992) Mischief (1993) And All Through the House (1994) Romance (1995) Nocturne (1997) The Big Bad City* (1999) The Last Dance* (2000) Money, Money, Money* (2001) Fat Ollie's Book** (2003)

THE MATTHEW HOPE NOVELS

Goldilocks (1978) Rumpelstiltskin (1981) Beauty & the Beast (1982) Jack & the Beanstalk (1984) Snow White & Rose Red (1985) Cinderella (1986) Puss in Boots (1987) The House That Jack Built (1988) Three Blind Mice (1990) Mary, Mary (1993) There Was a Little Girl (1994) Gladly the Cross-Eyed Bear (1996) The Last Best Hope (1998)

OTHER NOVELS

The Sentries (1965) Where There's Smoke • Doors (1975) Guns (1976) Another Part of the City (1986) Downtown (1991) Driving Lessons (2000) Candyland* (2001)

ED

A NOVEL OF THE **87**TH PRECINCT

McBAIN

THE HECKLER

POCKET BOOKS

New York London Toronto Sydney Singapore

The sale of this book without its cover is unauthorized. If you purchased this book without a cover, you should be aware that it was reported to the publisher as "unsold and destroyed." Neither the author nor the publisher has received payment for the sale of this "stripped book."

This book is a work of fiction. Names, characters, places and incidents are products of the author's imagination or are used fictitiously. Any resemblance to actual events or locales or persons, living or dead, is entirely coincidental.

 POCKET BOOKS, a division of Simon & Schuster, Inc.
1230 Avenue of the Americas, New York, NY 10020

Copyright © 1960 by Ed McBain
Copyright renewed © 1988 by Evan Hunter
Afterword copyright © 2003 by Hui Corp.

All rights reserved, including the right to reproduce
this book or portions thereof in any form whatsoever.
For information address Pocket Books, 1230 Avenue
of the Americas, New York, NY 10020

ISBN: 0-7434-6307-2

First Pocket Books printing March 2003

10   9   8   7   6   5   4   3   2   1

POCKET and colophon are registered trademarks of
Simon & Schuster, Inc.

For information regarding special discounts for bulk purchases,
please contact Simon & Schuster Special Sales at 1-800-456-6798
or business@simonandschuster.com

Front cover photo by Brian Velenchenko

Printed in the U.S.A.

*This is for my father-in-law
Harry Melnick—
who inspired it*

The city in these pages is imaginary.
The people, the places are all
fictitious. Only the police routine is based
on established investigatory technique.

THE
HECKLER

1.

SHE CAME IN like a lady, that April.

The poet may have been right, but there really wasn't a trace of cruelty about her this year. She was a delicate thing who walked into the city with the wide-eyed innocence of a maiden, and you wanted to hold her in your arms because she seemed alone and frightened in this geometric maze of strangers, intimidated by the streets and the buildings, shyly touching you with the pale-gray eyes of a lady who'd materialized somehow from the cold marrow of March.

She wandered mist-shrouded through the city, a city that had become suddenly green in exuberant welcome. She wandered alone, reaching into people the way she always does, but not with cruelty. She touched wellsprings deep inside, so that people for a little while, sensing her approach, feeling her come close again, turned a soft vulnerable pulsing interior to her, turned it outward to face the harsh angles of the city's streets and buildings, held out tenderness to be touched by tenderness, but only for a little while.

And for that little while, April would linger on the walks of Grover Park, linger like white mist on a mountain meadow, linger on the paths and in the budding trees, spreading a delicate perfume on the air.

And along the lake and near the statue of Daniel Webster below Twelfth Street, the cornelian cherry shrubs would burst into early bloom. And further west, uptown, facing Grover Avenue and the building which housed the men of the 87th Precinct, the bright yellow blossoms of forsythias would spread along the park's retaining wall in golden-banked fury while the Japanese quince waited for a warmer spring, waited for April's true and warm and rare and lovely smile.

For Detective Meyer Meyer, April was a Gentile.

Sue him; she was a Gentile. Perhaps for Detective Steve Carella April was a Jewess.

Which is to say that, for both of them, April was a strange and exotic creature, tempting, a bit unreal, warm, seductive, shrouded with mystery. She crossed the avenue from Grover Park with the delicate step of a lady racing across a field in yellow taffeta, and she entered the squadroom in her insinuating perfume and rustling petticoats, and she turned the minds of men to mush.

Steve Carella looked up from the filing cabinets and remembered a time when he was thirteen and experiencing his first kiss. It had been an April night, long, long ago.

Meyer Meyer glanced through the grilled windows at the new leaves in the park across the street and tried to listen patiently to the man who sat in the hard-backed chair alongside his desk, but he lost the battle to spring, and he sat idly wondering how it felt to be seventeen.

The man who sat opposite Meyer Meyer was named Dave Raskin, and he owned a dress business.

He also owned about two hundred and ten pounds of flesh which was loosely distributed over a six-foot-two-inch frame garbed at the moment in a pale-blue tropical suit. He was a good-looking man in a rough-hewn way, with a high forehead and graying hair which was receding above the temples, a nose with the blunt chopping edge of a machete, an orator's mouth, and a chin which would have been completely at home on a Roman balcony in 1933. He was smoking a foul-smelling cigar and blowing the smoke in Meyer's direction. Every now and then Meyer waved his hand in front of his face, clearing the air, but Raskin didn't quite appreciate the sublety. He kept sucking on the soggy end of his cigar and blowing smoke in Meyer's direction. It was hard to appreciate April and feel like seventeen while swallowing all that smoke and listening to Raskin at the same time.

"So Marcia said to me, you work right in his own precinct, Meyer's," Raskin said. "So what are you afraid of? You grew up with his father, he was a boyhood friend of yours, so you should be afraid to go see him? What is he now, a detective? This is to be afraid of?" Raskin shrugged. "That's what Marcia said to me."

"I see," Meyer said, and he waved his hand to clear the air of smoke.

"You want a cigar?" Raskin asked.

"No. No, thank you."

"Good cigars. My son-in-law sent them to me from Nassau. He took my daughter there on their honeymoon. A good boy. A periodontist. You know what that is?"

"Yes," Meyer said, and again he waved his hand.

"So it's true what Marcia said. I did grow up with your father, Max, God rest his soul. So why should I be afraid to come here to see his son, Meyer? I was at the *briss,* would you believe it? When you were circumcised, *you,* I was there, *me.* So I should be afraid now to come to you with a little problem, when I knew your father we were kids together? I should be afraid? You sure you don't want a cigar?"

"I'm sure."

"Very good cigars. My son-in-law sent them to me from Nassau."

"Thank you, no, Mr. Raskin."

"Dave, Dave. Please. Dave."

"Dave, what seems to be the trouble? I mean, why *did* you come here? To the squadroom."

"I got a heckler."

"What?"

"A heckler."

"What do you mean?"

"A pest."

"I don't think I understand."

"I've been getting phone calls," Raskin said. "Two, three times a week. I pick up the phone and a voice asks, 'Mr. Raskin?' and I say, 'Yes?' and the voice yells. *'If you're not out of that loft by April thirtieth, I'm going to kill you!'* And then whoever it is hangs up."

"Is this a man or a woman?" Meyer asked.

"A man."

"And that's all he says?"

"That's all he says."

"What's so important about this loft?"

"Who knows? It's a crumby little loft on Culver Avenue, it's got rats the size of crocodiles, you should see them. I use it to store dresses there. Also I got some girls there, they do pressing for me."

"Then you wouldn't say it was a desirable location?"

"Desirable for other rats, maybe. But not so you should call a man and threaten him."

"I see. Well, do you know anyone who might want you dead?"

"Me? Don't be ridiculous," Raskin said. "I'm well liked by everybody."

"I understand that," Meyer said, "but is there perhaps a crank or a nut among any of your friends who might just possibly have the foolish notion that it might be nice to see you dead?"

"Impossible."

"I see."

"I'm a respected man. I go to temple every week. I got a good wife and a pretty daughter and a son-in-law he's a periodontist. I got two retail stores here in the city, and I got three stores in farmers' markets out in Pennsylvania, and I got the loft right here in this neighborhood, on Culver Avenue. I'm a respected man, Meyer."

"Of course," Meyer said understandingly. "Well, tell me, Dave, could one of your friends be playing a little joke on you, maybe?"

"A joke? I don't think so. My friends, you should pardon the expression, are all pretty solemn bastards.

I'll tell you the truth, Meyer, no attempt to butter you up. When your dear father Max Meyer died, God rest his soul, when your dear father and my dear friend Max Meyer passed away, this world lost a very great funny man. That is the truth, Meyer. This was a hilarious person, always with a laugh on his lips, always with a little joke. This was a very funny man."

"Yes, oh yes," Meyer said, and he hoped his lack of enthusiasm did not show. It had been his dear father, that very funny man Max Meyer who—in retaliation for being presented with a change-of-life baby—had decided to name his new son Meyer Meyer, the given name to match the surname. This was very funny indeed, the gasser of all time. When Max announced the name at the *briss* those thirty-seven years ago, perhaps all the guests, including Dave Raskin, had split a gut or two laughing. For Meyer Meyer, who had to grow up with the name, the humor wasn't quite that convulsive. Patiently he carried the name like an albatross. Patiently he suffered the gibes and the jokes, suffered the assaults of people who decided they didn't like his face simply because they didn't like his name. He wore patience as his armor and carried it as his standard. *Omnia Meyer in tres partes divisa est:* Meyer and Meyer and Patience. Add them all together, and you got a Detective 2nd/Grade who worked out of the 87th Squad, a tenacious cop who never let go of anything, who doggedly and patiently worried a case to its conclusion, who used patience the way some men used glibness or good looks.

So the odd name hadn't injured him after all. Oh

yes, it hadn't been too pleasant, but he'd survived and he was a good cop and a good man. He had grown to adult size and was apparently unscarred. Unless one chose to make the intellectual observation that Meyer Meyer was completely bald and that the baldness could have been the result of thirty-seven years of sublimation. But who the hell wants to get intellectual in a detective squadroom?

Patiently now, having learned over the years that hating his father wasn't going to change his name, having in fact felt a definite loss when his father died, the loss all sons feel when they are finally presented with the shoes they've wanted to fill for so long, forgetting the malice he had borne, patiently reconstructing a new image of the father as a kind and gentle man, but eliminating all humor from that image, patiently Meyer listened to Raskin tell about the comedian who'd been his father, but he did not believe a word of it.

"So it isn't a man trying to be funny, believe me," Raskin said. "If it was that, do you think I'd have come up here? I got nothing better to do with my time, maybe?"

"Then what *do* you think, Dave? That this man is really going to kill you if you don't get out of the loft?"

"Kill me? Who said that?" It seemed to Meyer in that moment that Dave Raskin turned a shade paler. "*Kill* me? *Me?*"

"Didn't he say he was going to kill you?"

"Well yes, but—"

"And didn't you just tell me you didn't think this was a joke?"

"Well yes, but—"

"Then apparently you believe he *is* going to kill you unless you vacate the loft. Otherwise you wouldn't be here. Isn't that correct?"

"No, that's not correct!" Raskin said with some indignation. "By you, maybe, that is correct, but not by me. By me, it is not correct at all. Dave Raskin didn't come up here he thinks somebody's going to kill him."

"Then why did you come up, Dave?"

"Because this heckler, this pest, this shmuck who's calling me up two, three times a week, he's scaring the girls who work for me. I got three Puerto Rican girls they do pressing for me in the Culver Avenue loft. So every time this bedbug calls, if I don't happen to be there, he yells at the girls, *'Tell that son of a bitch Raskin I'm going to kill him unless he gets out of that loft!'* Crazy, huh? But he's got the girls scared stiff, they can't do any work!"

"Well, what do you want me to do?" Meyer asked.

"Find out who he is. Get him to stop calling me. He's threatening me, can't you see that?"

"I see it, all right. But I don't think there's enough here to add up to extortion, and I can't— This guy hasn't made any *real* attempts on your life, has he?"

"What are you gonna do?" Raskin asked. "Wait until he kills me? Is that what? And then you'll make a nice funeral for me?"

"But you said you didn't think he was serious."

"To kill me, I don't think so. But *suppose*, Meyer. Just suppose. Listen, there are crazy people all over, you know that, don't you?"

"Yes, certainly."

"So suppose this crazy nut comes after me with a shotgun or a butcher knife or something? I get to be one of those cases in the newspaper where I went to the police and they told me to go home and don't worry."

"Dave—"

" 'Dave, Dave!' Don't 'Dave' me. I remember you when you was in diapers. I come here and tell you a man said he's going to kill me. Over and over again, he's said it. So this is attempted murder, no?"

"No, this is not attempted murder."

"And not extortion, either? Then what is it?"

"Disorderly conduct," Meyer said. "He's used offensive, disorderly, threatening, abusive, or insulting language." Meyer paused and thought for a moment. "Gee, I don't know, maybe we have got extortion. He *is* trying to get you out of that loft by threatening you."

"Sure. So go pick him up," Raskin said.

"Who?" Meyer asked.

"The person who's making the calls."

"Well, we don't know who he is, do we?"

"That's simple," Raskin said. "Just trace the next call."

"Impossible to do in this city," Meyer said. "All our telephone equipment is automatic."

"So what do we do?"

"I don't know," Meyer said. "Does he call at any specific time?"

"So far, all the calls have come in the afternoon, late. Just about closing time, between four and five."

"Well, look," Meyer said, "maybe I'll stop by, this afternoon or tomorrow. To listen in on the calls, if any come. Where's the loft?"

"Twelve thirteen Culver Avenue," Raskin said. "You can't miss it. It's right upstairs over the bank."

In the streets, the kids were yelling "April Fool!" as the punch line to their first-of-April jokes. And they chased each other into Grover Park the way kids will always chase each other, leaping the stone walls and cavorting along the path and ducking behind trees and bushes.

"Watch out, Frankie! There's a tiger on that rock!" and then they shouted "April Fool!"

And then dashing off again to duck behind another rock or another tree, the punch line old and clichéd by this time, but delighting them nonetheless each time it was shouted.

"Over your head, Johnny! An eagle! *April Fool!*"

Running over the close-cropped grass and then one of the boys ducking into the trees again, and his voice coming from somewhere in the woods, a voice tinged with shock and awe, reaching out for the path.

"Frankie! There's a dead guy in here!"

And this time no one shouted "April Fool!"

2.

THE GENTLEMAN THEY FOUND in Grover Park had been dressed for the approaching summer. Or perhaps *undressed* for it, depending on how you chose to view the situation. No matter how you chose to view it, he was wearing only a pair of black shoes and a pair of white socks, and that's about as close to being naked as you can come in the streets of any big city. Not that this gentleman was overly worried about arousing the ire of the law. This gentleman was dead.

He had, in fact, if a summary glance at the wounds in his chest meant anything, been killed by a shotgun at fairly close range. He lay on his back under the trees and a small knot of experts in death surrounded the body and made faces indicative of disgust and empathy and boredom and indifference, but mostly of pain. Steve Carella was one of the policemen who looked down at the body of the naked man. Carella's eyes were squinted almost shut even though there was no sunshine under the canopy of the trees. There was a sour look on Carella's face, a look of disapproval and anger laced with discomfort. He looked at the man and he thought *Nobody should die in April,* and he noted automatically the shotgun wounds on the man's chest and, just as automatically, he noticed that there was a single large entrance wound and several zones of small satellite perforations produced by pellets which scattered from the main charge. The large entrance wound told him that the gun had been fired anywhere from one to three yards away from the victim. Up to a yard's distance, the shotgun would have produced a wound with a lot of tattooing, burning, and blackening. And beyond three yards, the shot would have dispersed, and formed constellationlike patterns on the victim's skin. Knowing this, and not knowing much more than this at the moment, Carella's mind made the associations unconsciously and unemotionally while another part of him looked down at this person who had once been a man and who was now a ludicrously naked, loosely jointed pile of fleshy, angular rubbish—no longer a man; simply something soft and spongy, but not a man. Life had been robbed from this mass of flesh, and now there was nothing but death housed in the skin case. Carella wiped a hand across his mouth even though he was not sweating.

It was cool in the copse of trees where the policemen worked. Flashbulbs popped around the dead man. A powdered chalk line was sprayed onto the ground, outlining the body. The laboratory technicians searched the bushes for footprints. The men stood about in uneasy clusters, discussing the world's heavyweight champion fight, the pennant race, the nice weather they'd had this past week, anything but death which stared up at them from the ground. And then they finished their work, all the work they could do for the time being. They hoisted the corpse onto a stretcher and carried it to the path, and then out of the park and over to the curb where an ambulance was waiting. They slid the corpse into the back of the meat wagon, and took it to General Hospital where the autopsy would be performed. Carella thought for a moment about the stainless-steel autopsy table which was laced with troughs like a carving board's troughs to catch the blood—the table slightly tilted—and channel it toward the basin at the far end, he thought of that goddam unemotionally sterile stainless-steel table, and he thought of scalpels and he tightened his fists in anger and again he thought *Nobody should die in April,* and he walked out to the police sedan parked at the curb and drove back to the precinct house. He could not find a parking space closer than two blocks away. He parked the car on Grover Avenue and walked back to the building facing the park.

Somehow the mottled stone front of the ancient building seemed to blend with April. The gray assumed a softer tone when juxtaposed to the vibrant blue sky beyond it. The hanging green globes captured something of the blue, and the white numerals "87" on each globe picked up a touch of the clouds that hung fat and lazy in the early spring sky. The similarity ended the moment Carella climbed the low flat steps of the front stoop and passed into the muster room. High-ceilinged, bare except for the muster desk and Sergeant Dave Murchison who sat behind it, the room resembled nothing more than the cheerless, featureless face of an iceberg. Carella nodded to the sergeant and followed the pointing white wooden hand which told him—in

case he didn't know after all these years—where to find
the DETECTIVE DIVISION. Where to find it was upstairs.
He mounted the iron-runged steps, noticing for the first
time what a clatter his shoes made against the metal,
turned left into the upstairs corridor, passed the two
benches flanking the hallway, and was passing the men's
lavatory when he almost collided with Miscolo who
came out of the room zipping up his fly.

"Hey, you're just the man I want to see," Miscolo
said.

"Uh-oh," Carella answered.

"Come on, come on, stop making faces. Come into
the office a minute, will you?"

The office he referred to was the Clerical Office,
labeled with a hand-lettered sign in the corridor, a
cubbyhole just outside the slatted, wooden railing
which divided the corridor from the detective squadroom. Alf Miscolo was in charge of the Clerical
Office, and he ran it with all the hard-fisted, clear-
headed mercilessness of an Arabian stablekeeper. His
horses, unfortunately, were usually a handful of
patrolmen who had pulled twenty-fours, duty as
records clerks. But if Miscolo had been given, let us
say, a hundred men with whom to run his clerical
office, all crime in that fair city would have been eliminated in the space of two days. In conjuction with the
police laboratory downtown on High Street, and the
Bureau of Criminal Identification, Miscolo's dossier
on criminals would have made it absolutely impossible
to commit a crime without risking immediate capture
and incarceration. Or so Miscolo fantasied.

The Clerical Office, at the moment, was empty. Its green filing cabinets lined the right-hand wall of the room, facing the two desks opposite it. At the far end of the room, a single huge window, covered on the outside with wire mesh and the grime of a decade, was opened to the fragrance of April.

"What a day, hah?" Miscolo said. He wagged his head in appreciation.

"All right, what's on your mind?" Carella said.

"Two things."

"Shoot."

"First, May Reardon."

"What about her?"

"Well, you know, Stevie, Mike Reardon worked here for a long time before he got killed. And I liked Mike. I mean, everybody did. You did, too."

"I did," Carella admitted.

"And he left May and two kids. That ain't no picnic, Stevie. So she makes the precinct beds, but what the hell does that give her? Enough to feed two kids? Stevie, this is a tough pull. You got a wife, you got kids. God forbid, suppose something should happen to you, you want Teddy living on what precinct beds get her? Do you?"

"No," Carella said. "What do you want?"

"I thought we could all chip in. The guys on the squad, and the patrolmen, too. Just a little something more each week to boost that bed money. What do you say, Stevie?"

"Count me in."

"Will you talk to the other bulls?"

"Now, listen—"

"I'll talk to the patrolmen. What do you say?"

"I'm a lousy salesman, Miscolo."

"Aw, this ain't like selling nothing, Stevie. This is giving that little girl a break. Did you ever see that little girl, Stevie? She's so goddam Irish, you want to cry."

"Why?"

"I don't know. Irish girls make me want to cry." He shrugged. He was not a handsome man. His nose was massive, and his eyebrows were bushy, and there was a thickness about his neck which created the impression of head sitting directly on shoulders. He was not a handsome man. And yet, in that moment, as he said what he had to say about Irish girls, as he shrugged boyishly afterwards, there was an enormous appeal to the man. He realized in an instant that Carella was staring at him, and he turned away in embarrassment and said, "What the hell do I know why? Maybe the first girl I laid was Irish—how do I know?"

"Maybe," Carella said.

"So, will you talk to the other bulls or not?"

"I'll talk to them," Carella said.

"Okay. Jesus, to get something done around here, you got to go around pulling teeth."

"What was the second thing?"

"Huh?"

"The second thing. You said there were two—"

"Yeah, that's right, I did." Miscolo frowned. "I can't think of the other thing right now. It'll come to me."

"That's it, then?"

"Yeah. You just come up from the street?"

Carella nodded.

"How's it look out there?"

"Same as always," Carella said. He sat for just a moment longer and then waved at Miscolo and went out of the office into the corridor. He pushed through the gate in the railing, threw his Panama at the hat rack, missed, and was heading to pick it up when Bert Kling stooped for it.

"Thanks," Carella said. He began taking off his jacket as he walked to Meyer's desk.

"What was it?" Meyer asked.

"Looks like a homicide," Carella answered.

"Man or woman?"

"Man."

"Who?"

"No identification," Carella said. "He got shot at close range with a shotgun, that's my guess. All he was wearing was shoes and socks." Carella shrugged. "I better make out a report. I didn't see anybody from Homicide there, Meyer. Suppose they've given up on us?"

"Who knows? They only like to make noise, anyway. They know the stiff officially belongs to whichever precinct is lucky enough to find it."

"Well, this one belongs to us," Carella said, wheeling over a typing cart.

"They doing an autopsy?" Meyer asked.

"Yeah."

"When do you suppose we'll have the report?"

"I don't know. What's today?"

Meyer shrugged. "Bert! What's today?"

"April first," Kling said. "Steve, some dame phoned about—"

"Yeah, but what *day*?" Meyer asked.

"Wednesday," Kling said. "Steve, this dame called about an hour ago, something about a dry-cleaning store and a counterfeit bill. You know anything about it?"

"Yeah, I'll call her back later," Carella said.

"So when do you think we'll have the report?" Meyer asked again.

"Tomorrow, I suppose. Unless the M.E.'s office got an unusually large number of stiffs today."

Andy Parker, who was sitting by the water cooler with his feet up on the desk, threw down a movie magazine and said, "You know who I'd like to get in the hay?"

"Anybody," Carella answered, and he began typing up his report.

"Wise guy," Parker said. "I been looking over these movie stars, and there is only one girl in this whole magazine who'd be worth my time." He turned to Kling who was reading a paper-backed book. "You know who, Bert?"

"Quiet, I'm trying to read," Kling said.

"I wish some of you guys would try to *work*," Meyer said, "This goddam squadroom is beginning to resemble a country club."

"I *am* working," Kling said.

"Yeah, I can see that."

"These are stories about the deductive method."

"The what?"

"Of detection. Haven't you ever heard of Sherlock Holmes?"

"Everybody's heard of Sherlock Holmes," Parker said. "You want to know which of these broads—"

"I'm reading a very good story," Kling said. "You ever read it, Meyer?"

"What's it called?"

" 'The Red-headed League,' " Kling said.

"No," Meyer answered. "I don't read mysteries. They only make me feel stupid."

THE AUTOPSY REPORT did not arrive at the squadroom until Friday afternoon, April 3. And, as if by black magic, a call from the assistant medical examiner came at the exact moment the Manila envelope bearing the report was placed on Carella's desk.

"Eighty-seventh Squad, Carella," he said.

"Steve, Paul Blaney."

"Hello, Paul," Carella said.

"Did that necropsy report get there yet?"

"I'm not sure. A man with hospital pallor just dumped an envelope on my desk. It may be it. Want to hang on a second?"

"Sure," Blaney said.

Carella opened the envelope and pulled out the report. "Yeah, this is it," he said into the phone.

"Good. I'm calling to apologize. We just had a full house, Steve, and first things came first. Yours was the shotgun murder, wasn't it?"

"Yeah."

"I hate shotgun wounds," Blaney said. "Shotgun wounds really look like gun wounds, have you ever noticed that? Especially when they're fired at close range."

"Well, a forty-five doesn't leave a very pretty hole, either," Carella said.

"Or a thirty-eight, for that matter. But there's something more lethal about a shotgun, I don't know. Did you see the size of the hole in your customer?"

"I did," Carella said.

"It's worse in contact wounds, of course. Jesus, I've seen cases where guys have stuck the barrel of a shotgun into their mouths and then pulled the trigger. Man, that is not nice to look at. Believe me."

"I believe you."

"All the goddam explosive force of the gases, you know. In contact wounds." Blaney paused, and for a moment Carella could visualize the man's violet eyes, eyes which seemed somehow suited to the dispassionate dismemberment of corpses, neuter eyes that performed tasks requiring neuter emotions. "Well, this wasn't a contact wound, but whoever did the shooting was standing pretty close. You know how a shotgun cartridge works, don't you? I mean, about the wad of coarse felt that holds the powder charge at the base of the cartridge?"

"Yes."

"Well, the goddam cartridge wad was driven into the track together with the pellets."

"What track? What do you mean, track?"

"Of the cartridge," Blaney said. "The track. The path of the pellets. Into the guy's chest. Into his body. The track."

"Oh."

"Yeah," Blaney said, "and the goddam felt wad had followed the pellets into the guy's chest. So you can imagine the force of the blast, and how close the killer was standing."

"Any idea what gauge shotgun was used?"

"You'll have to get that from the lab," Blaney said. "I sent over everything I dug out of the guy, and I also sent over the shoes and socks. I'm sorry about being so late on the report, Steve. I'll make it up to you next time."

"Okay, thanks, Paul."

"Looks like another nice day, doesn't it?"

"Yeah."

"Okay, Steve, I won't keep you. So long."

"So long," Carella said. He put the phone back into its cradle, and then picked up the report from the Medical Examiner's office. It did not make very pleasant reading.

3.

THREE OF THE MEN in the poker game were getting slightly p.o.'d. It wasn't so much that they minded losing—the *hell* they didn't mind!—it was simply that losing to the fourth man, the man with the hearing aid, was somehow degrading. Perhaps it was the cheerlessness with which he played. Or perhaps it was the air of inevitability he wore on his handsome features, a look which told them he would ultimately triumph, no matter what skill they brought to the game, no matter how often fortune smiled upon them.

Chuck, the burliest of the four men, looked at his cards sourly and then glanced across the table to where the deaf man sat. The deaf man was wearing gray flannel slacks and a navy-blue blazer over a white dress shirt open at the throat. He looked as if he had just got off a yacht someplace. He looked as if he were waiting for a butler to serve him a goddam Martini. He also looked like a man who was sitting with four cards to a high straight.

The game was five-card stud. Two of the players had dropped out on the third card, leaving only the deaf man and Chuck in the game. Looking across at the deaf man's hand, Chuck saw the three exposed cards: a jack of spades, a queen of clubs and a king of diamonds. He was reasonably certain that the hole card was either a ten or an ace, more probably a ten.

Chuck's reasoning, to himself, seemed sound. He was sitting with a pair of aces and a six of clubs exposed. His hole card was a third ace. His three-of-a-kind had the deaf man's possible straight beat. If the deaf man's hole card was a ten, he was sitting with a four-card straight, both ends of which were open. The chances of filling it seemed pretty slim. If his hole card was the ace, his straight was open on only one end, and the chances of filling it were narrower. Besides, there was always the possibility that Chuck would catch either a full house or four-of-a-kind on that last card. His bet seemed like a safe one.

"Aces bet a hundred," he said.

"Raise a hundred," the deaf man answered, and Chuck had his first tremor of anxiety.

"On what?" he asked. "All I see is three cards to a straight."

"If you looked more closely, you'd see a winning hand."

Chuck nodded briefly, not in agreement with the deaf man, but with an inner conviction of his own. "Raise *you* a hundred," he said.

"That's fair," the deaf man said. "And once again."

Chuck studied the deaf man's hand once more. Three cards to a straight showing. The fourth card to the straight obviously in the hole. Whether it was open on one end or both, it still needed a fifth card.

"*And* a hundred," Chuck said.

"Be careful now," the deaf man advised. "I'll just call."

He put his chips into the pot. Chuck dealt the next card. It was the ten of hearts.

"There's your goddam straight," he said.

He dealt his own card. The four of diamonds.

"Aces still bet," the deaf man said.

"I check," Chuck said.

"I'll bet a hundred," the deaf man said, and Chuck's face fell.

"Yeah," he answered. "I'll see you."

The deaf man turned over his hole card. Sure enough, it was the ace.

"Straight to the ace," he said. "I think that beats your three aces."

"How'd you know I had three aces?" Chuck asked, watching the deaf man pull in his winnings.

"Only from the force of your betting. I don't think you'd have bet so heavily with two pair. So I assumed you already had your third ace."

"And you raised three aces? On the strength of a *possible* straight?"

"On the strength of percentages, Chuck," the deaf man said, stacking his chips into a neat pile. "On the strength of percentages."

"Some percentages," Chuck said. "Luck, that's all. Dumb luck."

"No, not quite. I was sitting with four cards to a one-ended straight: the jack, queen, king and ace. In order to make my straight, I needed a ten—any ten. And this was the only possible way of improving my hand to beat your three aces. I had to catch that ten. If *not,* if for example I simply paired one of my cards, I couldn't possibly beat you. Am I right? So what were my chances of completing the straight? My chances against making it were nine to one, Chuck."

"Well, those seem like pretty damn steep odds to me."

"Do they? Consider the fact that no tens had appeared at any time during the game. Of course, either you—or our friends before they dropped out— could have been holding tens in the hole. But I knew you had an ace in the hole, and I took a chance on our friends."

"The odds were still too steep. You should have dropped out."

"But then I'd have lost, wouldn't I? And your own odds against improving your hand were even steeper."

"How could they be? I had you beat to begin with! I had three aces!"

"Yes, but how could you improve them? In one of two ways. Either by catching a fourth ace or by catching another six to give you a full house. I knew you *couldn't* catch the fourth ace because I was sitting with it in the hole. In any case, the odds on catching it, even if I *hadn't* been holding it, would have been thirty-nine to one. Considerably higher than nine to one, don't you think?"

"What about the possibility of a full house? I could have caught that other six."

"True, you could have. The odds against it, though, were fourteen and two thirds to one. Which, again, is higher than the nine to one odds I was bucking. And, weighted against this was the fact that our two friends were both showing sixes when they dropped out. This means there was only one six left in the deck, and it further means that the odds on catching that last six were essentially the same as they'd be for catching the fourth ace—thirty-nine to one. Get it, Chuck? My odds were nine to one. Yours were thirty-nine to one."

"You're forgetting something, aren't you?"

"I never forget anything," the deaf man said.

"You're forgetting that *neither* of us could have improved our hands. And if neither of us improved, I'd have won. Three aces beats an incompleted straight."

"That's true. But it's not something I forgot. It was simply a calculated risk. Remember, Chuck, that your pair of aces didn't turn up until the fourth card had been dealt. If your first two exposed cards had been aces, I'd have dropped out immediately. Up to that point, we were both on equal footing more or less. You had an ace and a six showing on the board. I had an ace in the hole, and a king and queen showing on the board. My hand seemed just about as strong as yours. I suspected you had a pair of aces but, considering my own ace in the hole, I thought you might be bluffing a strong bet on a pair of sixes. And *any* pair I caught would have beat those. I think I played the hand correctly."

"I think it was luck," Chuck maintained.

"Perhaps." The deaf man smiled. "But *I* won, didn't I?"

"Sure. And since you won, you can come on real strong about how you figured it all out beforehand."

"But I did, Chuck."

"You only *say* you did. If you'd have lost, it'd be a different story. You'd have been making excuses all over the lot to explain away your mistakes."

"Hardly," the deaf man said. "I am not a person who admits to mistakes. The word *mistake* isn't even in my vocabulary.

"No? Then what do you call it?"

"Deviation. Truth is a constant, Chuck. It is only the observation of truth which is a variable. The magnitude of error depends on the difference between the unchanging truth and the faithfulness of the observation. And so error can only be defined as deviation, not mistake."

"Bullshit," Chuck said, and the other men around the table laughed.

"Precisely," the deaf man said, laughing along with them. "Bullshit. Error is simply the amount of bullshit attached to any true observation. Do you want to deal, Rafe?"

The tall thin man on Chuck's left raised his gold-rimmed spectacles and wiped the tears from his eyes. He took the cards and began shuffling them.

"One thing I've got to say is that this is gonna be the goddammedest caper there ever was." He shoved the deck at Chuck. "You want to cut?"

"What's the use?" Chuck said petulantly. "Run them."

The man sitting opposite Rafe said, "What's the

game?" He put the question tentatively because he was a newcomer to the group, and not yet too sure of his standing. Nor was he yet too certain as to exactly who his predecessor had been or why he'd been dropped from the quartet. He possessed only one quality which could be considered useful to the group, and he had stopped considering that a quality some ten years ago. This quality was the making of bombs. Bombs, that is. You know, bombs. The old man sitting at the table with the other three had been quite adept at fashioning lethal exploding devices. He had lent his talents at one time to a certain foreign power and had spent a good many years in prison regretting this peccadillo, but his early political affiliations had not been questioned by the deaf man when he'd been hired. The deaf man was content to know he could still put together a bomb if called upon to do so. He was particularly interested in learning that the old man could put together incendiary bombs as well as the exploding garden variety. His versatility seemed to please the deaf man immensely. Pop couldn't have cared less either way. All he knew was that he was being hired to do a job—and as far as he could tell, the only qualification he possessed for that job was his ability to make bombs.

He could not have known, not at this stage of the game, that his second qualification was his age. Pop was sixty-three years old, and that was just young enough, just old enough; that was perfect.

"This is seven-card stud," Rafe told him. "Deuces wild."

"I don't like these bastardized versions of poker," the deaf man said. "They throw off the percentages."

"Good," Chuck said. "Maybe we'll stand a chance of winning. You play poker as if you're out to slit your mother's throat."

"I play poker as if I'm out to win," the deaf man said. "Isn't that the right way to play?"

Rafe began laughing again, his blue eyes misting behind their gold-rimmed eyeglasses. He dealt the cards, said, "King bets," and put the deck down on the table.

"Twenty-five," the old man said hesitantly.

"Call," Chuck said.

"I'll see you," Rafe said.

The deaf man studied his cards. He was holding a six in the hole, together with a jack. His exposed card was a five. He glanced around the table quickly, and just as quickly pulled his cards together.

"I fold," he said.

He sat just a moment longer and then rose suddenly, a tall good-looking man in his late thirties who moved with the economy and grace of a natural athlete. His hair was blond and cut close to his skull. His eyes were a dark blue. They flicked now to the street outside, through the plate-glass window of the store front and the inverted legend:

CHELSEA POPS, INC.

The street side of the store was quiet. An old woman struggled past with a full shopping bag and then moved out of sight. Behind the store, at the back of it, all was chaos. Bulldozers, steam shovels, construction crews swarmed over the vast leveled lot.

"You'd better make this the last hand," the deaf man said. "We've got lots of work to do."

Rafe nodded. Chuck raised the pot, and the old man dropped out.

"Want to come with me a minute?" the deaf man asked him.

"Sure," he said.

He pushed back his chair and followed the deaf man to the door leading down to the cellar. The cellar was cool and moist. The smell of fresh earth clung to the walls. The deaf man walked to a long table and opened a box there. He pulled out a gray garment and said, "You'll be wearing this tonight, Pop. While we work. Want to try it on?"

Pop took the garment and fingered it as if he were making a purchase in a men's clothing store. His fingers stopped suddenly, and his eyes widened.

"I can't wear that," he said.

"Why not?" the deaf man asked.

"I won't put it on. Not me."

"Why not?"

"There's blood on it," Pop said.

For a moment, for a brief moment in the still, earth-smelling coolness of the basement, it seemed as if the deaf man would lose his temper, as if he would flare into sudden undisciplined anger at the old man's rebellion. And then he smiled suddenly, radiantly.

"All right," he said. "I'll get a new one for you."

He took the gray garment from the old man and put it back into the box.

4.

A PICTURE OF THE unidentified dead man ran in three of the afternoon tabloids on Thursday, April 9. The papers hit the stands at about twelve noon, one of them carrying it on the front page, the others relegating it to page four, but all of them running the shrieking headline DO YOU KNOW THIS MAN? The man in the photo seemed to have his eyes closed, and a police artist had sketched a pair of swimming trunks over his exposed genitalia. If anything, the black shoes and white socks looked even more ludicrous now that they were accompanied by the trunks.

"DO YOU KNOW THIS MAN?" the reader read and then looked at this picture of an old duffer who'd undoubtedly been snapped sleeping at a public beach, one of those fellows whose soles are tender and who wears shoes while traversing the sand, some sort of publicity stunt probably, and then the reader saw the copy under the picture, and the copy under the picture informed one and all that this old duffer was not asleep, that he was deader than a mackerel and that the smear on his chest was not a printer's smudge but a bona fide shotgun wound which has been carelessly left there by a man with urticaria of the trigger finger.

The papers hit the stands at about twelve noon.

At twelve-fifteen, Cliff Savage showed up in the muster room of the 87th Precinct. Spotlessly dressed, a tan Panama shoved onto the back of his head, a white handkerchief peeking from the breast pocket of a brown Dupioni silk suit, Savage sauntered up to the desk and said, "My name's Savage. I'm a reporter." He threw the picture of the unidentified dead man onto the desk. "Who's handling this case?"

Sergeant Dave Murchison looked at the photo, grunted, looked at Savage, grunted again, and then said, "What did you say your name was?"

"Cliff Savage."

"And what newspaper are you from?"

Savage sighed and pulled a press card from his wallet. He put the card into the desk top, alongside the newspaper photo of the dead man. Murchison looked at it, grunted, and said, "Steve Carella's on the case. How come your name sounds familiar, Mac?"

"Beats me," Savage said. "I'd like to see Carella. He in?"

"I'll check."

"Don't bother. I'll just go straight up," Savage said.

"The hell you will, mister. You just hold your horses. That press card don't give you the run of the station house." Murchison picked up one of the wires protruding from the switchboard and plugged it in. He waited a moment, and then said, "Steve, this is Dave downstairs. A guy named Cliff Savage is here, says he's a reporter, wants to— What? Okay." Murchison pulled out the wire. "Says you should go drop dead, Mr. Savage."

"He said that?"

"Word for word."

"What the hell kind of an attitude is that?" Savage wanted to know.

"I gather he don't like you too much, is what I gather," Murchison said.

"Can you plug in and let me talk to him?"

"Steve wouldn't like that, Mr. Savage."

"Then get me Lieutenant Byrnes."

"The lieutenant ain't in today."

"Who's catching up there?"

"Steve."

Savage frowned, picked up the press card and, without another word, walked out of the muster room. He walked down the low flat steps onto the sidewalk and then he turned right and walked two blocks in the April sunshine to a candy store on Grover Avenue. He made change at the counter, walked to the telephone booth at the rear of the shop, dug a small black address book from his back pocket, and searched for an 87TH PRECINCT listing. There was none. He looked up BYRNES, PETER, and found a number for the precinct, FRederick 7-8024. He put his dime into the slot and dialed it.

"Eighty-seventh Precinct, Sergeant Murchison," a voice on the other end said.

"You ran a picture of a dead man in the newspaper today," Savage said.

"Yeah? What about it?"

"I know who he is. I'd like to talk to the detective handling the case."

"One moment, sir," Murchison said.

Savage nodded, grinned, and then waited. In a moment, another voice came onto the line.

"Eighty-seventh Squad, Detective Carella."

"Are you the cop in charge of the case involving the man they found in the park?"

"That's right," Carella said. "Who's this, please?"

"Are you the cop who sent the pictures out to the newspapers?"

"That's right. Sir, the desk sergeant tells me—"

"Why didn't you send one to my paper, Carella?"

"Wha—" There was a long pause on the line. "Is that you, Savage?"

"Yeah, this is me."

"Didn't you get my message?"

"It would be inconvenient for me to drop dead at the moment."

"Look, Savage, I'm not a polite feuder. I'm not interested in mixing clever talk with you. You almost got my wife killed once, you son of a bitch, and if you ever show your face around here I'll throw you out the window. Does that make it clear?"

"The Commissioner might like to know why every other paper in the city—"

"The hell with you and the Commissioner both! Goodbye, Savage," Carella said, and he hung up.

Savage held the dead receiver in his hand for just a moment, then he slammed it onto the hook and stormed out of the booth.

* * *

THE PUERTO RICAN GIRL'S name was Margarita. She had been in the city for only six months, and she didn't speak English too well. She enjoyed working for Mr. Raskin because he was a nice cheerful man who did not shout too much. It was important to Margarita that the person for whom she worked did not shout. Margarita reported for work at nine o'clock each morning. The Culver Avenue loft was only five blocks from her house, and she enjoyed the walk to and from work each day. Once she got to the loft, she went into the bathroom and changed from her street clothes to a smock which she wore while pressing. Since she lived so close to the loft, someone had once suggested to her that she wear the smock to work rather than changing after she got there. But Margarita felt that the smock was not suitable attire for the street. And so every morning she put on a sweater and a skirt and then changed to the smock after she got to the loft. She never wore anything under the smock. She pressed dresses all day long, and it got very hot in that loft and she didn't want the bother of panties and brassiere.

She was a very well-formed girl, Margarita, and as she hefted that steam iron her breasts frolicked beneath the loose smock in time to the accompanying jiggle of her buttocks. Which was another thing she liked about Mr. Raskin. Mr. Raskin never came up behind her and pinched her. She had worked for another man before him, and he was always pinching her. Mr. Raskin was a very cheerful man who kept his hands to himself and who didn't mind the girls telling jokes in Spanish every now and then. So long as they got the work done.

There were two other girls besides Margarita, but Margarita was the unofficial foreman of the group. Each morning, when all the girls had had their second cup of coffee and changed into their smocks and fixed their makeup, Margarita would roll over the dollies with the cartons of dresses which Mr. Raskin had bought in wholesale lots, and she would turn them over to the girls who would press out all the wrinkles. Margarita would work right alongside them, that iron flashing over the creased skirts and bodices, those breasts jutting and bouncing. Then she would have a consultation with Mr. Raskin about pricing the dresses, and then she and the girls would mark each of the dresses and that evening Mr. Raskin would take them to the retail stores or to the farmers' markets, depending on which outlets needed merchandise. It was a very smooth-running operation. Sometimes, when she discussed prices with Mr. Raskin, he would try to see into the low front of her dress because he knew she wore nothing underneath, but she didn't mind him looking because he never touched. He was a gentleman, and she liked working for him. As far as Margarita was concerned, David Raskin was the nicest man in the world.

Which is why she couldn't understand the threatening calls.

Why would anyone in the world want to threaten Mr. Raskin? And especially over so stupid a thing as a dirty loft? No, Margarita could not understand it, and each time the caller phoned again, she would feel frightened for her boss, and she would say a silent prayer in Spanish.

She was not frightened on the afternoon of Thursday, April 9 when the delivery man entered the loft.

"Anybody here?" he called from the door at the opposite end.

"Jus' a mini'," Margarita said, and she put down her steam iron and then ran the length of the loft to the entrance doorway, forgetting that she was wearing nothing beneath the smock, and puzzled by the goggle-eyed expression on the delivery man's face when she reached him.

The delivery man took a handkerchief from his back pocket and wiped his forehead with it.

"You know something?" he said breathlessly.

Margarita smiled. "What?"

"You ought to be in burlesque, sister. I mean it. Burlesque is crying for you."

"What eees thees bul-esk?"

"Oh, sister. Oh, sister." The delivery man sighed and rolled his eyes. "Look, where do you want these cartons?" he asked, his eyes swinging back to the low-cut front of the smock. "I've got about fourteen cartons of stuff downstairs, so tell me where you want it, and it's yours."

"Oh, I don' know," Margarita said. "My boss, he is no' here ri' now."

"I only want to know where you want it dumped, sister."

"What ees it, anyways?" Margarita asked.

"Don't know, sister, I only work for the trucking company. Come on, choose a spot. Go down to the other end of the loft again, and then run down this way and choose a spot as you come, okay?"

Margarita giggled. "Why I got to run for?" she asked, knowing full well what he was referring to. "You put them inside here, near the door, okay?"

"Okay, sister." The delivery man winked. "Sssssss," he said, as if he were a steam radiator. He wiggled his eyebrows, rolled his eyes and then went downstairs. He came up a few moments later with another man, carrying a heavy carton between them. Together they began setting it down just inside the door. The first man gestured with his eyebrows toward Margarita who was stooping to pick up a hanger. The second man almost crushed his fingers as they put down the carton. It took them an hour and a half, what with the various distractions provided by Margarita, to carry thirteen of the cartons upstairs. They were carrying the fourteenth and final carton into the loft when Dave Raskin arrived.

"So what's all this?" he asked.

"Who are you?" the delivery man said. "Mr. Minsky?" He winked at Raskin. Raskin didn't get the joke, so he didn't wink back. Margarita had gone back to her pressing and was throwing herself into her work with wild abandon. The second delivery man was leaning against one of the cartons and wishing he had a better seat and a box of popcorn.

"Who is Mr. Minsky?" Raskin said: "Who, in fact, are *you*? And what is all these boxes, would you mind telling me?"

"Are you David Raskin?"

"I am he."

"Darask Frocks, Inc.?"

"Yes?"

"Then these are yours, mister."

"*What* is mine?"

"Search me. We're only truckers, mister. What does it say on the cartons?"

Raskin studied the bold black lettering on the side of one of the cartons. "It says 'Sandhurst Paper Company, New Bedford, Massachusetts'!" Raskin scratched his head. "I don't know any Sandhurst Paper Company in New Bedford, Massachusetts. What is this?"

The delivery men were in no hurry to leave. Margarita at the table was pressing up a storm, and it was a delightful storm indeed.

"Why don't you open one of the cartons?" the first man suggested.

The second man nodded in vague abstraction and said, "Sure, why don't you?"

"Will that be all right?" Raskin asked.

"Sure. It's addressed to you, so open it."

"Sure," the second man said.

Raskin began struggling with the carton. The two delivery men sat on the edge of his desk and watched Margarita's monumental bout with the steam iron. Finally, Raskin managed to pry loose two of the staples holding the carton closed. He tore the cardboard flap open, ripped the opening still larger and reached into the carton where he found a horde of smaller boxes resembling shoe boxes. He pulled one of these out, placed it on his desk top, and then lifted the lid.

The box was full of envelopes.

"Envelopes?" Raskin said.

"That's what they are," the first man said.

"That's what they are, all right," the second man said.

"Envelopes? But who ordered . . . ?" and Raskin suddenly stopped talking. He pulled one of the envelopes from the box and turned it over so that he could read the printing on the flap. It read:

> David Raskin
> The Vacant Loft, Inc.
> 30 April Avenue
> Isola

"Is that a new store you're opening?" the first man asked.

"Take these back," Raskin said. "I didn't order them."

"Hey, we can't do that, mister. You already opened—"

"Take them back," Raskin said, and he pulled the telephone to him.

"Who you calling?" the second man said. "The manufacturer?"

"No," Raskin answered. "The police."

TEDDY CARELLA was in a robe when her husband came home from work that night. He kissed her as he crossed the threshold of the big monstrous house they lived in, and didn't truly realize she was so attired until they'd gone into the kitchen together. Then, surprised because the house was so still at six-thirty in the evening, surprised that Teddy was wearing high-heeled bedroom slippers with the robe—her *silk* robe, at that—he asked first, "Where are the children?"

Teddy's hands moved in silent answer. *Asleep*.

"And Fanny?" he asked.

Her fingers moved again. *Thursday*.

"Oh yeah, her day off," and suddenly it was all very clear to him. He did not acknowledge that he'd tipped to her plans or her preparations. He pretended he did not see the bottle of white wine resting on its side in the refrigerator when she opened the door to take out the melon. He pretended that he didn't notice the exaggeratedly female way in which Teddy moved this evening, or the fact that she was wearing a subtly penetrating perfume, or that she had made up her eyes, startlingly wide and brown in her oval face, but that her lips carried not a trace of lipstick, her lips seemed more than anxious to be kissed—he pretended he noticed none of these things.

He went into the bathroom to wash, and then he took off his holster and gun and put them into the top drawer of their dresser, and then he put on a tee shirt and threw his soiled white shirt into the hamper, and then he came downstairs. Teddy had set the table outdoors on the patio. A cool breeze rustled through the grape arbor, crossed the patio, lifted the skirt of her robe to reveal the long lissome curve of her leg. She did not move to flatten the skirt.

"Guess who I ran into today?" Carella said, and then realized that Teddy's back was to him, and that she could not hear him. He tapped her gently and she turned, her eyes moving instantly to his lips.

"Guess who I ran into today" he repeated, and her eyes followed each muscular contraction and relaxation of his mouth so that—though she was born a deaf mute—she could almost hear each separate word as it rolled from his tongue. She raised her eyebrows in question. There were times when she used sign language to convey her thoughts to her husband; other times, when there was no real necessity for a formal language between them, when the simple cocking of an eye or nuance of mouth, sometimes a glint, sometimes the rarest of subtle expressions served to tell him what she was thinking. He loved her most during those times, he supposed. Her face was a beautiful thing, oval and pale, with large brown eyes and a full sensuous mouth. Black hair curled wildly about her head, echoing the color of her eyes, setting the theme for the rest of the woman who was Teddy Carella, a theme of savagery which sprang through the blatant curve of her breast and the ripe swelling of hip and thigh and splendid calf, narrow ankles, narrow waist, a woman with the body of a barbarian and the gentle tenderness of a slave. And never was she more lovely than when her face explained something to him, never more lovely than when her eyes "spoke." She raised her eyebrows in question now, and fastened her eyes to his mouth again, waiting.

"Cliff Savage," he said.

She tilted her head to one side, puzzled. She shrugged. Then she shook her head.

"Savage. The reporter. Remember?"

And then she remembered all at once, and the light broke over her face and her hands moved quickly, bursting with questions. *What did he want? My God, how many years has it been? Do you remember what that fool did? We weren't even married then, Steve. Do you remember? We were so young.*

"One at a time, will you?" Carella said. "He was beefing because I'd sent that I.D. photo to every newspaper but his." Carella chuckled. "I thought that'd get a rise out of the bastard. And it did. Man, was he steaming! Do you know something honey? I don't think he even realizes what he did. He doesn't even know he could have got you killed."

Carella shook his head.

What Savage had done, actually, was run a story in his newspaper several years back, a story which had strongly hinted that a detective named Steve Carella had confided to his fiancée, a girl named Theodora Franklin, some suspicions he had about a series of cop killings. In addition, Savage had also listed Teddy's address in the newspaper, and he could not have fingered her more effectively than if he'd led the killer to her apartment in person. The news story had indeed smoked out the killer. It had also damn near got Teddy killed.

Do you remember? she said with her hands again, and an expression of total sadness crossed her face and Carella remembered what she had said to him not a moment ago, *We were so young,* and he wondered what she'd really meant and suddenly he took her into his arms.

She came to him desperately, as if she had been waiting for his arms all day long. She clung to him, and he was not surprised to find her hot tears on the side of his neck.

"Hey, what's the matter?" he said. Weeping, she kept her face buried against the side of his neck so that she could not "hear" him. He twisted his right hand in her hair and pulled back her head. "What's the matter?"

She shook her head.

"Tired of your humdrum existence?" he asked.

She did not answer.

"Bored by the four walls?"

Still she would not answer.

"Long for a life of romantic adventure?" Carella paused. "What's the matter, honey? Look, your eyes are running all over your face, and after you spent so much time making them up."

Teddy sat bolt upright in his lap, an expression of shocked outrage on her face. Her black brows swooped down. Her right hand darted up in front of his face. Rapidly the fingers spelled out their message.

My eyes!

"Well, honey—"

Then you did notice! And you probably noticed everything else, too! The—

"Honey, what are you getting all—?"

Shut up! Get away from me!

She tried to get off his lap, but his hands slid up under the robe, and though she struggled to free herself, his hands were strong upon her and at last she relaxed in his arms, and his hands roamed beneath the loose gown, touching her belly and her smooth flanks, stroking her gently as he spoke, his lips moving beneath her listening fingers.

"So sometimes you feel like an old matron," he said. "Sometimes you roam this big shell of a house in your dirty dungarees and you wipe runny noses all day long and keep cigarette butts out of the twins' mouths, and wonder when the hell your adventuresome husband is coming home. And sometimes you long for it to be the way it used to be, Teddy, before we were married, when every time was like the first time and the last time rolled into one, when my eyes went up like butane every time I saw you, when it was young, Teddy, when it was new and shining and young."

She stared at her husband in solemn wonder because there were times when he seemed to be such an insensitive lout, times when he seemed to be only the uncouth slob who told dirty jokes in a detective squadroom and who brought all of his grubbiness home with him, times when she felt alone in her silent world without even the comfort of the person who had been to her the one shining spark in her life, and then suddenly—suddenly there he was again, the person she had known all along, her Steve, the person who knew the things she was feeling, who had felt them himself, and who could talk about them until, until. . . .

"And you want it to be that way again, honey, that wild crazy young flying way that was for kids, Teddy, but we're not kids, anymore. So you dressed yourself up for me tonight. It's Fanny's day off, so you rushed the kids into their beds, and you put on your black shorty nightgown—I saw it when the wind caught your robe—and your good silk robe and your fancy high-heeled slippers, and you put that shadow all round your eyes, and you left your lips naked and Teddy, Teddy baby, I love you anywhich way you are, in a potato sack, or digging in the back yard, or right after you had the babies and they rolled you in all sweaty and stinking on the maternity table, or taking a bath, or cooking, or swimming, dressed, naked, reading, weeping, baby, baby I love you and it only gets better all the time and I'll be goddamned if I'm going to cater to your silly back-to-seventeen movement and get all excited because you're in a nightgown and high-heeled pumps, especially, especially when I've been planning on *exactly* this all day long, all goddam day long! Take your fingers off my mouth, I want to kiss you."

He kissed her, and he didn't ask her afterward whether or not there was any of that flying jazz they had known as kids, or whether or not the world went up in neon, and whether or not Mongolian gongs and bugles went off—he didn't ask her. Instead he slipped the robe from her shoulders, lowered it to her waist, kissed the full rich globes of her breasts, felt her trembling beneath his fingers, and carried her to the new grass lining the patio. And then he held her to him naked, and he didn't ask her anything, and she didn't say anything, and whereas neither of them flew and whereas there was no flash of neon and no crashing of gongs or bleating of bugles, he had the distinct impression that the sky was crumbling and that he was about to fall off the edge of the earth. And, from the way she clung to him so desperately, he knew she was experiencing the same odd sensation.

5.

THE SQUADROOM WAS JAMMED to capacity on that Friday, April 10. Sometimes it just happened that way. There were days when the man who was catching barely had anyone to talk to. Everybody else on the team was out preventing crime or collecting graft or some damn thing. But on that Friday, April 10, that old squadroom was just the most bustling old place on Grover Avenue. Detectives, patrolmen, the lieutenant, the captain, messengers from downtown, citizens making complaints—everybody seemed to be in the room that morning. Telephones rang and typewriters clattered and the place had the air of a thriving, if small, business concern.

At the desk closest to the grilled windows that faced the street, Meyer Meyer was on the telephone talking to Dave Murchison, the desk sergeant.

"That's right, Dave," he said. "Sandhurst Paper Company in New Bedford, Massachusetts. What? How the hell do I know where New Bedford is? Right next to Old Bedford and Middle Bedford, I guess. That's the way it usually works, isn't it?" he paused. "Right. Buzz me when you've got them." He hung up to find Andy Parker standing alongside the desk.

"There's also," Parker said, "East Bedford and West Bedford."

"And Bedford Center," Kling put in.

"You guys got nothing to do but clown around?" Meyer asked. "Come on, look alert. Suppose the Chief of Detectives should walk in here?"

"He can't," Parker said. "He's downtown running the lineup. He wouldn't come visit no grubby squad-room like this. Downtown, they give him a micro-phone and a bunch of bulls who have to laugh at his crumby jokes every morning."

"Except Fridays, Saturdays and Sundays," Kling said. "Today is Friday."

"That's right," Meyer said. "So you see, he just *might* walk in here and find you with your thumb up your behind."

"The fact is," Parker said, "I only come in here to see if there was any messages for me. Because maybe you didn't notice it, but I'm dressed for a plant, and in exactly"—he shoved back his cuff and looked at his wrist watch—"in exactly forty-five minutes, I'll be leaving you gentlemen to take up my position in the candy store."

"What are you supposed—"

"So don't make no cracks about my working or not working. I go on at ten-thirty, and that's that."

"Yeah, but what are you supposed to be dressed *as*?" Meyer asked.

In truth, the question was not put in jest. For whereas Andy Parker may have felt he'd donned a cos-tume for his candy store plant, the fact was that he looked much the same as he always looked. Which was to say, he looked like a slob. There are people, you know, who always look like slobs. There's simply nothing to be done about it. This tendency toward sloppiness first exhibits itself when the subject is still a child. Dress him for a birthday party and five minutes later he will look as if he'd been ran over by a steamroller. Nor will he look that way because he's run through a mud puddle or anything. Oh, no. He will simply look that way because he has within him, inside his beating little heart, the makings of a true slob. It is not good to discourage slobs. They will become slobs anyway.

Andy Parker was a true slob. Five minutes after he'd shaved, he looked as if he needed a shave again. Ten minutes after he'd tucked his shirttail into his trousers, the shirttail was hanging out again. Fifteen minutes after he'd shined his shoes, his shoes were scuffed again. Listen, that was the way he was. Did this necessarily make him a bad cop? Absolutely not. His being a bad cop had nothing whatever to do with his being a slob. He *was* a slob, and he *was* a bad cop—but the two phenomena were not at all related.

In any case, Lieutenant Byrnes had planted Andy Parker in a candy store on North Eleventh with the idea of getting him to smell out the alleged pushers who were peddling their lovely little packets of junk in that spot. Andy Parker was supposed to look like a junkie. It hardly seems necessary to explain, in this communications-enlightened day and age, that a junkie is not a man who buys and sells scrap iron. A junkie is a person who buys junk. Junk is dope. A junkie, in short, is a drug addict—as if you didn't know. Now, Parker had seen a great many junkies throughout his career and it could be assumed that he knew what a junkie looked like. But if the casual observer took his "costume" as an indication, that observer would be forced to conclude that a junkie looked like Andy Parker. For although Meyer Meyer was studying him quite closely, Andy Parker seemed to be dressed the way he always dressed. Which was like a slob.

"Don't tell me what you're supposed to be," Meyer said. "Let me guess." Meyer wrinkled his brow. "A floorwalker in a department store. Am I right?"

"That's what he's supposed to be," Kling said. "Only, Andy, you forgot a carnation in your lapel."

"Come on, don't kid me," Parker said seriously.

"Then what could he be?" Meyer said. "Just a minute, I've got it! An usher at a fancy wedding!"

"Come on, come on," Parker said, just as Lieutenant Byrnes pushed his way through the slatted-rail divider and into the office.

"Mark my words," he said, "this precinct is going to have the biggest traffic problem in the city as soon as that damn shopping center is finished. I just drove through there and even the *workmen's* cars are causing a bottleneck. You can imagine what it's going to be like when all those stores are finished." Byrnes shook his head and said to Parker, "I thought you were supposed to be in that candy store."

"Ten-thirty," Parker said.

"Won't kill you to get there a little early," Byrnes said.

"I already established that I'm a late sleeper."

"You established that the minute you began working for this squad," Byrnes said.

"Huh?"

"I'm telling you, Frick's gonna have to detail six squad cars to that shopping center," Byrnes said, dismissing Parker's puzzled look. "Did you see the big sign they've got up, listing all the stores? There's gonna be a bakery, and a movie house, and a supermarket, and a bank, and a delicatessen, and a department store, and—"

"That's why he's the lieutenant around here," Meyer said. "Because he's so observant."

"The hell with you," Byrnes said, grinning, and he went into his office to the left of the divider. He paused at the door and said, "Steve in yet?"

"Not yet," Meyer said.

"Who's catching?"

"I am," Kling answered.

"Let me know when Steve gets in, will you?"

"Yes, sir."

The telephone on Meyer's desk rang. He picked up the receiver quickly. "Eighty-seventh Squad, Meyer. Oh yes, Dave, put it right through." He covered the mouthpiece and said to Kling, "My New Bedford call," and then waited.

"Detective Meyer?" a voice asked.

"Yes?"

"I have your party on the line. One moment, please."

Meyer waited.

"Go ahead, please," the operator said.

"Hello?" Meyer said.

A static-filled voice on the other end said, "Sandhurst Paper Company, good morning."

"Good morning," Meyer said. "This is Detective Meyer of the Eighty-seventh Detective Squad down in—"

"Good morning, Detective Meyer."

"Good morning, I'm trying to trace an order that was placed for—"

"One moment please, I'll give you our Order Department."

Meyer waited. In the promised moment, a man's voice came onto the line.

"Order Department, good morning."

"Good morning, this is Detective Meyer of the Eighty-seventh Squad, in—"

"Good morning, Detective Meyer."

"Good morning. I wonder if you can help me. A man named David Raskin here in Isola received several cartons of envelopes and stationery from your company, but he did not place an order for this material. I wonder if you could tell me who *did*."

"What was his name again, sir?"

"David Raskin."

"And the address?"

"Darask Frocks, Inc., Twelve thirteen Culver Avenue here in the city."

"And when was the order delivered, sir?"

"Just yesterday."

"One moment, please."

Meyer waited. While he waited, Steve Carella came into the squadroom. Meyer covered the mouthpiece and said, "Steve, the loot wants to see you."

"Right. Did the lab call?"

"Nope."

"Any luck on the photo so far?"

"Not a peep. Give it time. It only ran yester— Hello?"

"Detective Breyer?" the voice on the phone said.

"Yes?"

"That order *was* placed by Mr. Raskin."

"When was this, please?"

"Ten days ago. It usually takes us a week to ten days to fill an order."

"Then that would be on April first, is that right?"

"March thirty-first, to be exact, sir."

"Was it a mail order?"

"No, sir. Mr. Raskin called personally."

"He called and ordered the material, is that right?"

"Yes, sir, he did."

"What did he sound like?"

"Sir?"

"What kind of a voice did he have?"

"A very nice voice, I think. It's difficult to remember."

"Is there anything you *do* remember about him?"

"Well, not really. We handle a great many orders each day, you understand, and—"

"I understand. Well, thank you very much for—"

"There *was* one thing."

"What was that, sir?"

"He asked me to talk a little louder, Mr. Raskin did. During the conversation. He said, 'Excuse me, but would you talk a little louder? I'm slightly deaf, you know.' "

"I see," Meyer said, shrugging. "Well, thanks again."

The telephone on the desk nearest Meyer's rang. Andy Parker, who was doing nothing but killing time, picked up the receiver.

"Eighty-seventh Squad, Detective Parker," he said.

"Carella there?" the voice on the other end asked.

"Yeah, just a second. Who's this?"

"Peter Kronig at the lab."

"Just a second, Kronig." Parker put down the phone and bellowed, "Steve, for you!" He looked around the squadroom.

"Where the hell's Carella? He was here a minute ago."

"He went in to see the loot," Kling said.

Parker picked up the phone again. "Kronig, he's in with the lieutenant. You want him to call back, or you want to give it to me?"

"This is just a report on those shoes and socks the mortuary sent over. You got a pencil?"

"Yeah, just a second," Parker said sourly. He hadn't hoped to become involved in any work this morning before heading for his candy store, and he silently vowed never to pick up a ringing telephone again unless it was absolutely necessary. He sat on the edge of the desk and reached over for a pad and pencil. He wiped one finger across his nose, said, "Okay, Kronig, shoot," into the telephone and leaned over the desk with the pencil poised over the pad and the receiver propped against his ear.

"The socks can be had anywhere, Parker. Just a blend of sixty per cent dacron and forty per cent cotton. We could have narrowed it down to four or five trade names, but there didn't seem much sense to doing that. You can pick the damn things up in the five and ten, if you like."

"Okay," Parker said. "That it?" On the pad he wrote simply, "Socks—No make."

"No, there're the shoes," Kronig said. "We may have run into a bit of luck there, though we can't figure out how it ties with the morgue's description of the body."

"Let me have it," Parker said.

"The shoes are simple black shoes, no perforation on the top, quarter or heel. No decorations anywhere. We checked them through and found out they're manufactured by the American T. H. Shoe Company in Pittsburgh. This is a pretty big outfit, Parker, and they put out a huge line of men's shoes and women's play shoes, casual stuff, you know?"

"Yeah," Parker said, and still he wrote nothing on the pad. "So what about this particular pair of shoes?"

"Well, this outfit makes shoes for the U.S. Navy. Just a single model. A plain black shoe."

"Yeah," Parker said.

"You got it?"

"I got it. This is the shoe, right?"

"Right. So how does that check out against the morgue's description?"

"What do you mean?"

"They said the guy was sixty-five years old! You know any sixty-five-year-old sailors?"

Parker thought for a minute. "I'll bet there are some sixty-five-year-old admirals," he said. "They're sailors, ain't they?"

"I never thought of that," Kronig said. "Well, anyway, that's it. They make the shoe for the Navy, and it can only be purchased from Navy ship's services. Eight ninety-five the pair. Think an admiral would wear such a cheap shoe?"

"I don't know any admirals," Parker said. "Also, this is Carella's headache, not mine. I'll pass it on to him. Thanks for calling."

"Don't mention it," Kronig said, and he hung up.

"Do admirals wear shoes that cost only eight ninety-five?" Parker asked no one.

"*I* wear shoes that cost more than that," Meyer said, "and I'm only a cop."

"I read someplace that J. Edgar Hoover doesn't like cops to be called cops," Kling said.

"Yeah? I wonder why that is?" Parker scratched his head. "We're cops, ain't we? If we ain't cops, what are we then?"

Captain Frick pushed his way through the gate in the railing and said, "Frankie Hernandez here?"

"He's in the john, Captain," Meyer said. "You want him?"

"Yeah, yeah," Frick said. There was a pained and harried expression on his face, as if something dreadful had happened and he didn't quite know how to cope with it. If the truth were known, of course, there weren't very many things that Captain Frick could cope with. He was technically, in charge of the entire precinct, although his actual command very rarely extended beyond the uniformed force. In any case, he hardly ever offered any advice to Lieutenant Byrnes who ran the detective squad quite capably and effectively. Frick was not a very bright man, and his approach to police work was perhaps comparable to the approach of an old woman toward a will to be settled. He allowed the actual settling to be handled by those better qualified to handle it, and then he reaped the rewards. And yet, all the while it was being handled for him, he fretted and fussed like a hen sitting on a laggard egg.

He fretted and fussed now while he waited for Frankie Hernandez to come out of the men's room. He would have followed him into the room but Frick firmly believed that police business should be conducted in dignified surroundings. So he paced back and forth just inside the railing, one eye on the closed men's room door, waiting for the appearance of the detective. When Hernandez did come out of the room, he went to him immediately.

"Frankie, I've got a problem," he said.

"What is it, Captain Frick?" Hernandez asked. He was drying his hands on his handkerchief. He had, in fact, been heading for the Clerical Office to tell Miscolo there were no more paper towels in the bathroom when Frick intercepted him.

"There's a boy who keeps getting into trouble, a

nice kid, but he keeps swiping things from the fruit carts, little things, nothing to get upset about, except he's done it maybe seven, eight times already, he's a Puerto Rican kid, Frankie, and I think you know him, and I think we can save both him and the law a lot of headaches if somebody talks to him right now, which is why I'm coming to you, I'm sure you know the kid, his name is Juan Boridoz, would you talk to him please, Frankie, before he gets himself in trouble? His mother was in here yesterday afternoon and she seems like a nice hardworking lady, and she doesn't deserve a kid who'll wind up in the courts. He's only twelve, Frankie, so we can still catch him. Will you talk to him?"

"Sure, I will," Hernandez said.

"You know the kid?"

Hernandez smiled. "No," he said, "but I'll find him." It was a common assumption among the men of the 87th that Frankie Hernandez knew every single person of Spanish or Puerto Rican descent in the precinct territory. He had, it was true, been born and raised in the precinct, and he *did* know a great many of the residents therein. But there was more to the assumption of the other men than a simple recognition of his birthplace. Frankie Hernandez was a sort of liaison between the cops and the Puerto Ricans in the precinct. The other cops came to him when they wanted advice or information. Similarly, the people came to him whenever they needed protection, either from criminal elements or from the law. There were people on both sides of the fence who hated Frankie

Hernandez. Some men in the department hated him because he was Puerto Rican and, despite department edicts about the prevalence of brotherhood among the men in blue, these men simply felt a Puerto Rican had no right being a cop and certainly no right being a detective. Some people in the streets hated him because he had flatly refused to square any raps for them, raps ranging from speeding tickets to disorderly conduct, or sometimes assault, and on several occasions burglary. Hernandez wanted no part of it. He let it be known quickly and plainly that, old neighborhood ties be damned, he was a cop and his job was enforcing the law.

For the most part, Frankie Hernandez was a highly respected man. He had come out of the streets in one of the city's hottest delinquency areas, carrying the albatross of "cultural conflict" about his youthful neck, breaking through the "language barrier" (only Spanish was spoken in his home when he was a child) and emerging from the squalor of the slums to become a Marine hero during the Second World War, and later a patrolman ironically assigned to the streets which had bred him. He was now a Detective 3rd/Grade. It had been a long hard pull, and the battle still hadn't been won—not for Frankie Hernandez, it hadn't. Frankie Hernandez, you see, was fighting for a cause. Frankie Hernandez was trying to prove to the world at large that the Puerto Rican guy could also be the *good* guy.

"So will you talk to him, Frankie?" Frick asked again.

"Sure I will. This afternoon some time. Okay?"

Frick's mouth widened into a grateful smile. "Thanks, Frankie," he said, and he clapped him on the shoulder and went hurrying off down the corridor to his office downstairs. Hernandez opened the door to the Clerical Office and said, "Miscolo, we're out of towels in the bathroom."

"Okay, I'll get some," Miscolo said, without looking up from his typing. Then, as an afterthought, he wheeled from the machine and said, "Hey, Frankie, did Steve mention about May Reardon "

"Yeah."

"You in?"

"I'm in."

"Good, good. I'll get a fresh roll of towels later."

Hernandez went into the squadroom. He was just about to sit at his desk when the telephone rang. He sighed and picked it up.

Behind the closed door marked LT. PETER BYRNES, Steve Carella watched his superior officer and wished this were not quite as painful for Byrnes as it seemed to be. The lieutenant clearly had no stomach for what he was doing or saying, and his reluctance to carry out an obviously unpleasant task showed in his face and in the set of his body and also in the clenching and unclenching of his hands.

"Look," Byrnes said, "don't you think I hate that son of a bitch as much as you do?"

"I know, Peter," Carella said. "I'll do whatever—"

"You think I enjoyed that call I got from Detective Lieutenant Abernathy yesterday afternoon? Right after you left, Steve, the phone buzzes and it's a patrolman in the Public Relations Office downtown on High Street, and he asks me to hold on a moment for a call from Lieutenant Abernathy. So Abernathy gets on the phone and he wants to know if a man named Steve Carella works for me, and did I know that this man had sent out photos to all the newspapers except one and that if the police department was to expect co-operation from the press in the future, it would have to show equal consideration to *all* of the city's newspapers. So he demanded that I give this Carella a reprimand and that a copy of the photo go out to Cliff Savage's paper immediately, together with a note from Carella apologizing for his oversight. Abernathy wants to see a copy of the note, Steve."

"Okay," Carella said.

"You know I hate that son of a bitch Savage."

"I know," Carella said. "I should have sent him the picture. Kid stuff never gets anybody anyplace."

"You sore at me?"

"What the hell for? The order came from upstairs, didn't it?"

"Yeah." Byrnes shook his bullet-shaped head and pulled a sour face. "Just write a little note, Steve. Sorry I overlooked your paper, something like that. The day we have to kiss Savage's ass is the day I turn in my buzzer."

"Okay," Carella said. "I'll get on it right away."

"Yeah," Byrnes said. "You get any make on that picture yet?"

"Not yet," Carella said, and he opened the door. "Anything else, Pete?"

"No, no, go ahead. Get back to work. Go ahead."

Carella went out into the squadroom. Hernandez came over to him and said, "There was a call for you while you were with the loot, Steve."

"Oh?" Carella said.

"Yeah. Some guy saw the picture of the stiff in the papers. Said he recognized him."

6.

THE MAN WHO HAD PHONED the 87th to identify the photograph of the stiff was named Christopher Random. He was a man in his early sixties, and he had only four teeth in his mouth, two upper front and two lower front. He had told Detective Hernandez that he could be found in a bar called Journey's End, and it was there indeed that Carella and Hernandez found him at eleven-thirty that morning.

Journey's End may have been just that for a good many of the bar's customers. They were all wearing wrinkled and soiled gray suits. They were all wearing caps. They were all past fifty, and they all had the veined noses and fogged eyes of the habitual drinker.

Christopher Random had that nose and those eyes, and in addition he had only those four teeth, so that he looked like a remarkable specimen of something preserved in alcohol. Carella asked the bartender which of the men in the gray wrinkled suits was Random, and the bartender pointed him out and then he and Hernandez went to the end of the bar and Carella flashed the tin at Random, who blinked, nodded and casually threw off the shot of whiskey which rested on the bar before him.

He burped and the fumes damn near killed Carella and Hernandez.

"Mr. Random?" Carella said.

"That's me," Random said. "Christopher Random, scourge of the Orient."

"What makes you say that?" Carella asked.

"I beg your pardon? Say what?"

"Scourge of the Orient."

"Oh." Random thought for a few moments. "No reason," he said, shrugging. "Just an expression."

"You called the precinct, sir, to say you knew who that dead man was, is that right?"

"That is right, sir," Random said. "What is your name, sir?"

"Carella. And this is Detective Hernandez."

"Nice to meet you two gentlemen," Random said. "Would either of you care for a little refreshment, or are you not allowed to imbibe while wearing the blue?" He paused. "That's just an expression," he said.

"We're not allowed to drink on duty," Carella said.

"That is a shame," Random said. "Sir, that is a crying shame. Barkeep, I would like another whiskey, please. Now then, about that photograph?"

"Yes, sir, what about it?" Carella said. "Who was he?"

"I don't know."

"But I thought—"

"That is to say, I don't know what his name is. Or, to be more precise, I don't know what his full name is. I do know his first name."

"And what's that?" Hernandez asked.

"Johnny."

"But Johnny what, you don't know?"

"That is correct, sir. Johnny what, I do not know. Or even Johnny Who." Random smiled. "That's just an expression," he said. "Ahh, here's my whiskey now. Drink hearty lads, this stuff here puts hair on your clavicle it does, arghhhhh!" He smacked his lips, set the glass down again and asked, "Where were we?"

"Johnny."

"Yes, sir. Johnny."

"What about him? How do you happen to know him?"

"I met him in a bar, sir."

"Where?"

"On The Stem, I believe."

"The Stem and where?"

"North Eighteenth?"

"Are you asking us or telling us?" Carella said.

"I don't know the street exactly," Random said, "but I do know the name of the bar, it is called, sir, the Two Circles, does that help you?"

"Maybe," Carella said. "When did this meeting take place?"

"Let me think," Random said. His brow wrinkled. He sucked spit in around his four teeth and made horrible noises with his mouth. "I think better with a bit of refreshment before me," he said subtly.

"Bartender, another whiskey," Carella said.

"Why, thank you, sir, that's good of you," Random said. "I think I met him a few nights before the

beginning of the month. March twenty-ninth or thirtieth, something like that. It was a Saturday night, I
remember."

Carella flipped open his wallet and pulled a small
celluloid calendar from one of the compartments.
"Saturday was the twenty-eighth," he said. "Was that
the date?"

"If it was the last Saturday in March, yes sir."

"There were no Saturdays in March after that one,"
Carella said, smiling.

"Then that, sir, was the date, yes, sir. Ahhh, here's
my whiskey now. Drink hearty, lads, this stuff here
puts hair on your clavicle it does, arghhhh!" He
smacked his lips, set the glass down again and asked,
"Where were we?"

"Johnny," Hernandez said. "Met him in a bar called
the Two Circles up on The Stem on Saturday night,
March twenty-eighth. Go on."

"Did you write all that down, sir?" Random asked.

"I did."

"Remarkable."

"How old would you say the man was?" Carella
asked. "This fellow Johnny."

"In his sixties, I would say."

"In good health, would you say?"

Random shrugged. "I don't know. I'm not a physi-
cian, you understand."

"I know. But was he coughing or anything? Did he
look pale or run-down? Did he have any tics or nervous mannerisms? Did he—"

"He seemed to be in perfectly good health," Random said, "as far as I could tell. You understand, I didn't ask him to take off his clothes so I could give him a physical examination, you understand, sir. I am saying only that, on the surface, looking at him with my naked eye, and without the benefit of a medical education, I would say this fellow Johnny was as fit as a fiddle." Random paused. "That's just an expression," he said.

"Okay," Carella said, "he told you his first name was Johnny. Did he mention his last name?"

"No, sir, he did not. Sir, with all due respect to the Police Department, any extended conversation makes me exceedingly thirsty. I do wish I could . . ."

"Bartender, another whiskey," Hernandez said. "He didn't give you his last name, correct?"

"Correct."

"What did he say?"

"He said he was on his way to work."

"Work? What kind of work?"

"He didn't say."

"But this was the nighttime, wasn't it?"

"That is correct, sir. It was a Saturday night."

"And he said he was going to work?"

"Yes, sir, that is exactly what he said."

"But he didn't say what kind of work?"

"No, sir," Random said. "Of course, he was wearing the uniform."

"Uniform?" Carella said.

"Uniform?" Hernandez echoed.

"Was it a sailor's uniform?" Carella asked. "Was he a sailor, Mr. Random?"

"Ahhhh," Random said, "here's my whiskey now. Drink hearty, lads, this stuff here puts hair on your clavicle, it does, arghhhhh!" He smacked his lips, set the glass down again and asked, "Where were we?"

"The uniform. Was it a sailor's uniform?"

"A sailor's uniform? On a man well into his sixties? Now, sirs, that's pretty silly, if you ask me."

"Well what kind of a uniform was it?"

"It was gray," Random said.

"Go on."

"It could have been a postman's uniform," Random said.

"*Was* it?"

"I don't know. Or a bus driver's."

"Well, which was it? A postman's or a bus driver's?"

"I don't know. To tell you the truth, I wasn't feeling too well that night, you understand. I was having a little trouble with my eyes, you understand. Focusing, you understand. So all I can remember is that it was a gray uniform, with a uniform cap and all."

"It wasn't a chauffeur's uniform, was it?"

"No, sir, it was gray. *Gray*. Not black. No, not a chauffeur's uniform." Random paused. "But he *was* working for somebody. I remember that. So I guess that would let out the post office, wouldn't it? Unless he was talking about his foreman, that's a possibility, isn't it?"

"He mentioned his employer's name?" Carella asked.

"Well, no, not exactly," Random said. "Only indirectly."

"What did he say?"

"He said he had to get to work or the deaf man would be angry. That's what he said."

"The who?" Carella asked. "The *dead* man?"

"No, no, the *deaf* man. Deaf. You know. Hard of hearing. Deaf. Of course, that may have been just an expression."

"You're sure that's what he said?" Carella asked.

"Yes, sir."

"Anything else about this deaf man?"

"No, sir."

"Or about where he was going to work?"

"No, sir. Not a word."

"You're sure you're remembering this correctly, Mr. Random?" Hernandez asked.

"Of course I remember it," Random said. "Why shouldn't I?"

"Well, you said you were a little out of focus."

"Yes, but—"

"What you meant was that you'd had a little too much to drink, isn't that right?" Hernandez asked.

"Well, yes, but—"

"What you meant was that you had a couple of sheets to the wind, isn't that right?" Hernandez asked.

"That's just an expression," Carella said quickly. "*Were* you kind of loaded, Mr. Random?"

"I suppose so," Random said philosophically.

"But in spite of that, you do remember what happened?"

"I do, sir," Random said.

"What do you think?" Hernandez asked.

Carella nodded. "I believe him."

THE MAN WAS WEARING a chauffeur's uniform. He stood in the doorway of the haberdashery, and he looked around at the fedoras and derbies and caps and Homburgs, and he held his own hat in his hands and stared into the shop, waiting. One of the salesmen spotted him and walked over instantly.

"Yes, sir," he said. "May I help you?"

"Mr. Lombardo, please?" the chauffeur said.

"Just a moment. He's in the back. I'll get him for you."

The salesman went into the back of the store and returned a moment later with Mr. Lombardo, the owner. Lombardo wore a dark-gray suit and a beautiful white shirt with a gray foulard necktie. A cat's-eye ring glistened on his pinky.

"Yes, sir?" he said to the chauffeur. "May I help you?"

"Mr. Lombardo?" the chauffeur said.

"Yes?" Mr. Lombardo frowned. Perhaps he already knew what was coming.

"The car's waiting, sir," the chauffeur said.

"You don't say?"

"Yes, sir."

"*What* car, may I ask?"

"The car you ordered, sir." The chauffeur looked puzzled. "I'm from Carey Cadillac, sir." He nodded his head, as if that simple statement explained everything.

"Carey Cadillac?" The chauffeur kept nodding. "The car? It's outside? Waiting?"

He nodded again, studied Lombardo's scowl, and desperately plunged ahead. "You said twelve noon, sir, and its twelve noon now. So I'm ready and waiting, sir." He tried a grin which evaporated the moment he saw Lombardo's scowl deepen. Finally, completely routed, he returned to his original statement, delivering it with cold hauteur. "The car's waiting, sir."

"I didn't order any car," Lombardo said calmly.

"But you did, sir. James Lombardo, Lombardo's Haberdashery, eight thirty-seven—"

"I did not order any automobile!" Lombardo said, his voice rising.

"It's that lunatic again, Mr. Lombardo," the salesman said.

"I know it!"

"Call the police, Mr. Lombardo," the salesman advised. "This has gone too far. Those telephone threats and all these—"

"You're right," Lombardo said. "This has gone far enough." And he started for the telephone.

"Hey, what about the car?" the chauffeur wanted to know.

"I didn't order it," Lombardo said, dialing. "Some madman has been trying to get me to vacate my store. This is just another one of his stunts."

"Well, look—"

"I did not order it!" Lombardo shouted. Into the telephone, he said, "Operator? Get me the police."

The chauffeur shrugged, stared at Lombardo for a

moment, and then put on his cap and went out of the haberdashery. The black Cadillac was parked at the curb, but he didn't go directly to it. Instead, he went to the plate-glass front of the store next door to the haberdashery. And, longingly, he studied the sapphires and rubies and emeralds and diamonds which were spread on black velvet in the window.

Sighing, he went back to the car and drove away.

7.

THE DEAF MAN AND RAFE had been sitting in the ferry-house waiting room for close to a half hour, watching the people who came and went, watching especially the number of policemen patrolling the docks or hanging around the waiting room, or coming on and off the ferry itself. A huge clock was at one end of the pale-green room, and the deaf man looked up at the clock occasionally, and occasionally he studied the ferry schedule in his hands. The inside of the schedule looked like this:

ISOLA TO MAJESTA Daylight Saving Time Schedule symbols should be checked carefully against "REFERENCES" in center of tables.		REFERENCES	MAJESTA TO ISOLA Daylight Saving Time Schedule symbols should be checked carefully against "REFERENCES" in center of tables.	
Lve Isola	Arr Majesta		Lve Majesta	Arr Isola
	12:15 AM	12:45 AM	A—Will run on Saturdays only.		1:00 AM	1:30 AM
A	12:45	1:15		A	1:45	2:15
	1:45	2:15	B—Will run on Sundays only.		2:30	3:00
A	2:15	2:45		A	3:15	3:45
	2:45	3:15	C—Will run on Saturdays and Sundays only.	B	4:45	5:15
B	3:45	4:15		C	5:00	5:30
C	4:15	4:45	D—Will run on weekdays.		6:45	7:15
	6:05	6:35			8:15	8:45
D	7:30	8:00	E—Will run only on May 30, July 4, and September 7.	D	8:30	9:00
D	8:00	8:30		D	8:45	9:15
	9:05	9:35			10:00	10:30
	11:00	11:30	Authorized and distributed by the River Harb Ferry Company, not responsible for errors, all times subject to change without notice, all fares ten cents additional if tickets are purchased on boat.		11:45	12:15 PM
	12:30 PM	1:00 PM			1:30 PM	2:00
	2:15	2:45			3:00	3:30
	4:05	4:35			5:00	5:30
	5:45	6:15		D	5:30	6:00
	6:05	6:35			6:30	7:00
E	7:15	7:45			8:00	8:30
	8:45	9:15			9:30	10:00
	9:15	9:45			10:00	10:30
	9:45	10:15			10:20	10:50
	11:00	11:30			11:35	12:05AM

The deaf man studied the timetable, made a mental note and then walked to the nearest ticket booth.

"Good morning," he said to the ticket seller in his gentle voice, smiling.

"Morning," the ticket seller said, not looking up. The ticket seller seemed to be counting something. All ticket sellers always seem to be counting something no matter when you approach their windows. They are either counting money, or new tickets, or cancelled tickets, or stamps, or schedules, or sometimes they are counting their big toes, but they are always counting something, and they are always too busy with what they are counting to look up at you. This one was no exception. The deaf man was smiling his most powerful smile and talking in his most persuasively gentle voice, but the ticket seller went right on counting whatever it was he was counting, and he didn't look up once during the entire conversation.

"Does your ferry carry trucks?" the deaf man asked.

"Depends on how big."

"Well, I wasn't thinking of a trailer truck," the deaf man said, gently, his blue eyes twinkling.

"Well, what kind of a truck *were* you thinking of?"

"An ice-cream truck."

"Ice-cream truck, huh? You mean like Good Humor? Like that?"

"Yes. Not Good Humor, but a truck of that size. That's exactly what I meant."

"We carry 'em."

"What was that? I'm sorry, I'm a little deaf."

"I said we carry 'em. Ice-cream trucks."

"Do I need a ticket in advance, or can I buy it on the ferry?"

"You buy it on the ferry."

"Would you mind looking at this ferry schedule, please?" the deaf man said, and he shoved the schedule under the barred window. The ticket seller did not look up. His eyes shifted toward the schedule, but he continued counting, and he would not look up at the deaf man.

"What about it?"

"It says it's effective April 13. That's next Monday."

"That's right. What about it? We still got some old schedules over there, if you want them."

"No, no, this is just what I want. But will these arrivals and departures be in effect for a while?"

"Absolutely. Don't put out a new schedule until June sometime. And even that'll be the same, actually, except it makes people feel better when they see new dates on a timetable."

"Then these times will be in effect throughout April and May, is that right?"

"June, too," the ticket seller said. "*And* July, for that matter. *And* August. Schedule don't change again until we go off daylight-saving time. That's in September sometime."

"I see, thank you. And I can buy a ticket for the truck after I have boarded the ferry with it, is that also correct?"

"Yes, that's right."

"Should I get here very far in advance, or can you

usually accommodate all the vehicles that want passage?"

"We got room for twenty-five cars. Seldom get more'n a dozen. Plenty of room aboard the old tub. Not many people want to go to Majesta. Sure, it's nice and quiet there, but it ain't exactly anybody's idea of city life, if you know what I mean."

"Well, thank you very much," the deaf man said. "What time does the next ferry leave?"

The ticket seller did not stop counting, nor did he look up at the clock or down at his wrist watch. He simply said, "Eleven o'clock."

"Thank you," the deaf man said. He walked away from the window, nodded pleasantly at a uniformed cop standing near the newspaper stand, and strode rapidly to where Rafe was sitting on the bench. He sat beside him unobtrusively.

"I'll be going over to Majesta," he said. "You have some phone calls to make, don't you?"

"Yes, I do," Rafe said, nodding. The sight of the uniformed cop made him somewhat anxious. He did not like policemen. He had spent five years in prison because of policemen.

"I just checked the schedule," the deaf man told him. "We'll plan on catching the 5:45 P.M. boat on the evening of the caper. The one after that is at 6:05. That gives us a twenty-minute leeway, should anything go wrong."

"Do you think anything will go wrong?" Rafe asked. He was a tall thin man with a mild manner, a manner accentuated by the gold-rimmed eyeglasses and sandy-blond hair.

"No," the deaf man said confidently. "Nothing will go wrong."

"How can you be sure?"

"I can be sure because I have studied the probabilities. And I can be sure because I know exactly what we are dealing with."

"And what's that?"

"An outmoded police force," the deaf man said.

"They weren't so outmoded when they sent me to jail," Rafe said quietly, glumly.

"Examine the Police Department, if you will," the deaf man said. "There are approximately thirty thousand cops in this sprawling metropolis. And this figure includes all of them, inspectors, deputy inspectors, detectives, patrolmen, veterinarians, policewomen, everything. The total police force numbers thirty thousand. That's it."

"So?"

"So there are approximately ten million people in this city. And it is the task of those thirty thousand policemen to see that those ten million people do not commit various criminal acts against each other. If we divide the number of potential lawbreakers by the number of policemen, we can say—roughly—that each cop is responsible for the conduct of about three hundred thirty-three people, am I right?"

Rafe did some laborious long division. "Yes, that's about right."

"Now, obviously, one cop—even assuming he is armed with the most modern weapons—couldn't possibly control three hundred thirty-three people should they, for example, decide to commit three hundred thirty-three crimes in three hundred thirty-three places at the same time. It would be physically impossible for one cop to prevent all of those crimes because he couldn't possibly be in two places at the same time, one of the basic laws of physics. But, of course, there are a vast number of policemen who, in combination, can be brought into action against a multitude of simultaneous criminal explosions. But even these men, in combination, could not cope with, if you will, ten million people committing ten million crimes simultaneously. Despite the permutations."

"I don't understand you," Rafe said.

"Permutations," the deaf man said. "The number of possible ways—well, let's take a deck of cards. You'll be more at ease with cards than with policemen. There are fifty-two cards in the deck. If we want to know how many possible ways there are of arranging those fifty-two cards, we start with the simple permutation, written this way." He took a slip of paper from his pocket and quickly jotted: 52p52.

"I still don't understand," Rafe said.

"That's simply the mathematical way of writing the permutations of 52. We call *all* the arrangements we can make by selecting all the numbers of a group 'simple permutations.' The equation becomes . . ." And he wrote: 52p52=52!

"That tells us how many possible ways there are of arranging a deck of 52 cards."

"What's the exclamation point for?" Rafe asked.

"It's not an exclamation point. There are no interjections in mathematics. It simply indicates that the number must be multiplied by every whole number below it until we get to 1. For example, the number four followed by that symbol simply means 4 times 3 times 2 times 1."

"So how many ways *can* you arrange a deck of cards?"

"52! ways—or 52 times 51 times 50 times 49 times—well, all the way down until you reach the figure 1. It would take all day to multiply it out. But at the risk of making you nervous again, let's get back to something of more concern to us, policemen. And, specifically, the detectives of the Eighty-seventh Squad. There are normally sixteen men on the squad. But when we pull our job, two will be on vacation and two will be in Washington taking an FBI course."

"That leaves twelve," Rafe said.

"Right. Let's try to figure how many possible combinations those twelve men can arrange themselves into, shall we? The equation would be this." He wrote: 12p12=12!

"Which means," he went on, "12 times 11 times 10, and so on. Let's see what that comes to." Quickly, he began multiplying figures on his sheet of paper. "Well, here you are," he said. "All the possible combinations for twelve men, 12 times 11 times 10 down through 1, is 479,001,600. It sounds staggering, doesn't it?"

"It sure does. Even *one* cop sounds staggering to me," Rafe said.

"Of course, detectives usually work in pairs, and

not in teams of twelve or eight or six or what have you. And this would automatically limit the number of possible combinations. Besides, we need not concern ourselves with the permutations of those twelve men. We need only to abstract a theory about law enforcement and crime prevention. It seems to me, Rafe, that the police operate on their own limited theory of probability. Obviously, with their inadequate force of thirty thousand, they cannot possibly hope to be everywhere at once. This is a damned big city and a great many people in it are practicing criminals. So the police operate against percentages. They figure in this fashion, more or less: A certain number of criminals must escape detection *for the moment* because we can't possibly hope to be where they are when a crime is being committed or because we can't successfully investigate every crime even after it's been committed; however, *in the long run,* we will one day catch a previously undetected criminal because we will be in the right place at the right time or because the situation for a successful investigation will present itself. *'In the long run'*—those are the key words in probability."

"I think I'd better go make my phone calls," Rafe said. "Besides, your ferry's coming in."

"Just a moment, Rafe. *'In the long run.'* Remember those words. If you flipped a penny five times in succession, the first five flips might come up tails. If you stopped flipping right there, you might come to the conclusion that a penny will come up tails one hundred per cent of the times it is flipped. Deviation, remember? The difference between observation and reality. Actually, the longer you kept flipping that penny, the closer you would come to the truth. Which is, of course, that it will turn up heads fifty per cent of the time and tails the remaining fifty per cent. So the cops are playing the long run. They've got this rather cute, quaint, antiquated, friendly, bumbling law enforcement machine and *in the long run,* through a combination of choice and chance, they will make their arrests and maintain order—primarily because the percentages are on their side. Most citizens, you see, are law-abiding. But tell me something, Rafe."

"What?" Rafe asked.

"What happens when someone comes along and screws up the percentages? What happens when the police are forced to cope with something the likes of which they've never encountered before? What happens when they're pushed into dealing with the *short* run?"

"I don't know," Rafe said. "What happens?"

"We'll walk off with two and a half million bucks," the deaf man said. "That's what."

THE REAL ESTATE AGENT in Majesta was quite taken with his caller. The man was tall and good-looking, with pleasant blue eyes and a manner reminiscent of the Old South. At the same time, the man knew what he wanted and he wasted no time in stating his needs.

"A small house with a garage," the deaf man said. "It needn't be close to the ferry, and I shall only need it for a few weeks. The garage must be large enough to hold two cars; a sedan and a small truck."

"I see, sir," the agent said. "And the house? How large a house need it be?"

"It should accommodate four adults," the deaf man said. He grinned pleasantly. "My colleagues and I are working on a screenplay which will be shot in the city streets this summer. We want two weeks of uninterrupted work, no telephones, no visitors. That's why we thought of Majesta."

"I see," the agent said. "You're a screen writer then, is that right?"

"That's right."

"Well, I knew you were *something* right off the bat. I could tell."

"Well, thank you," the deaf man said.

"Sure. And I think I've got just the house for you." He paused. "What movie company do you work for?"

"An independent outfit," the deaf man said quickly.

"You write anything else besides movie scripts?"

"Oh yes, a great many things."

"Would I know your name?" the agent asked.

"Perhaps."

"Well, what is it? I'll need it for our records, anyway."

"Thomas Wolfe," the deaf man said.

"Oh, sure," the agent said, smiling. "Sure. I think I even read a few of your books. Sure."

SITTING IN THE PHONE BOOTH, Rafe put a small tick mark alongside the tenth number on his list. There were fifteen numbers after that one, and all of the exchanges were for locations on the south side of the city, or—to be more precise—on the south side of the territory under the command of the Eighty-seventh Precinct. David Raskin's phone number was among those on the list. So was James Lombardo's. Dave Raskin ran a dress loft. Jim Lombardo ran a haberdashery. The two men had nothing at all in common. Unless one wished to comment on the fact that Dave's loft was over a bank and Jim's hat store was next door to a jewelry concern. Otherwise, there was no similarity.

Of the twenty-five numbers on the list, six belonged to clothing stores, eight belonged to restaurants, one belonged to Raskin, one belonged to Lombardo, three belonged to candy shops, two belonged to leather goods stores, one belonged to a travel agency, two belonged to shoe stores, and the last belonged to a tie shop.

Very innocent-looking concerns.

But Dave Raskin's loft was over a bank. And Jim Lombardo's hat shop was next door to a jewelry concern. Thirteen more of the stores on that list were next door to banks. Six were next door to rather fancy jewelry shops. One was next door to a firm which made money loans. Another was next door to a firm which sold silverware. The twenty-fourth store on the list was a Chinese restaurant which was located on the second floor of a building which housed a quaint little shop on the ground floor; the shop had close to five hundred thousand dollars' worth of Oriental jade in the window. And the twenty-fifth store was next door to a company which dealt in foreign exchange and which kept huge sums of cold cash in its safe.

Rafe dialed the eleventh number on his list and waited for the phone to be picked up on the other end. When the voice came on, he asked, "Mr. Carmichael?"

"Yes?" the man said.

"Get out of that store, Mr. Carmichael!" Rafe shouted. "Get out before the thirtieth, or I'll kill you!"

8.

"CAR TWENTY-THREE, car twenty-three, signal thirteen, signal thirteen."

"This is twenty-three."

"Signal thirteen, seven three five Gramercy Street, repeat seven three five Gramercy Street, complainant Sergei Rosnakoff, stink bomb in incinerator, signal thirteen. Car thirty-six, car thirty-six, signal eleven, signal—"

"This is thirty-six. Go ahead."

"This is twenty-three, what was that address again?"

"Hold it, thirty-six. I gave it to you twice, twenty-three. What the—"

"This is thirty-six, thirty-six, over."

"That's seven three five Gramercy. You got that, twenty-three?"

"Seven three five Gramercy, Roger."

"Car thirty-six, car thirty-six, come in car . . ."

CENTRAL COMPLAINT DESK REPORT

TIME	DATE	RECEIVED BY
9:12 AM	APR 13	PTL. JACOBS
CITY SECTION	PRECINCT	DESK OFFICER
BETHTOWN	HQ COMMAND	SGT. EDWARDS

ADDRESS **735 GRAMERCY STREET** FLOOR **GROUND**

NAME OF COMPLAINTANT **SERGEI ROSNAKOFF**

CRIME REPORTED **DISORDERLY CONDUCT (?)**

DETAILS **STINK BOMB IN INCINERATOR. BUILDING SUPER SMELT SOMETHING STRANGE. SAYS SOMEBODY THREW A STINK BOMB DOWN THE INCINERATOR. DISPATCHED TO BETHTOWN MOTOR PATROL.**

DISPATCHER NO. **12** TIME **9:15 AM**

C.R.D. 16
5900L-60464 C505 MB

POLICE DEPARTMENT
Case Report

For   *Captain Charles Hendriks*

CLASSIFICATION   *Investigation of Complaint*

Officer Assigned *Ptl. Ralph Allora* Shield No. *35-416*

Place of Occurrence *735 Gramercy Street*

Date of Occurrence *April 13* Time of Occurrence *9:00 AM*

Date Reported   *April 13*   Time Reported   *9:12 AM*

BRIEF OUTLINE OF CRIME

Super of the building said somebody threw a stink bomb into the garbage incinerator. Investigated claim, found what caused smell, but it was no stink bomb. Removed same from incinerator room.

WITNESSES (Name, Address, and Nature of Testimony)

Sergei Rosnakoff

735 Gramercy Street

     Super of bldg, man who made complaint

EVIDENCE (Quantity, Form, and Relationship to Crime)

     Burnt clothing and tobacco pouch.

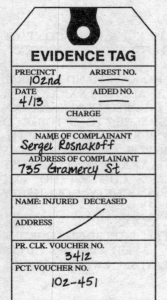

EVIDENCE TAG

PRECINCT   ARREST NO.
102nd

DATE   AIDED NO.
4/13

CHARGE

NAME OF COMPLAINANT
Sergei Rosnakoff

ADDRESS OF COMPLAINANT
735 Gramercy St

NAME: INJURED DECEASED

ADDRESS

PR. CLK. VOUCHER NO.
3412

PCT. VOUCHER NO.
102-451

NAME OF DEFENDANT

ADDRESS OF DEFENDANT

NATURE AND DESCRIPTION
OF EVIDENCE

Burnt material
found in
incinerator

ARRESTING OFFICER
Ptl. Ralph Allora

TIME AND PLACE
COURT EXAMINATION

Pr Clk 2a

IF DELIVERY URGENT BUT PICKUP & HOLD CONTACT
RIVERHEAD PCT (*(*(* 98TH PCT 98TH XXXXXXXX
XXXXXXXXXX
INFORMATION REQUEST HQ COMMAND GENERAL
REQUEST ALL PCTS ALL PCTS ALL PCTS XXXXXXXXX
PRECINCTS GEN REQUEST INFORMATION XXXXXXX
MAN'S UNIFORM GREY BRASS BUTTONS TOBACCO
POUCH FOUND REMAINS BURNT CHARRED BETH-
TOWN APT BLDG INCINERATOR XXX SUSPECT POSS
POWDER BURNS ON CLOTH XXXXX INFO OR ASSIST
UNSOLVED SHOOTING CASES CONTACT HQ XXX
HQ COMMAND DET LT DOUGHETY DOUGHERTY
DOUGHERTY XXXXXXXX
      X   XXXXXX   XXXXX   XXX
APRIL 13 GENERAL ALARM ALL PCTS BE ON LOCKOUT
WOMAN BLONDE AGE 24   5 FEET 4 INCHES 110 LBS
EXTREMELY ATTRACTIVE LAST SEEN WEARING BLUE S

POLICE DEPARTMENT
Police Headquarters Command
89 High Street, Isola

BY MESSENGER

TO: **BY MESSENGER**

Detective Stephen Louis Carella
87th Detective Squad
87th Precinct
711 Grover Avenue
Isola

Enclosed herewith is laboratory report received on the charred scraps of uniform garment taken from Bethtown incinerator, and forwarded as per your request received at 3:07 P.M. this afternoon.

Please note that report is preliminary and incomplete concerning matchbook discovered in pocket of uniform coat, but laboratory tests should be complete by tomorrow Tuesday April 14 and suggest you contact Lieutenant Samuel Grossman at that time should you desire further information in your case.

Sincerely,

Albert N. Dougherty

Det/Lt. Albert N. Dougherty
Headquarters Command

AD/rl
cc: Lt. Samuel Grossman

POLICE LABORATORY
89 High Street
Isola

LABORATORY REPORT

PR. CLK. VOUCHER NO.	3412
PCT. VOUCHER NO.	102-451
LABORATORY REPORT NO.	L-9034
TECHNICIAN	Peter Kronig
DATE RECEIVED	4/13
DATE THIS REPORT	4/13

NATURE OF EVIDENCE:

Burnt xx material and tobacco pouch found in
incinerator of apartment building

CONCLUSIONS:

1) Material is 60% nylon, 40% wool, apparently
   a xxx man's garment, grey in color, with
   brass buttons, no labels or identtags, no
   mfg name on buttons. Suggest that garment is
   uniform of some type.

2) For most part, garment burnt and charred by
   incinerator fire but indication xx of powder
   burn and the similar shotgun markings portion
   below left breast pocket. Metal stple in
   pocket xxx ashes indicates possible presence
   of matchbook. Tests to be concluded.

3) Tobacco pouch remains among ashes leather
   and rubber, smoldering rubber caused smell
   precipitating complaint. Tobacco scraps
   prwsent in untouched portion of pouch xxx
   mixture tradename Smoker's Pipe, Forale
   Moralco Tobacco, North Carolina; nationally
   distributed, soft pack and in tin.

4) Hair oil or other grease stain portion of
   garment which seems to be lapel, but tests
   run prove negative for compo or make.

REMARKS:

Should staple prove to have come from match
folder, report on same will follow.

9.

LIEUTENANT SAM GROSSMAN was one of those rare and vanishing individuals who take extreme pride in their work. As one of these, he was not the type of man who would wait for someone to call for information once that information was available. He had worked all day Monday on the matchbook remains which had been found with the charred uniform material in the incinerator. He was in receipt of a carbon copy of Dougherty's letter, and so he knew that Steve Carella was interested in the case. But even if the interested party hadn't been someone Grossman knew and liked, even if it had been an obscure patrolman pounding a beat on Majesta, Grossman's attitude would have remained the same. He was now in possession of information which could prove extremely valuable to the man investigating the case. He'd be damned if he was going to wait for that man to call him.

Nor had Grossman come into possession of this possibly valuable information through a stroke of luck, or even through the performance of a few simple laboratory tests. There are, you know, some laboratory tests which are extremely simple and which require no patience or perseverance. The reconstruction of burnt paper, unfortunately, does not fall into this category.

To begin with, the matchbook found with the material was contained by what the lab assumed to be the breast pocket of the jacket. The presence of the matchbook would not have been suspected at all had not one of Grossman's capable assistants noticed the glint of metal among the commingled ashes. Upon study, the metal turned out to be a tiny staple of the kind that holds matches to an outside cover. And once the presence of the remains of a matchbook had been determined, the real work lay just around the corner.

There were possibly four or five methods which could have been used to reconstruct the burnt matchbook, all of which required the patience of Job, the steadiness of Gibraltar, and the perseverance of Senator McCarthy. The method best suited to this particular document was discussed by Grossman and his assistants and, when they'd agreed on the proper approach, they rolled up their sleeves and got to work.

The first thing they did was to prepare a hot solution of one per cent gelatin in water. They then placed this solution in a flat developing pan. Then, with his assistant holding a glass plate as close to the ash as he could get, Grossman delicately and gingerly fanned the ash out onto the plate. No one breathed. Inching the plate toward the gelatin solution, the men slowly submerged it so that the solution just covered the surface of the plate. The ash had now been moistened, and the difficult and painstaking job of flattening it without destroying it remained to be done. Finally another glass plate was pressed into place above the first one, and both were squeezed together to dispel any air bubbles. The plates sandwiching the ash were then put into a printing frame and the suspect matchbook was photographed on an orthochromatic plate and printed on compression paper.

Simple.

It took five hours.

At the end of that time, the men went home.

On Tuesday morning, Sam Grossman called Steve Carella.

"Hello, Steve," he said. "I hate to barge in, but I've got a report on that match folder, and I couldn't see any good reason for waiting for you to call me. You don't mind, do you?"

"Not at all, Sam. How've you been?"

"Fine, thanks. I'm sorry that report on the uniform wasn't more helpful, Steve."

"It was a pretty good one."

"Not really. What the hell good is a report on a uniform if we can't tell you what kind of a uniform it was? Who cares whether it was nylon or wool or horse manure? You want to know whether it belonged to a bus driver or a mailman or whatever, am I right?"

"That's right, Sam. But some of that other stuff in the report—"

"Side effects and not really important. The folder may be something else again, though."

"Something good?"

"Considering what we had to work with, I think we did an amazing job."

"What have you got, Sam?"

"Well, to begin with, your suspect is twenty-three years old and probably a college graduate."

"Huh?"

"He has, at some time during the past year, smoked a marijuana cigarette and gone to bed with a blonde between the ages of nineteen and twenty-two."

"What!" Carella said, astonished.

"Yes," Grossman said. "And from this match folder ash, we were able to determine that our suspect served in the U.S. Cavalry as a gunner in a tank during the Korean War. In addition to that—"

"You got all this from that burnt matchbook?" Carella asked, and Grossman began laughing. The dawn broke slowly. Carella, holding the phone close to his violated ear, began to grin. "You bastard," he said. "I believed you for a minute there. What *did* you get from the matchbook?"

"The name of a hotel," Grossman said.

"Here? This city?"

"Yep."

"Shoot."

"The Hotel Albion. It's on Jefferson and South Third."

"Thank you, Sam."

"Don't thank me yet. You can probably pick up these matches in any cigar store in the city."

"Or maybe not, Sam. Maybe they're private hotel stock. The Albion, the Albion. That's not one of those big chain jobs like Hilton runs, is it?"

"No. It's a small quiet place right on Jefferson."

"That's what I thought. So maybe this *is* a break. In any case, I'll check it out. Thanks again, Sam."

"Right. How's Teddy?"

"Fine."

"And the twins?"

"Growing."

"Good. I'll be talking to you," Grossman said, and he hung up.

Carella looked at the hotel name he'd jotted onto the pad on his desk. He nodded, pulled the phone to him, and dialed the number of his home in Riverhead.

"Hello?" a sprightly voice answered.

"Fanny, this is Steve," he said. "Is Teddy still there, or did I miss her?"

"She's upstairs taking a bath. What is it, Steve? I was just feeding the twins."

"Fanny, I'm supposed to meet Teddy at three o'clock outside Bannerman's and I thought I'd be able to make it, but it doesn't look that way now. Would you just tell her I'll meet her for dinner at six at the Green Door? Have you got that? Six o'clock at—"

"I heard it the first time. Your son is screaming his head off at me, would you mind if I— Oh, holy mother of God!"

"What's the matter?"

"He's just thrown his spoon at April and hit her right in the eye with it! I don't know why I stay on in this madhouse. It seems to me—"

"Aw, you love us, you old bag," Carella said.

"An old bag is what I'll be before the year is out. Me who used to provoke street whistles not two months ago."

"Will you give her my message, dearie?" Carella asked, imitating her thick Irish brogue.

"Yes, I'll give her your message, dearie. And will you take a message from me, dearie?"

"What is it, dearie?"

"In the future, don't be calling at twelve noon because that is the time your darling little twins are being fed. And I've got my hands full enough with *two* Carellas not to have a third come bothering me. Is that clear, sir?"

"Yes, dearie."

"All right, I'll give your wife the message. Poor darling, she's been rushing about like a mad fool so that she'd meet you on time, and now you call with—"

"Goodbye, dearie," Carella said. "Go take the spoon out of April's eye."

He hung up, smiling, wondering how he and Teddy had ever managed to run a household without Fanny. Of course, he told himself, before Fanny there hadn't been the twins, either. In fact, had the twins not been born, Fanny would not have been hired as a two-weeks, postnatal nurse. And then when they'd moved into the new house, the monster which was on the market for back taxes, and Fanny's two weeks were up—well, it was difficult to say exactly what had prompted her to stay on at practically no salary, unless it was the fact that she had come to think of the Carellas as her own. Whatever her motive, and Carella never thought too much about motive except when he was working on a case, he was damned grateful for her existence. He sometimes had qualms that his children would grow up speaking with an Irish brogue since, by necessity, it was her speech they imitated and not the nonexistent speech of their mother. And only last week, he was nearly shocked out of his skin when young Mark said, "Dammit, dearie, I don't want to go to bed yet." But all in all, things were working out fine.

Carella stood up, opened the top drawer of his desk, took his gun and holster from it, and clipped it to the right side of his belt. He took his jacket from where it was draped over the back of his chair, put it on, and then tore the top page from the pad and stuck the sheet into his pocket.

"I probably won't be back for the rest of the day," he told Parker.

"Where you going?" Parker asked. "A movie?"

"No, a burlesque," Carella said. "I dig naked broads."

"Ha!" Parker said.

THEY'RE TEARIN DOWN the whole damn city, Meyer thought as he passed the building site of the new shopping center on Grover Avenue and the huge sign announcing that the work was being done by the Uhrbinger Construction Company. In truth, his observation was slightly in error since what they were doing was not tearing down the whole damn city but building up a major portion of it. As Lieutenant Byrnes had reported so accurately, the new shopping center would be a self-contained commercial operation with a large parking lot and with a conglomeration of services designed to lure housewives from everywhere in the city. The new stores were set in a low modern building which clashed violently with the surrounding grimy fingers of the slum tenements but which nonetheless presented an open area of clean space where the city dweller felt as if he could once again breathe while picking up his package of Wheaties or while cashing a twenty-dollar bill at the bank. Of course, entering the bank or the supermarket was still some weeks away from reality. The sites of these enterprises still crawled with workmen in overalls and sweat-stained shirts, so that perhaps Meyer's observation was not too far from the truth after all. The men rushing about with wooden beams and copper pipes *did* seem to be a demolition crew rather than a construction gang.

He sighed heavily, wondering how he would ever adjust to this new image of a neighborhood he had come to know quite well over the years. It was odd, he thought, but a person very rarely looked at the neighborhood where he spent his entire working day, until they began to make changes there. And then, quite suddenly, the old way, the old buildings, the old streets seemed to become very dear and the new way seemed to be an encroachment upon something private and familiar.

What the hell's the matter with you? he thought. *You like slums?*

"Yeah, I like slums.

Besides, the 87th Precinct isn't a slum. Part of it is a slum, yes. But you couldn't call the apartment houses lining Silvermine Road a slum. And some of the shops on The Stem were actually pretty fancy. And Smoke Rise, along the river, was as elegant as anything you were likely to find anywhere. So, all right, I'm rationalizing. For the most part, this is probably the crumbiest neighborhood in the city, and we've undoubtedly got the highest crime rate and our fire department is probably the busiest in the world, but I guess I like it here. I've never asked for a transfer and God knows there have been times when I was pretty damned disgusted, and yet I've never asked for a transfer, so I guess I really like it here.

Which, again, answers your question.

Yeah, I like slums.

I like slums because they are alive. I hate them because they breed crime and violence and filth—but I like them because they are alive.

It was twelve noon, and Meyer Meyer walked the streets of this slum that was alive, passing the construction site on Grover Avenue and then cutting up Thirteenth and walking north. The neighborhood was a rich amalgam of color, the color of flesh tones ranging from the purest white through the myriad shades of tan and brown and into the deepest brown, a brown bordering on black. Color, too, in the April finery of the precinct citizens, and color in the shop windows, bolts of blue silk and pink taffeta, and color on the sidewalk stands, the rich scarlet of ripe apples, and the subtle sunshine of bananas, and the purple bruise of grapes. And color, too, in the language of the streets, the profanity interlaced with the pseudo-musical jargon, the English of the underprivileged, and the bastardized Spanish, the Jewish peddler shouting his wares with a heavy Yiddish accent, the woman on the street corner wailing psalms to the indifferent blue sky of April. And all of it alive, all of it bursting with the juice of life, all of it raw and primitive somehow, stripped of all the nonsense of twentieth century ritual, that is what he meant by alive, this is what Meyer Meyer meant. For perhaps it was uncouth and uncivilized, but there was no question here of which fork to pick up first at the dinner table, and no question here of the proper way to introduce a duchess to a marquis, no question here of the little civilities, the little courtesies that separate us from the barbarians and at the same time steal from us our humanity. The precinct was as basic as life itself—and as rich.

And so he walked the streets there without fear even though he knew that violence could erupt around him at any moment. And he walked with a spring to his step, and he breathed deeply of air which stank of exhaust fumes but which was, nonetheless, the heady air of April, and he felt very glad to be alive.

The loft which David Raskin occupied was directly over a bank.

Mercantile Trust was the name of the bank. The name was engraved onto two bronze plaques, one of which decorated either side of the huge bronze bank doors which were open to admit the noonday traffic. A sign stuck to one of the open doors advised any interested party that the bank was changing quarters on April thirtieth and would be ready for business at its new location on May first. Meyer passed the bank, and the sign, and then climbed the steps to David Raskin's loft. A thumb-smeared sign hanging to the left of a huge fireproof door advised Meyer Meyer that he had located

DARASK FROCKS, INC.
*Women's Garments Of
Distinction*

Meyer did not knock. He went into the loft, stared down at the front of Margarita's low-cut smock for a second or two, asked for Dave Raskin and was ushered to the back of the loft where Raskin himself, standing in his undershirt and sweating profusely, was working with the girls pressing dresses. Raskin seemed to be in excellent high spirits.

"Hallo, hallo, Meyer!" he shouted. "What a day for pressing dresses, hah? A beautiful April day, what a day! It's nice out, hah, Meyer?"

"Beautiful," Meyer replied.

"April, that's the only time of the year. April is just right for everything, and I mean *everything*, Meyer, even an old man like me could say it, *everything*, Meyer!"

"You seem very happy today," Meyer said.

"Yes, yes, I'm happy like a little lark. You know why? I'll tell you why. To begin with, my crazyman hasn't called since Friday. Already this is Tuesday, and thank God nothing has come for me, no stationery, nothing, and no telephone calls, either." Raskin beamed. "So I'm happy. My girls aren't frightened, and I'm not pestered by this *meshugenuh* heckler. Also, I'm making money like a crazy thief."

"Good," Meyer said. "Maybe he's given up the game, huh? Figured he wasn't getting enough of a rise out of you, maybe." Meyer shrugged. "I'm glad to hear there've been no incidents since Friday, Dave. And of course I'm glad to hear your business is going so well."

"It couldn't be better. I got six dozen summer dresses yesterday for—guess what? Guess how much?"

"I don't know. How much?"

"A dollar each dress! Can you imagine something like that? These beautiful little summer things, sleeveless you know, and a little tight across the backside, I'll sell them like hot cakes, they'll come running all the way from Bethtown to buy these, I can sell them for four dollars each and they'll snap them up! I'm telling you, Meyer, I'll make a fortune. You saw the bank downstairs when you were coming in?"

"Yes," Meyer said, grinning.

"Okay. Right under where we're standing, right here under my feet, they got their vault. And into this vault, Meyer, I'm going to place thousands and thousands of dollars!"

"You'd better do it in a hurry," Meyer said, "because the bank is moving at the end of the month."

"Slow or in a hurry," Raskin said, chuckling, "I'll do it. I'll be known as the sultan of sexy garments, the lama of ladies' coats and dresses, the monarch of maternity clothes, the king of Culver Avenue! Me, David Raskin! If I keep buying dresses at a dollar each—*oi gevalt,* what a steal!—a dollar apiece and selling them for four dollars, Meyer, I could build my *own* bank! I won't need already the vault downstairs! Meyer, I'll be a millionaire! Can't you see me now? I'll only—"

The telephone rang. Raskin walked to it, still talking to Meyer, not breaking his conversational stride—

"—drive a Cadillac car, nothing else, and I'll wear silk underwear and in Miami Beach I'll be known as—"

He picked up the receiver.

"Hello—the biggest tipper on Collins Aven—"

"You son of a bitch!" the voice said. "Get out of that loft before the thirtieth, or I'll kill you!"

10.

THE HOTEL ALBION was on Jefferson Avenue near
South Third Street. A narrow green canopy stretched
from the hotel entrance to the street, and a doorman
wearing a green uniform and watching the girls strut
by in their April cottons, sprang to attention as Carella
approached, promptly pulled open one of the brass-
bound doors for him, and damn near threw a salute.

"Thank you," Carella said.

"You're-welcome-sir!" the doorman shouted smartly.

Carella raised his eyebrows appreciatively, went into
the lobby, and felt immediately that he had left the city
somewhere far behind him. The lobby was small and
quiet. Rich dark woods dominated the ceilings and the
walls. A thick Persian carpet covered the floor. The furniture was upholstered in vibrant red-and-green velvet,
and a huge cut-glass chandelier dominated the ceiling.
He felt that he was no longer in the United States, felt
somehow that Venice must look like this, rich and
vibrant and somehow decadent, somehow out of place
with the bustling twentieth century, a city misplaced in
time. He had never been to Venice, never indeed been
outside of America except during the war, and yet he
knew instinctively that this hotel would have fit into

that waterlogged city with uninhibited ease. He took off his hat and walked to the main desk. There was no one behind it. The hotel, in fact, seemed to be deserted, as if news of an impending atom bomb blast had sent everyone creaking downstairs to the wine cellar. A bell rested on the counter. He reached out with one hand and tapped it. The bell tinkled in the small lobby, cushioned by the velvet chairs and the Persian rug and the thick draperies on the windows, muffled by the overwhelming soddenness of the surrounding materials.

Carella heard the shuffle of soft-soled slippers sliding over steps. He looked up. A small thin man was coming down from the first floor. He walked with a slight stoop, a man in his sixties wearing a green eye shade and a brown cardigan sweater which had been knitted for him by a maternal aunt in New Hampshire. He looked like that Yankee-type fellow who plays the small-town hotel clerk in all the movies or the small-town postmaster, or the one the convertible pulls alongside to ask directions of, that guy, you know the one. He looked exactly like him. For a moment, listening to his creaky tread on the steps, watching him come into the cloistered silence of the lobby, Carella had the feeling that he was in a movie himself, that he would speak a line which had been written for him by some Hollywood mastermind and would be answered in turn with another scripted line.

"Hello, young feller," the Yankee-type said. "Can I be of some assistance?"

"I'm from the police," Carella said. He reached into his back pocket, pulled out his wallet, and opened it to where his shield was pinned to the leather.

"Um-hum," the Yankee said, nodding. "What can I do for you?"

"I don't believe I caught your name, sir," Carella said and knew instantly that the man would reply "Didn't throw it young feller," and almost winced before the words left the old-timer's mouth.

"Didn't throw it, young feller," the Yankee said. "But it's Pitt. Roger Pitt."

"How do you do, Mr. Pitt. My name is Detective Carella. We found the remains of a—"

"Carella, did you say?"

"Yes."

"Carella?"

"Yes."

"How d'do?" Pitt said.

"Fine, thank you. We found the remains of a uniform in an incinerator, sir, and we also found a matchbook from your hotel, the Hotel Albion, and there's the possibility that this uniform might tie in with a case we are investigating, and so I wondered—"

"*You* investigating the case?"

"Yes, sir."

"You a detective?"

"Yes, sir."

"Well, what was it you wanted to know?"

"To begin with, do you know anyone named Johnny?"

"Johnny what?"

"We don't know. But he might have been the person who was wearing this uniform."

"Johnny, huh?"

"Yes. Johnny."

"Sure."

The lobby was silent.

"You know him?" Carella asked.

"Sure."

"What's his last name?"

"Don't know."

"But . . ."

"Lotte's feller," Pitt said.

"Lotte?"

"Lotte Constantine. Lives right upstairs. He's been by here a lot, Johnny."

"I see. And this Lotte Constantine is his girl friend, is that right?"

"That's right," Pitt said.

"How old a man would you say this Johnny was?"

"Was?" Pitt asked quickly, his eyes narrowing. "In his sixties, I guess."

Carella reached into his inside jacket pocket. He pulled out a photograph encased in lucite. He put it face up on the counter. It was the photo of the dead man which had run in the metropolitan dailies.

"Is that the man you're thinking of?" Carella asked.

Pitt studied the photo. "Course," he said, "I never seen him in a bathing suit. Or asleep."

"But is that him?"

"It could be. This ain't a very good picture, is it?"

"Perhaps not."

"I mean, it looks like Johnny, and yet it don't. There seems to be something missing."

"There is," Carella said.

"What's that?"

"Life. The man in that picture is dead."

"Oh." Pitt seemed to wash his hands of the matter quite suddenly. "Look, maybe you better ask Lotte. I mean, she'd know better than me."

"Where can I reach her?"

"She's right upstairs. I'll give her a ring, and maybe she'll come on down to the lobby."

"No, that's all right, I'll go up. I wouldn't want—"

"Won't take a second to buzz her," Pitt said. He went to the switchboard and plugged in one of the rubber snakes there. Holding the earpiece to his right ear, he waited a moment and then said, "Lotte? This is Roger downstairs. There's a feller here asking questions about Johnny. Yes, that's right, *your* Johnny. Well I thought maybe you wouldn't mind talking to him. Well, he's from the police, Lotte. Now, Lotte, there's no need to go getting upset. No, he seems to be a very nice young feller. Okay, I'll tell him."

Pitt put down the headset, pulled out the plug, and said, "She'll be right down. She got a little upset when she heard you was a cop."

"Everybody gets upset when they hear that," Carella said, smiling.

He leaned against the counter and waited for the arrival of Miss Lotte Constantine. If there was one thing he disliked, he supposed it was interrogating old people. Actually, there were a great many things he disliked, and a great many people who would testify to the fact that Steve Carella was, on occasion, a god-dammed crab. So it was an understatement to say, "If there was *one* thing he disliked." But, among his other dislikes, interrogating oldsters took high priority, and interrogating old *women* particularly annoyed him. He had no idea why he disliked old women unless it had something to do with the fact that they were no longer young. In any case, he found talking to them trying to his patience, and he was not now looking forward to meeting Miss Lotte Constantine, the girl friend of a man who had been in his sixties.

He watched a luscious redhead in a very tight skirt as she navigated her way down the carpet-covered steps from the first floor. Because the skirt was so tight, the girl had lifted it above her knees, and she walked downstairs with her head slightly bent, watching the steps, a hank of red hair falling over one eye.

"Here she is now," Pitt said, and Carella turned to look into the lobby, saw no one there, and then looked up the steps beyond the redhead, still seeing no one, and then the redhead was swiveling over to the desk with a lubricated hip and thigh movement that made him seasick, and she extended a hand tipped with scarlet claws and she said in the sexiest voice since Mae West was a girl, "Hello, I'm Lotte Constantine."

Carella swallowed hard and said, "You? Are? Miss Constantine?"

The girl smiled. Her lips moved back from her teeth like tinted clouds pulling aside to let the sunshine through. A dimple appeared in either cheek. Her green eyes flashed. "Yes," she said. "And you are . . . ?"

"Detective Carella," he said, struggling to regain some of his composure. He had expected a woman in her late fifties and when he'd been confronted with a *zaftig* redhead who'd seemed at a distance, to be in her early thirties, he'd been flabbergasted, to say the least. At close range, however, he realized this girl was no older than twenty-three, bursting all over the place with youth and vitality and abundant flesh that threatened every stitch of clothing she wore. So he automatically thought of the old man who had been Johnny Something-or-other, and then he automatically thought of *Middle of the Night,* and Oh my, he thought, oh my, oh my.

"Could we sit down and talk a little, Miss Constantine?" he asked.

"Certainly," she said. She smiled shyly, as if she were unused to sitting with strange men. Her lashes fluttered. She sucked in a deep breath and Carella turned away, pretending to look for a chair.

"We can sit over there," Lotte said, and she began leading the way. Carella walked behind her. Married man and all, he had to admit this girl had the plumpest, most inviting bottom he had seen in a dog's age. He was tempted to pinch her, but he restrained himself. I'm much too young for her, he thought, and he grinned.

"Why are you smiling?" the girl asked, sitting and crossing her legs.

"I was only thinking you're a lot younger than I imagined you would be."

"What did you imagine?"

"Truthfully?"

"Of course," Lotte said.

"A woman in her fifties."

"Why?"

"Well . . ." Carella shrugged. He took the picture from his pocket again. "Know this man?"

She glanced at the picture and nodded immediately. "Yes," she said. "What's happened to him?" She did not blench or gasp or wince or blush or grimace. She simply said, "Yes," and then, matter-of-factly and just as quickly, said, "What's happened to him?"

"He's dead," Carella said.

She nodded. She said nothing. Then she gave a tiny shrug of her shoulders, and then she nodded again.

"Who was he?" Carella asked.

"Johnny."

"Johnny who?"

"Smith."

Carella stared at her.

"Yes, Smith," she said. "John Smith."

"And who are you? Pocahontas?"

"I don't think that's funny. He told me his name was John Smith. Why shouldn't I believe him?"

"Why shouldn't you indeed? How long had you known him, Miss Constantine?"

"Since January."

"When did you see him last?"

"Last month sometime."

"Can you remember when last month?"

"The end of the month."

"Were you and he very serious?"

Lotte shrugged. "I don't know," she said wistfully. "What's serious?"

"Were you . . . more than just friends, Miss Constantine?"

"Yes," she said abruptly. She nodded, as if lost in thought, as if alone in the silent lobby that reminded Carella of Venice. "Yes." She nodded again. "Yes, we were more than just friends." She lifted her eyes and then tossed her head and brushed a long strand of red hair away from her forehead. Defiantly she said, "We were lovers."

"All right," Carella said. "Any idea who'd want him dead, Miss Constantine?"

"No," She paused. "How—how did he die?"

"I was wondering when you'd get to that."

Lotte Constantine looked Carella straight in the eye. "What the hell are you?" she asked. "A tough cop?"

Carella did not answer.

"Do I *have* to want to know how he died?" she said. "Isn't it enough that he's dead?"

"Most people would be curious," Carella said.

"I'm not *most* people," she answered. "I'm me. Lotte Constantine. You're a great one, aren't you? A regular little IBM machine, aren't you? Punch-punch, put in the card and out comes the right answer. You come here telling me Johnny is dead and then you start asking a lot of fool questions and then you tell me what the reaction of *most* people would be, well the hell with you, Detective Whatever-your-name-is, *most* twenty-two-year-old girls wouldn't fall in love with a man who's sixty-six years old, yes, sixty-six, don't look so goddamned surprised, that's how old Johnny was, so don't go telling me what *most* people would do, you can take *most* people and drown them, for all I care."

"He was shot at close range with a shotgun," Carella said, and he did not take his eyes from her face. Nothing crossed that face. No expression, not the slightest nuance of emotion.

"All right," she said, "he was shot at close range with a shotgun. Who did it?"

"We don't know."

"*I* didn't."

"Nobody said you did."

"Then what the hell are you doing here?"

"We're only trying to make a positive identification, Miss Constantine."

"Well, you've made it. Your dead man is John Smith."

"Would you say that name was a great deal of help, Miss Constantine?"

"What the hell do you want from me? It was *his* name, not mine."

"And he never told you his real name?"

"He said his name was John Smith."

"And you believed him?"

"Yes."

"Suppose he'd told you his name was John Doe?"

"Mister, I'd have believed him if he told me his name was Joseph Stalin. Now how about that?"

"That's how it was, huh?" Carella asked.

"That's how it was."

"What'd he do for a living?" Carella asked.

"Retired. He was getting social security."

"And the uniform?"

"What uniform?" Lotte Constantine asked with wide open eyes.

"The uniform. The one somebody stripped off of him and dumped into an incinerator."

"I don't know what you're talking about."

"You never saw him in a uniform?"

"Never."

"Did he have any job? Besides the retirement money. Did he run an elevator or anything?"

"No. I gave him—" Lotte stopped suddenly.

"Yes?"

"Nothing."

"You gave him money? Is that what you were about to say?"

"Yes."

"Where did he live, Miss Constantine?"

"I . . . I don't know."

"What do you mean, you—"

"I don't know where he lived. He . . . he came here a lot."

"To stay?"

"Sometimes."

"For how long?"

"The . . . the longest he ever stayed was . . . was for two weeks."

"Pitt know about this?"

Lotte shrugged. "I don't know. What difference does it make? I'm a good customer. I've been living in this hotel ever since I came to the city four years ago. What difference would it make if an old man—" She caught herself, stopped speaking, and returned Carella's level gaze. "Stop staring at me as if I was Lolita or something. I loved him."

"And he never mentioned a uniform, is that right? Or a job?"

"He mentioned a deal."

"What kind of a deal?" Carella asked, leaning forward.

The girl uncrossed her legs. "He didn't say."

"But he did mention a deal?"

"Yes."

"When was this?"

"The last time I saw him."

"What did he say?"

"Only that he had a deal cooking with the deaf man."

They were sitting in velvet chairs around a small coffee table in an ornate lobby which suddenly went as still as death.

"The deaf man?" Carella said.

"Yes."

He sucked in a deep breath.

"Who's the deaf man?"

"I don't know."

"But Johnny had some kind of a deal with him, right?"

"Yes. That's what he said. He said he had a deal with the deaf man, and that he'd be very rich soon. He was going—We were going to get married."

"The deaf man," Carella said aloud. He sighed heavily. "Where can I reach you if I need you, Miss Constantine?"

"Either here or at The Harem Club."

"What do you do there?"

"I'm a cigarette girl. I sell cigarettes. That's where I met Johnny. At the club."

"He bought cigarettes from you?"

"No. He smokes—he *smoked*—a pipe. I sold him pipe tobacco."

"Smoker's Pipe?" Carella asked. "Was that the brand?"

"Why . . . why, yes. How—"

"Here's my card, Miss Constantine," Carella said. "If you should think of anything else that might help me, give me a call, won't you?"

"Like what?"

"What do you mean?"

"Like what do you want me to call you about? How do I know what'll help you?"

"Well, any further information about this deaf man would—"

"I don't know anything else about him."

"Or anything Johnny might have said regarding this deal of hi—"

"I told you everything he said."

Carella shrugged.

"You want your card back?" Lotte Constantine asked.

THAT NIGHT, the deaf man celebrated.

Perhaps things were going well at the ice-cream store behind the construction site. Or perhaps he was simply anticipating what would begin happening the next day. Perhaps, like a good general, he was drinking a symbolic toast on the eve of battle.

The symbolic toast, in this case, was the taking of a nineteen-year-old girl whose attributes were surely not mental.

But the deaf man, you see, was an economical man and a man who never lost sight of his goals. He was not interested, that evening, in a discussion of mathematics. Nor was he interested in learning about the ambitions or tribulations or strivings for independence or strugglings for realization of self of any member of the opposite sex. He was interested in making love, pure and simple. He had been casing his love partner in much the same way he'd have cased the site of a future robbery. He had been casing her for two weeks, attracted by her obvious beauty at first—the girl was a brunette with luminous brown eyes and a full pouting mouth; her breasts, even in the waitress uniform she wore, were large and inviting; her legs beneath the hem of the white garment were splendidly curved to a trim ankle—and attracted, too, by the smooth-skinned freshness of her youth.

But youth and beauty were not, to the deaf man,

qualities which when taken alone would assure a good bed partner. He had explored the girl further.

He had noticed that her luminous eyes carried a challenge, and that the challenge was directed toward any man who walked into the restaurant. He was surprised to find such blatancy in the eyes of a nineteen-year-old, and he tried to evaluate it. He did not want a nymphomaniac. He knew that satisfaction could be multiplied to infinity when allowed to ricochet off the simultaneous pleasures of two, and he had no desire to become involved with an insatiable woman. At the same time, he did not want an uninitiated girl who would allow the evening to dissolve into a literal shower of blood, sweat and tears. The challenge in this girl's eyes boldly stated that she had been had, and that she could be had again, and that the taking might well be worth the efforts of whoever successfully met the challenge. Pleased with what he saw, he continued his surveillance.

The girl's breasts, while admittedly comfortable-looking, could have amounted to nothing more than so much excess fat imbued with a nonexistent sexuality by a culture with an obsessive mammary fetish—were it not for the way the girl carried them. She knew they were there. She never once took them for granted. Her every motion, her every step indicated an extreme awareness of the rich curve below her throat. He was sure that her awareness was sensual, an awareness so total could be nothing else. And, observing her secure knowledge, he never once doubted her potential passion.

Her legs, too, indicated a promising sensuality. They were well-shaped, with a full, curving calf that dropped with surprising grace and swiftness to a narrowness of ankle and a sharpness of arch. The girl was a waitress, and her expected footgear should have been flat-soled shoes. But she chose to emphasize the shape of her leg, and whereas she did not commit the folly of wearing a bona fide high-heeled spike she nonetheless wore a pump with a French heel that was both flattering and promising. She used her legs in two ways. One was strictly utilitarian. They were strong legs, and they carried her from table to table with speed and directness. The other use was calculated and strictly decorative. She used her legs as pistons to manipulate her buttocks.

Casually, the deaf man struck up a conversation with her. The girl, as he'd suspected, would not qualify for a teaching position at Harvard. Their first conversation, as he later recalled it, went something like this. He had ordered a chocolate eclair for dessert.

The girl said, "I see you have a sweet tooth."

"Yes, indeed," the deaf man said.

She had cocked one eyebrow coquettishly. "Well, sweets for the sweet," she answered, and swiveled away from the table.

Slowly, he had engaged her in further conversations, strengthening his opinion of her potential. When he finally asked her out, he was certain she would accept immediately—and she did.

That evening, the fourteenth of April, he had dazzled her with his brilliance at dinner. She sat in wide-eyed wonder, contributing little to the conversation, fascinated with his speech. They walked under a star-scattered sky later, guided imperceptibly by the deaf man to an apartment on Franklin Street. When the deaf man suggested that they go up for a drink, the girl demurred slightly, and he felt a quickening of passion; this would not be a pushover; there would be a struggle and a chase to whet his appetite.

They did not talk much in the apartment. They sat on the modern couch in the sunken living room and the girl took off her shoes and pulled her knees up under her, and the deaf man poured two large snifters of brandy, and they sat rolling the glasses in their hands, the girl peeking over the edge of her glass the way she had seen movie stars do, the deaf man drinking the brandy slowly, savoring the taste of the lip-tingling alcohol, anticipating what he would do to this girl, anticipating his pleasure with a slow cruelty that began mounting inside him, a carefully controlled cruelty—control, he reminded himself, control.

By midnight, the girl was totally witless.

Half naked, she did not know what was happenng to her, nor did she care; she had no mind; she possessed only a body which was alive in his arms as he carried her down a long white corridor to the first of three bedrooms. Her stockings were off, she realized; he had taken off her stockings; firmly cradled in his arms, her skirt pulled back, she realized she was naked beneath the skirt, her blouse hung open; he had somehow removed her bra without taking off her blouse, she could see the white beating expanse below her neck and suddenly he was standing over her and she was looking up at him expectantly and seeing him and feeling sudden fear, the fear of true and total invasion, and then she knew nothing.

Nothing. She knew nothing. She was drawn toward a blazing sun, pulled away from it, he knew nothing inviolate, every secret place of her succumbed totally to his vicious onslaught, every aching pore of her was his to claim, she was drugged, she was not herself, she was not anyone she knew, she had been carried mindlessly to the edge of totality, violated and adored, cherished and possessed, worshiped and ravaged, there was no cessation, no beginning and no end, she would remember this night with longing and excitement, remember it too with shame and guilt as the night she surrendered privacy to a total stranger, with an abandon she had not known she'd possessed.

At three in the morning, he gave her a gift. He crossed the room and she was too weary to follow him even with her eyes, and suddenly he was beside her again, opening a long carton, pulling the filmy silk from within its tissue paper folds.

"Put this on," he said.

She obeyed him. She would have obeyed whatever command he'd given her. She rose and pulled the black gown over her head.

"And your shoes."

She obeyed. She felt somewhat dizzy, and yet she longed to be in his arms again. The short nightgown ended abruptly above her thighs. She felt his eyes upon her, sweeping the curve of her leg, the long accentuated curve dropping to the high-heeled spike.

"Come here," he said, and she went to him hungrily.

11.

WELL, THE FIFTEENTH was the middle of the month, and a hell of a month it was shaping up to be so far.

All things considered, and not even taking into account the petty little daily crimes which bugged every man working the squad, April so far—despite the lovely weather—was beginning to assume the characteristics of a persistent migraine. And no man on the squad had a bigger headache than Meyer Meyer.

Meyer, it seemed, had become the man officially assigned to the Heckler Case. That it was now a bona fide "case," there seemed to be no doubt. What had started with David Raskin as a simple series of threatening phone calls and foolish pranks had somehow mushroomed into something with the proportions of an epidemic. Slowly, bit by bit, the complaints had come in until the list of shop or restaurant owners reporting threatening calls and acts of harassment had grown to a total of twenty-two. Some of the complainants were truly terrified by the threats; others were simply annoyed by the disruption of their business. Meyer, taking the calls, became more and more convinced that one man, or group of men, was responsible for the heckling. In any case, the *modus operandi* seemed identical.

But what he couldn't understand was what the hell was so important about April thirtieth?

Or why these particular shops had been chosen? A haberdashery, a Chinese restaurant, a tie store, a leather goods shop, a candy shop—what was so important about these particular locations?

Meyer simply couldn't figure it.

Nor was Steve Carella much better off with his case, the case of the almost-naked dead man found in Grover Park. Why, he wondered, had anyone wanted old John Smith dead? Or, for that matter, why would the dead man have taken an assumed name? And such a phony one at that? John Smith! My God! How many hotel and motel registers in the United States carried that pseudonym daily? And who was this deaf guy? And why had twenty-two-year-old Lotte Constantine wanted to invest time and money in sixty-six-year-old John Smith? (The obvious alias rankled every time he thought of it.) The deaf man. Who? And he pulled a face at the ironies of fate. The one person who meant everything in the world to him was a deaf mute, his wife Teddy. And now his adversary was someone known only as the deaf man. The juxtaposition was irony with a knife-edge, but Carella was not amused. He was only puzzled. Truly and honestly puzzled.

And when it's going bad, you might expect the people who are causing you trouble to let up for a while, mightn't you? When two stalwart and intelligent detectives were struggling with two separate nuts which seemed uncrackable and which caused both men a considerable loss of sleep, when these two intrepid protectors of the innocent, these indefatigable investigators, these supporters of law and order, when these two darned nice fellows were trying their utmost to get out from under two miserable cases, wouldn't it have been decent and only cricket to leave them alone, to allow them a respite from their torments? Friends, wouldn't it have been the decent thing to do? Cop lovers of the world, wouldn't it have been the only nice way, the only good way, the only fair way?

Sure.

On April 15, which was a balmy spring day blowing fresh breezes off the River Harb to the north, the harassment began anew.

It began with a difference, however.

It seemed to be concentrated against Dave Raskin, as if all armies had suddenly massed on poor Raskin's frontiers and were pressing forward with their spring invasion. If you looked at this sudden offensive one way, you could assume the enemy was doing his best to plague Raskin and the cops. But if you looked at it another way, you could think of the concentrated attack as a guide, a signpost, a singling-out of the one store among twenty-five, a divine hand pointing, a divine voice saying, "Look and ye shall see; knock and it shall be opened unto ye."

Meyer Meyer looked, but he didn't see at first. Later on, when he knocked, it was truly opened unto him. And he didn't for a moment suspect that this was

what was desired of him, that the sudden spring offensive against Dave Raskin's loft was designed to alert a
police department which, with all due respect to those
stalwarts, seemed to be somewhat asleep. You can play
percentages only if your opponents are playing some
sort of percentages themselves. Whatever the deaf
man's plan, it wouldn't work if the cops didn't at least
suspect what he was up to. And so the tanks rolled
into high gear, churning through the spring mud, and
the dive bombers warmed up on the airfields and took
off into the chill early morning air and from across the
city, the big guns began thundering against poor Dave
Raskin's loft.

At ten o'clock on the morning of April 15, four
hundred and thirty folding chairs were delivered to
Raskin.

They were piled on the floor, and against the wall,
and on the tables, and in the hallway, and down the
steps, and some of them even overflowed onto the
sidewalk. David Raskin insisted that he had not
ordered any folding chairs, but the truck driver was a
persistent man who told Raskin he always delivered
what he was supposed to deliver and if Raskin had a
beef he could call the chair company and discuss it
with them. David Raskin called both the chair company and the 87th Squad, and then he paced the floor
of his loft waiting for the chair people to come pick
up the chairs again and waiting for Meyer Meyer to
do something. There was, naturally, nothing Meyer
Meyer could do except call the chair company who
confirmed the fact that David Raskin had ordered the

chairs sometime last week for delivery that day which, again naturally, David Raskin had not done.

So Meyer Meyer ran his hand over his bald head and cursed in pig Latin, a trick he had learned as a boy because his mother had not allowed swearing in her house. And David Raskin paced the floor of his loft and cursed in very loud English which, fortunately, his Puerto Rican girls did not understand too well.

At twelve-thirty on the nose, the caterers arrived.

The caterers arrived and with them they brought enough food to feed the entire Russian Army together with a few Yugoslavian partisans, or so it seemed. Actually they brought only enough food to feed the four hundred and thirty lunch guests who were to occupy the four hundred and thirty folding chairs. They brought little bottles containing Martinis and Manhattans, and they brought celery and olives and carrot sticks, and they brought onion soup, and they brought roast beef and turkey and candied sweet pota-toes and asparagus tips au gratin and coffee, tea or milk, and orange sherbet and chocolate layer cake and little mints and—man, David Raskin positively flipped! The caterers insisted that he had called them and ordered this veritable feast and Raskin told them he didn't know four hundred and thirty people in the entire world, let alone four hundred and thirty people he would care to invite for lunch, and the caterers said he had ordered the stuff, they had prepared all the food, what the hell were they supposed to do with it all, this wasn't folding chairs which you could return, this was food, food, FOOD, especially cooked and prepared for the occasion, who was going to pay the bill?

"The man who ordered this *megillah!*" Raskin shouted.

"*You* ordered it!" the caterers shouted back.

"I ordered nothing! Get it out of here! Get it out! Out! Out! Out!"

And that was when the orchestra arrived.

There were fourteen musicians in the orchestra, and they were all carrying their instruments, instruments like trombones and saxophones, and a bass drum, and a bass fiddle, and trumpets, and even a French horn or two. And they were also carrying music stands and they wanted to know where they should set up, and Raskin told the leader—a small man with a Hitler mustache and a personality to match—that he could go set up in the River Dix, just get the hell out of his loft, he did not order any damned orchestra! To which the man with the Hitler mustache said, "You came down to the union personally and left a twenty-dollar deposit when you hired the band!"

"*Me!*" Raskin shouted. "*I* came down to the *firshtunkenuh* union? I don't even know where your dirty union *is, I* came down? Get out of here with those drums!" and that was when the men returned to pick up the chairs, and the way Raskin finally got everybody out of the place was by calling Meyer again, who rushed over and tried to settle things as best he could.

That was on the fifteenth, and a jolly Wednesday that was, by George.

On Monday the twentieth, only four items arrived, and they were obviously a mistake.

The four items were:

2 PICKS
2 SHOVELS

David Raskin mopped his feverish brow.

"I didn't order these," he said.

The delivery boy shrugged and consulted the order slip. "Two picks and two shovels. Says so right here."

Patiently, Raskin said, "I didn't order them. You see, there's a crazy man who—"

"Two picks and two shovels," the delivery boy said firmly. "Deliver to the loft at twelve thirteen Culver Avenue. See? Says so right here. Can you read that, mister?"

"I can read it, but I didn't order—"

"Deliver to the loft at twelve thirteen Culver Avenue after Darask Frocks, Inc. has vacated the premises. Oh." The delivery boy's voice dropped as he continued reading. "Call FRederick 7-3548 before delivery. Oh."

"I got news for you," Raskin said. "That's my phone number, but I ain't never vacating these premises. So forget this delivery."

"They've already been paid for," the delivery boy said.

And suddenly, David Raskin felt extremely shrewd. Suddenly, David Raskin was confronted with the single clue which would split this mystery wide open, suddenly David Raskin was presented with that opportunity which comes to all men but once in a lifetime, the chance to solve something, the chance to be a hero.

"Tell me," he said casually, though his heart was pounding, *"who ordered the picks and shovels?"*

The delivery boy looked at his slip. "Here's the name of the man right here," he said.

"What is it? What is it?" Raskin asked excitedly.

"L. Sordo," the delivery boy replied.

NOW, WHEREAS Meyer Meyer, by his own admission, had not read "The Red-headed League," he *had* read a book by a gentleman known as Ernest Hemingway, and the title of that beautiful volume was *For Whom the Bell Tolls,* which is about a lovely guerilla girl laid in Spain. There is a memorable character called El Sordo in the book and, as any half-wit knows, *el sordo* in Spanish means "the deaf one" or, because of the masculine *o* ending, "the deaf man."

It seemed obvious to Meyer at this point that someone with a hearing deficiency was the person responsible for the various threats everyone had been receiving. The gentleman at the Sandhurst Paper Company in New Bedford, Massachusetts, had told Meyer not too long ago that the person who'd ordered the envelopes had said, "Excuse me, but would you talk a little louder? I'm slightly deaf, you know."

And now someone had ordered two picks and two shovels to be delivered *after* Darask Frocks, Inc. vacated the loft, but those picks and shovels had obviously been delivered by mistake *before* Raskin got out, and the man who'd ordered those tools was a man who called himself L. Sordo. So not only was there a strong possibility that this was the same man who'd ordered the Massachusetts envelopes but there was a sneaking suspicion on Meyer's part that this fellow wanted to be known, he wanted to be sure he was given credit for his handiwork, wanted to be certain his byline appeared on everything he created, El Sordo, The Deaf Man.

And sitting not three feet away from Meyer Meyer at his own desk was Detective Steve Carella who was fairly convinced that a person who'd used the alias of John Smith had had something cooking with someone known only as the deaf man, and that if he could get some sort of a lead onto this deaf man fellow, he would be a lot closer toward solving the case.

The trouble was, of course, that Meyer Meyer was working on a series of threatening phone calls and harassments and Steve Carella was working on a shotgun homicide and neither man saw fit to discuss his respective case with his colleague. That was the way things were going that April. In a squadroom where everyone generally was willing to discuss anything and everything involving police work, toilet training, marital technique and pennant races, nobody seemed too talkative that April. Even Bert Kling, who managed to finish his volume of Sherlock Holmes stories between phone conversations with his fiancée, failed to discuss any of the yarns with Meyer Meyer. That's the way things were going that April.

Well, on Monday of the following week, the advertisement appeared in the two morning dailies which carried classified advertisements. The ad read:

WANTED

Redheads! Redheads! Redheads! To model women's dresses in swank Culver Avenue showroom. No experience necessary. Apply 12 noon. Darask Frocks, Inc. 1213 Culver Avenue, Mr. Raskin. Redheads! Redheads! Redheads!

And, man, the redheads came out of the sewers that day! No one in the world would have believed there were so many redheads in the entire city. Rome is supposed to be the city of redheads, but at twelve noon on April 27 there were dozens, hundreds, thousands of redheads of every conceivable size, shape, and hue standing in a disorderly line in front of Dave Raskin's loft, trailing past the open doors of the bank and going around the corner. There were fat redheads and skinny redheads, tall ones and short ones, busty ones and flat-chested ones, hippy ones and straight ones, flaming redheads and auburn redheads, natural orange redheads and bleached scarlet redheads, and each and every one of them wanted to see Dave Raskin about this job of modeling women's dresses in the swank Culver Avenue showroom. The line sailed clear around the block and past the bank and into the open doorway alongside the bank and up the steps and into the loft where Dave Raskin frantically tried to explain he was not hiring any damn models that day.

And all of a sudden, the dawn broke.

All of a sudden, Meyer Meyer tipped to what was afoot.

Just the way he was supposed to.

12.

HE SLAMMED THE PHONE DOWN angrily and said,
"Raskin again! The heckler sent him thousands of redheads! I'm telling you, Bert, this is driving me nuts. All
of a sudden, he's concentrating on poor Dave. What
does he want from the guy? What's he after?"

Kling, working hard at his desk, looked up and
said, "What's a four-letter word for walking sticks?"

"Huh?"

"The puzzle," Kling said, tapping the newspaper on
his desk.

"Is that all you've got to do with your time?"

"What's a four-letter—"

"There are no four-letter words in my vocabulary."

"Come on. Walking sticks. A four-letter word."

"Legs," Meyer answered. "So what could that crazy
nut want from Raskin? Why does he want him out of
that loft?"

"You think it *could* be?"

"Could be what? What are you talk—"

"Legs."

"I don't know. Don't bother me. Why did he stop
calling all the other guys? Twenty-three stores by the
last count, and all of a sudden silence except for
Raskin. What does he want from him? His money?

But who keeps money in a loft? Where people keep money is in—"

Meyer stopped talking. A look of shocked recognition had crossed his face. His eyes had opened wide, and his mouth had dropped open in surprise. The word caught in his throat, refusing to budge.

"What's a four-letter word that means a slope or acclivity?" Kling asked.

"A bank," Meyer said breathlessly, pushing the word out of his mouth.

"Yeah, that's right. Like the bank of a riv—"

"A bank," Meyer said again, his mouth still hanging open, a dazed and glassy look in his eyes.

"I heard you the—"

"A bank!" he said. "The bank! The bank under the loft! The bank, Bert! The goddammed bank!"

"Huh? What?"

"That's why he wants Raskin out! He wants to chop through that loft floor and come through the ceiling of the bank vault! That's what those picks and shovels were for! But they were delivered too early by mistake! He's going to rob that bank, but he's got to do it before the thirtieth of April because the bank is moving then! *That's* why all the pressure on Raskin! Oh man, how could I have—"

"Yeah, that was a good story," Kling said, not looking up from his paper.

"*What* was a good story?" Meyer asked confused.

"The Red-headed League," Kling said.

Meyer shrugged. "Come on," he said. "I want to talk to the lieutenant.

He grabbed Kling's wrist and dragged him across the room. He almost forgot to knock on Byrnes's door.

THE SQUADROOM WAS EMPTY when Carella entered it not five minutes later. He looked around, yelled "Anybody home?" and went to his desk. "Hey, where is everybody?" he yelled again.

The door to Byrnes's office opened briefly. Meyer's bald head appeared. "In here, Steve," he said, and then closed the door again instantly.

Carella took off his jacket, rolled up his sleeves, and frowned again. He had begun frowning a lot lately. He knew exactly why.

Ever since he had learned the dead man's alias—the patently transparent "John Smith"—he had been going through the files of known criminals in an attempt to locate the man's real name. He had found nothing even resembling the dead man. It was now the twenty-eighth of April and he seemed no closer to identifying his man—much less solving his case—than he'd been on the day the body was discovered in the park. He supposed that set some sort of record for inept detection but, by Christ, he was really trying, and nothing seemed to jell. He had considered the possibility that the shapely Lotte Constantine had done in the old man herself, and he had assigned Bert Kling to a surveillance of the girl while he himself had tried to get a line on her. From what he could gather, the girl was perfectly clean. She had come to the city from Indiana some four years back. She had held a

series of unrelated jobs before landing the job as cigarette girl in the Harem Club two years back. She had never been in trouble with the police. Her employer at the Harem described her as "a lovely, quiet girl." Her affection for the dead "John Smith" had apparently been very real. Her co-workers at the club informed Kling that since she'd met the man who called himself "Johnny," she had not dated another man, even though men at the club were constantly asking her. Bert Kling, reporting on the girl's movements, stated that she generally slept late, went to dancing school on Mondays, Wednesdays and Fridays, dramatics classes on Tuesdays and Thursdays, and reported for work daily at the Harem at 8:00 P.M. where she donned her abbreviated costume and black net stockings, not removing them until three in the morning, at which time she went directly home. Kling had been tailing her since April eighteenth and this was the twenty-eighth. In one of his reports, Bert Kling wrote, *"She has a lovely behind, this girl, and I don't mind tailing her. But Steve, I think she's clean. I think I'm wasting my time."*

Carella was inclined to agree, but he decided to maintain the surveillance for at least a few more days.

But now, considering the seeming innocence of this girl, considering the fact that she and "John Smith" really did seem to be in love with each other, it occurred to him that the man might possibly have been telling her the truth. In fact, Carella could find no really good reason for assuming the man had lied. And, in thinking about the situation, Carella realized

that he had fallen into the trap of accepting the nearest and easiest conclusion without bothering to search
for the more elusive but perhaps more rewarding
answer. And, as frequently happened in such cases, the
real truth was as close to hand as was the *apparent*
truth. In this case, it was even closer.

John Smith was an obvious alias.

That was the apparent truth.

The girl Lotte Constantine had told Carella that
John Smith was retired, and living on his social security checks. Carella pulled the Isola telephone direc-
tory to him and looked up "UNITED STATES
GOVERNMENT" and, under that, "SOCIAL SECU-
RITY ADMIN." The small type advised Carella to
"See US Govt Health Educ&Welfare Dept of," so he
looked up "HEALTH EDUC & WELFARE DEPT OF"
on the same page but slightly to the left, under that he
found:

> Social Security Admin—
>   Bur of Old Age & Survivors Ins—
>   For Info Call The Office Nearest Your
>   Home—
>   Isola Dist Offices—

And beneath that were four listings for offices in
Isola, none of which were near his home (which happened to be in Riverhead) but one of which was fairly
close to the squadroom of the 87th Precinct, from
whence he was making the phone call. Carella asked
Murchison for an outside line, and he dialed the num-

ber. He identified himself, told the switchboard operator what information he was seeking, and was
promptly connected to a woman with a kindly voice
who said her name was Mary Goodery. Carella could
not have invented a better name to have gone with
that gentle voice. He told Mary Goodery what he
wanted, and Mary Goodery asked him to wait.

When she came back onto the line, she said, "Yes,
indeed, we do have records for a Mr. John Smith."

"You do?" Carella said, amazed because he was certain the thing could not be as simple as all that.

"Yes, sir, we do."

"This John Smith is how old, please?"

"Just one moment, sir," Mary Goodery said, and
she studied her record card, and then her voice came
back to the telephone, "Sixty-six in March. He has
been receiving Federal social security benefits for
more than a year now."

"Would you know if he was also working? I mean,
in addition to receiving his checks?"

"I wouldn't know, sir. You understand, don't you,
that anyone who earns more than one hundred dollars
a month—that's twelve hundred dollars for the year—
is automatically disqualified for social security benefits?"

"No, I didn't know that."

"Yes," Miss Goodery said.

"I see. But you wouldn't know whether or not he
was holding down a job which paid him less than a
hundred a month, would you?"

"I have no record of that, sir, no."

"Thank you, Miss Goodery."

"Not at all," she said, and she hung up.

Carella put the receiver back into the cradle and sat staring reflectively through the open window.

"Oh, my God!" he said suddenly, and he pulled the phone to him, got an outside line, and dialed rapidly.

"Social Security Administration," a voice said.

"Would you get me Miss Goodery, please?" Carella said.

"Just a moment, sir."

Carella waited, wondering how he'd ever got to be a detective, wondering how it happened that a *klutz* like him could manage to stay alive in a job which sometimes required quick thinking, wondering how . . .

"Miss Goodery," that good woman said.

"This is Detective Carella again," he admitted. "I forgot to ask you something."

"Yes?"

"Do you—do you have an address listed for John Smith?" Carella said, and he winced at his own stupidity.

"An address? Why, yes, I'm sure we do. If you'll just wait while I get his folder again."

"Certainly," Carella said, and he leaned back to wait.

In a few moments, Mary Goodery came back with the address for an apartment building on Franklin Street.

FANNY GOT HER IDEA that afternoon at lunch, and she moved on it as soon as she had discussed it with

Teddy. "Discussed" is perhaps the wrong word. For, whereas Teddy was perfectly capable of having a discussion, the conversation which took place at the kitchen table that afternoon was not a discussion but a monologue.

The twins had already been fed and put in for their nap. Fanny had made a batch of scrambled eggs and onions for herself and Teddy, and the two women sat at the kitchen table now, eating in silence, the strong aroma of onions and eggs and hot coffee filling the large kitchen. Both women wore slacks, Teddy's form-fitting and trim over a youthful body, Fanny's form-fitting over a body which was thick and solid and which had served its mistress well for more than fifty years. Teddy was shoveling a forkful of eggs into her mouth when Fanny said, out of the blue, "Why would they first strip the uniform off him and then throw it into an incinerator?"

Teddy looked up inquisitively.

"I'm talking about Steve's case," Fanny said.

Teddy nodded.

"Obviously, that uniform is pretty damned important, wouldn't you say? Otherwise, why bother to take it off the man? Whoever killed him left his shoes and socks on, isn't that right? Navy shoes, mind you, but apparently the Navy part didn't mean a damn or they'd have taken the shoes off of him, too. But they did take the uniform off. That they did. Now why? I'll tell you why. Because that uniform probably had some kind of a marking on it, something that would have told any interested party something very important about the man who was wearing it. And maybe something about why he was killed. So what kind of a uniform could it be?"

Teddy shrugged and continued eating her eggs.

"Did you ever see a man in his sixties delivering mail, or driving a bus? I never did," Fanny said. "But I *have* seen men in their sixties working as bank guards, or night watchmen, or elevator operators. And didn't Steve say this John Smith was on his way to *work* the night Random met him in the bar? Isn't that what Steve said? Sure, it is. So why hasn't Steve thought of it before this? That man was a night watchman, or I'll eat my hat. And for some reason, that uniform would identify the place where he was a watchman, and whoever killed the man doesn't want that spot to be identified. Now that's what I'm betting, Teddy, and I'm going to tell Steve the minute he gets here." Fanny nodded emphatically. "In fact, I'm going to call and tell him right now."

She went to the telephone and dialed FRederick 7-8024.

"Eighty-seventh Precinct, Sergeant Murchison."

"This is Fanny Knowles. May I talk to Steve, please?"

"Fanny *who?*" Murchison said.

"Fanny Knowles, you dumb Irishman!" Fanny shouted. "Fanny Knowles who lives with the Carellas and who's only called that run-down station house a hundred times already in the past year and spoken to yourself, you big jerk sitting on your fat butt! Fanny Knowles, now get me Steve Carella, would you please, dearie?"

"One of these days, Fanny . . ."

"Yes, dearie?" she said sweetly.

"Never mind. I can't get you Steve because he's gone out, said he wouldn't be back until late this afternoon, if at all. Had an apartment on Franklin Street he wanted to check, and said it might take a bit of time."

"That's too bad," Fanny said. "I had an idea for him, about the case he's working on."

"Well," Murchison said with saccharine solicitude, "he'll just have to struggle along without your assistance, I guess. Was there any other cop you want to offer help to today? We got a whole squadroom of them upstairs."

"Go to the devil," Fanny said, and she hung up.

The whole squadroom of cops was really *none* of them at the moment. Carella had gone out to look up the address given him by Mary Goodery, Parker was still on his candy store plant, Hernandez was out interrogating a buglary victim, and Meyer and Kling were in the lieutenant's office. The squadroom was empty and stone silent. Anyone could have walked up there and marched out with all the typewriters and electric fans.

In Byrnes's office, Meyer was divulging his sudden brainstorm, his eyes aglow. Byrnes sat behind his desk, his fingers before him in a small cathedral. Kling leaned against the wall and listened skeptically.

"It's *obvious* that's what he's trying to pull," Meyer said. "I'm surprised I didn't see it before this."

"It's too obvious," Kling said dryly.

"What do you mean?" Meyer answered, annoyed. "Don't start telling me—"

"Let him talk, Meyer," Byrnes said.

"All I know is that a guy who's going to rob a bank isn't going to point a finger at it. He's not going to say, 'This is it, fellas, so please be waiting for me when I blast in, okay?' It's just too damn obvious."

"Then why were those shovels sent to the loft?"

"To let us *think* he was going to break into that bank," Kling said. "Aren't you forgetting something? He's been calling a bunch of *other* stores, too."

"Restaurants, clothing stores, a tie—"

"So what's Raskin's place? The Taj Mahal?" Kling said. "Raskin runs a wholesale dress business. What the hell does that matter? It's not Raskin's place he's calling attention to. It's the bank downstairs! Okay, how many of those other places are over banks, or next door to them?"

"I never thought of that," Meyer said. "Where's that list of stores?"

"On your desk," Kling said.

Meyer ran out of the room. Kling shook his head and said, "It looks like a smoke screen to me, sir. I may be wrong, but it smells to high heaven. The man couldn't be that stupid or that egotistical. He's pointed an obvious finger at Raskin's loft, right over the bank, and he's even had some picks and shovels delivered there, supposedly by accident. And the redheads today. It's just too obvious."

"What about the redheads?" Meyer asked, coming back into the room with his list. He went directly to the phone, got an outside line and began dialing.

"The A. Conan Doyle story," Kling said. " 'The Redheaded League.' "

"Stop *hocking* me with your damn mysteries," Meyer said. "We're trying— Hello?" he said into the phone. "Mr. Lombardo? James Lombardo? This is Detective Meyer of the Eighty-seventh Squad. Listen, could you please tell me what's next door to you? What? Oh, a lingerie shop. Well, thank y— What? *What's* on the other side? Oh, I see. Thank you, Mr. Lombardo. No, nothing yet. Thank you." He replaced the phone on its cradle.

"Well?" Byrnes said.

"A lingerie shop on one side of him, and a jewelry shop on the other."

"Jewelry," Kling said.

"Yeah." Meyer looked at his list again. "Let me try another one of these."

"Sure," Kling said. " 'The Red-headed League.' The son of a bitch is referring us to his source."

"What do you mean, Bert?" Byrnes asked. Meyer, standing alongside him, was dialing again.

"You know the story, don't you? These men run an ad in a London paper, advertising for redheads to fill a vacancy in the League. The idea is that the League will pay this man I-forget-how-many pounds a week for copying words from the encyclopedia, but the copying job must be done in the League's offices. Well, this redheaded man applies for the position and gets it, and every day he trots out to the office and copies words."

"It sounds implausible to me," Meyer said. Into the phone, he said, "Let me talk to Mr. Chen, please."

"Not implausible at all," Kling said. Meyer suddenly began talking again, so he shifted his attention to Byrnes. "The reason they want the redhead out of his shop, you see, is because they're digging a tunnel to the bank across the way. Finally, when they're ready to rob the bank, the man loses his job. He contacts Holmes to see if he can't do something about his being fired, and of course Sherlock figures out exactly what's going on."

"How the hell does he do that?" Meyer asked, hanging up. "That was the Chinese restaurant. It's over an antique shop. Rare jade mostly. I'm gonna call one more place." Rapidly, he began dialing again.

"So what's happened here?" Kling asked Byrnes. "This guy called God knows how many stores which are alongside banks and jewelry shops and—"

"We're not sure on *all* of them yet," Meyer said, waiting for someone to pick up the phone on the other end.

"We're pretty sure," Kling said. "He calls all these guys and he hopes one of them'll call the cops, or all of them. He wants them to call the cops. Why? Because there're twenty-three stores so far, and who knows how many others who didn't bother to call us. Then he directs attention to Raskin's loft because he wants us to think he's going to hit *that* bank. And today he takes out an ad for *redheads,* making sure we don't miss the significance of the Sherlock Holmes story. He draws a direct parallel. He wants us to tip, wants us to figure out he's going to rob the bank under Raskin's loft. Okay, why?"

Into the phone, Meyer said, "Thank you very much,

Mr. Goldfarb. Yes, thank you." He hung up. "The travel agency," he said. "It's next door to a bank."

"Sure," Kling said. "So you know why he's doing this?"

"Why?" Byrnes asked.

"Because he's not going to hit that bank under the loft at all. He's going to hit one of the other twenty-three. The rest are just his smoke screen."

"Which one is he gonna hit?" Meyer asked.

Kling shrugged. "That's the big question, Meyer."

"What do we do, Pete?"

"What's today?" Byrnes asked.

"The twenty-eighth."

"And his deadline is the thirtieth?"

"Yes."

"That gives us two days. I imagine we can put some men on."

"What do you mean?"

"We'll cover those shops. I'll have to get help from some of the other squads. One man to a shop. You say there are twenty-three of them?"

"So far."

"That's a hell of a lot of men to be throwing out of action," Byrnes said. He shook his head. "I'd better call Headquarters on this. I'm going to need more help than the squads can give. We can't put so many detectives out of action."

"Why not patrolmen?" Kling said.

"They'd never catch him. He'd spot the uniforms."

"Put them on special duty. Plainclothes. It's only for two days."

"That's a good idea," Byrnes said. "I'll talk to Captain Frick." He reached for the phone. "There's only one thing that puzzles me," he said.

"What's that?"

"If none of these shopowners move—if none of them yield to his threat to get out by the thirtieth—how in hell will he pull his job?"

The men stared at each other blankly.

They had just asked the two-and-a-half-million-dollar question.

And none of them knew the answer.

13.

THE FOUR MEN SAT on the hillside overlooking the
ice-cream factory. The factory was surrounded by a
cyclone fence and within that fence there were at least
thirty white ice-cream trucks lined up in three identical rows. Two smokestacks jutted up into the April
sky, and a huge sign straddled the stacks:

PICK-PAK ICE CREAM
The Big Lick on a Stick

The four men looked like a group of congenial bud-
dies who had been out for a late afternoon stroll,
who'd discovered this grassy hillock overlooking the
ice-cream plant, and who'd decided to sit and rest
their weary feet. There was certainly nothing sinister-
looking about any of the men. If they'd showed up at
Central Casting for parts in a grade-B gangster film,
each and every one of them would have been turned
down. And yet three of the four men had police
records, and two of the men were, at that very
moment, carrying guns. And even though their conversation was carried on in low and gentle tones,
accompanied by sincere facial expressions, these men
were discussing the future commission of a crime.

The deaf man was the tallest and handsomest of the four. He sat looking out over the rows of white trucks, a strand of grass between his teeth.

"That's where we get it," he said.

Chuck, sitting next to him, fished for a cigarette in the pocket of his jacket, pulling out a single cigarette while leaving the package inside the pocket. He took out a book of matches, lifted the cover, bent one match over from the rest so that it was close to the striking surface, closed the cover, and then struck the match, all with one hand, the match flaming but still attached to the folder.

"Plenty trucks," he said, and he blew out a stream of smoke.

"We only need one, Chuck," the deaf man said.

"That's for sure. When do we grab it?"

"Tomorrow."

"The day before, huh?"

"The *night* before," the deaf man corrected.

"What time?"

"I figured along about midnight. Rafe's been casing the lot for a week. Rafe, do you want to fill us in?"

Rafe adjusted his gold-rimmed glasses, let out a sigh and ran a busy hand through his straw-blond hair. He seemed reluctant to speak. It almost seemed as if speaking pained him physically.

"There's a simple padlock on the gate," he said, his voice very low, as if he had learned at an early age that people who speak softly are generally listened to. "I can open it with a bobby pin."

"He's speaking figuratively," the deaf man said. He grinned. "Aren't you, Rafe?"

"Sure, not a bobby pin, but this is a snap, believe me. Also, there's no watchman in the yard. So once we're in, we're in."

"Are the ignition keys left in the trucks?" Chuck asked.

"No. We'll have to cross the wires."

"No possibility of getting duplicates made?"

"I don't see how."

"That might be worth thinking about," Chuck said, turning to the deaf man. "I mean, we can't keep the thing running all the time, can we? And if the law shows, who wants to be fooling around with wires under the dash?"

"Once we get the truck away from here, I can rig a switch that works without an ignition key," Rafe said. "Don't worry about that."

"I'm not worried, I'm only thinking ahead. This isn't a penny-ante thing we're involved in here, Rafe."

"Nobody said it was."

"Okay. Is the fence wired?"

"No."

"Are you sure?"

"Positive. Apparently they're not too concerned about the trucks. There's an alarm for the plant, and there's also a watchman who—"

"Uh-oh," Chuck said.

"No, no, nothing to worry about," the deaf man assured him quickly. "He never comes out into the yard, and we won't make our play until he's up on the top floor of the building."

"How do we know when that is?" Chuck asked.

"It's at eleven P.M.," Rafe said. "He begins making his rounds at that time. Takes the elevator up to the sixth floor and then starts down on foot. We'll start working on the fence at eleven. We'll grab the truck when he reaches the top floor."

"And how will we know when he reaches the top floor?"

"You can see his flashlight as he walks around. It lights up the whole damn floor. Okay?"

"Sounds good so far. We grab the truck and we're out before he gets a chance to come all the way downstairs again, right?"

"Right."

"Then what?" Chuck asked.

"We drive the truck to the store."

"Think that's smart?"

"Why not? It says Chelsea Pops, Inc. right on our window, doesn't it?"

"Sure. But it says Pick-Pak Ice Cream on the side of the truck."

"The truck'll be in the back yard. Nobody's going to go looking there. Besides, Pop can keep away any visitors while we work on it."

Pop, who had not uttered a word thus far, cleared his throat and said, "Sure, I can do that. It's Rafe and Chuck who'll be taking the truck, is that right?"

"That's right, Pop," the deaf man said.

"And they'll drive it to the store where you and I'll be waiting, is that right?"

"That's right, Pop."

"Will I be dressed, or what?"

"Yes, of course," the deaf man said. "Your job is to keep any unwanted visitors away."

"Okay." The old man put a hand up to shade his eyes and squinted at the rows of white trucks in the lot below. "Is that tin covering the trucks?" he asked.

"It's a porcelainized metal of some sort," Rafe answered. "Why?"

"Will we have any trouble getting the new signs on it?"

"I don't think so. We've got an electric drill and carborundum bits. Those things can drill through *steel*."

"Mmm, that's good," the old man said, nodding.

"What about the license plate?" Chuck asked, sucking in on his cigarette.

"What about it?" the deaf man said.

"We're grabbing the truck the night before the job, aren't we?" he asked. He was truly an ugly man with the squat solidity of a gorilla, huge shoulders and long, dangling arms, massive hands, a square, shortsnouted head. And yet he spoke quietly, almost gently.

"Yes, the night before the job," the deaf man said.

"So they'll be looking for it, won't they? What I mean is, the watchman'll call the cops either as soon as he hears that truck taking off, or as soon as he realizes it's gone, depending on how much on the ball he is. Next thing you know a whole description is going out, you know how the cops work, don't you? So next thing you know, the license plate is being flashed to every squad car in the city. So where does that leave us? So that's what I meant when I asked about the plate."

"Naturally, the plate will be changed."

"But when? It's a long haul from here to the store. If that watchman is on the ball, the license plate number can be on the air in five minutes. I'll be driving this truck, you know."

"So what's your idea?"

"I say we change the plate right here in the lot, even before we start the truck. That's what I say."

"All right."

"Fine. And it can't be an ordinary plate, you know. You look at those trucks down there, you'll see they're not carrying ordinary plates. That's a special kind of commercial plate. We'll have to scout around for some between now and the thirtieth."

"We will," the deaf man said.

"The other thing that bothers me is working in the open, in the back yard, when we get to the store. You know what I mean? Even if the license plate isn't flashed, every cop in the city'll be looking for a Pick-Pak Ice Cream truck. So there we are drilling holes into the side of one. That doesn't smell so hot to me."

"What do you suggest?"

"Can't we build some kind of a temporary screen?"

"I'm afraid a screen would attract attention."

"Well, I don't like working in the back yard. This is too big a thing to take a risk like that."

"Could we take the truck to Majesta?" the old man asked. "Work on it there?"

"That would really be dangerous. A half-hour ferry ride? No, that would be out of the question."

"Why don't we rent a private garage somewhere near here?" Rafe asked. "We can drive to it as soon as we have the truck, make our changes, and then go over to the store. Once the changes are made, we're safe."

"I think that would be best," the deaf man said. "I'll contact some real estate agents tomorrow. This is a fairly rural section, so perhaps we'll have some luck. If not, we're simply going to have to chance working in the open."

"If we can't get a garage near here, I'd rather drive it to some dark street and do the job there instead of in that back yard."

"Let's not cross our bridges," the deaf man said. "It's agreed that I'll try to find a garage in this neighborhood tomorrow. Let's leave it at that for now."

"Okay," Chuck said.

"But we'll be taking the truck tomorrow, right?" the old man asked. He paused. "I don't like to ask too many questions, but I did get in this sort of late, and . . ."

"That's all right. Yes. We take the truck tomorrow night."

"And the big job?"

"The next day, of course. April thirtieth."

The old man nodded. "Who'll be driving on the day of the big job?"

"Rafe."

"Who'll be with him?"

"I will," the deaf man said.

"Have you got uniforms?"

"I've ordered them. I'm to pick them up tomorrow."

"Where will Chuck and I be?" Pop asked.

"After you deliver your packages?" the deaf man said, and he grinned.

"Yes."

"You'll go immediately to the house in Majesta. You should be finished by one o'clock or so. I expect you'll both catch the two-fifteen boat. Or, at worst, the four-oh-five."

"And you and Rafe? Which boat will you be on with the truck?"

"We're trying for the five-forty-five. If not, we'll catch the six-oh-five."

"And when's the one after that?"

"Seven-fifteen," Rafe said.

"We don't have to worry about any boat beyond the six-oh-five," the deaf man said. "We're starting the job at five o'clock, and it shouldn't take more than ten minutes to do the remaining work. Another ten minutes to load the cartons, and another ten to get to the ferry slip."

"With the loot," Pop said.

"I should hope so," the deaf man said, smiling.

"And when do we leave Majesta?"

"As soon as things begin to cool. We can work that out while we're there. We'll leave one at a time. Last man takes the car. The ice-cream truck stays behind, in the garage."

"You think of everything, don't you?" Chuck said, and there was a tinge of bitterness to his voice.

"I try to," the deaf man said flatly. "I find it's just as simple to think of everything as *not* to. And a hell of a lot safer."

"I hope you've thought of everything," Chuck said.

"I have, believe me." He looked at his watch. "We'd better get back to the store," he said. "I want to get to work again. We've got a lot to do before Thursday."

"Look, I hate to sound too cautious," the old man said.

"What is it?"

"I'm going to have to take another look at those maps you drew. I mean, I've got to know exactly where to plant those things."

"Certainly," the deaf man said, and he reached into his side jacket pocket. "I thought I had them with me," he said. "I guess I left them at the Franklin Street apartment. I'll stop by for them."

"Think that's safe?" Chuck asked, a worried look on his ugly features. "Going back to that apartment?"

"I think so, yes," the deaf man said. "As a matter of fact, I was there again just last night, entertaining a lady friend." He stared at Chuck defiantly. "I'll meet you back at the store. You can begin working again as soon as it's dark. Pop, you take up your usual post. We have to be finished by Thursday, remember that."

THE BUILDING ON Franklin Street was an elegant dwelling which, some twenty years ago, had been

among the most aristocratic of apartment houses. Time
and the vagaries of the taste makers, a fickleness which
shifted the desirability of neighborhoods from the
south side to the north side with the swiftness of summer lightning, had combined to render Franklin Street
no longer as desirable as the buildings to the south.
The local joke now was that no one went to the north
side unless it was to take a steamer to Europe, and the
bromide was not very far from the truth. But the buildings on Franklin Street had not succumbed to the
shoddy encroachments of the slums as had some of the
buildings within the territory of the 87th Precinct,
buildings which had once been princely and which had
slowly been strangled by the octopus of poverty. The
buildings on Franklin Street still had doormen and elevator operators. There were no profanities scrawled on
the walls of the entrance foyers. The rents in these
now-unfashionable buildings were still very fashion-
ably high.

Which led Carella to wonder how a man like John
Smith, who had been existing on his social security
checks, could afford to live in a joint like 457 Franklin
Street. Carella stood on the sidewalk underneath the
green canopy and looked into the entrance foyer. A
doorman standing just inside the glass entrance doors
stared out at him, opened one of the doors in anticipa-
tion, and came out onto the sidewalk.

"Help you, sir?" he asked.

"Yes. I'm trying to locate one of your tennants, a
man named John Smith."

"Yes, sir, he's one of our tenants," the doorman said. "But he ain't around right now. In fact, I ain't seen him for quite some time."

"For how long?"

"Oh, since last month some time."

"Mmm. How long has he been living here, would you know?"

"Just a few months, sir."

"When did he move in, would you say?"

The doorman studied Carella narrowly. "Are you a friend of his?" he asked.

"No, I'm a cop." He flashed the buzzer.

"Oh."

"Yes. When did he move in, can you tell me that?"

"The end of February, I think it was."

"And the last time you saw him was in March, that right?"

"That's right."

"Was he living alone?"

"I don't know. He was here quite a lot."

"But alone?"

"What?"

"Alone? Was he here alone?"

"Well, I just told you—"

"There were visitors?"

"Yes."

"Living with Smith?"

"Maybe. It don't matter to the building, you know. Long as a tenant don't disturb other tenants, it's his apartment, after all. So long as he don't play the radio late or make noise or do anything against—" The doorman's eyebrows went up quizzically. "The *law*?" he asked. "Is Mr. Smith in some kind of trouble?"

"Well, I wouldn't worry about it, if I were you. I'd like to take a look at the apartment. Think you can let me in?"

"I'd have to check that with the building manager. And he won't be here until later this afternoon."

"Call him," Carella said.

"Well, I—"

"It's very important," Carella said. He smiled. "Call him, won't you?"

The doorman seemed dubious for a moment. Then he smiled back at Carella and said, "Sure, I'll call him."

Carella followed him into the building. The lobby had been redecorated recently, the furniture looking shining and new and unused. The doorman went into a small office, made his call and returned to Carella, still smiling. "Miracles will never cease," he said. "The old bastard said okay. Only thing is we ain't got a pass key or anything. I mean, he said if you can get in, okay, he don't want any trouble with the police. But everybody buys their own locks, and we don't have keys to none of the apartments."

"Well, just take me up, and I'll try some of my keys, okay?" Carella said.

"You carry skeleton keys, huh?" the doorman said, grinning knowingly.

Carella winked slyly. Together they took the elevator up to the sixth floor, and then walked down the corridor to apartment 6C.

"There it is," the doorman said. "Nice apartment. Seven rooms. Very nice. It has this sunken living room."

Carella reached into his pocket and took out a ring of keys.

"Skeleton keys, how about that!" the doorman said, still grinning. The doorman watched him as he began trying the keys in the lock. There were, in addition to his own house keys, perhaps half a dozen skeleton keys hanging from the ring. He tried them all. Not one of them turned the lock.

"No good?" the doorman asked.

"Not very," Carella said, shaking his head. "How many floors to this building?"

"Nine."

"Fire escapes?"

"Sure."

"Think you can take me up to the roof?"

"You going to come down the fire escape?" the doorman asked.

"I'm going to try," Carella said. "Maybe Smith left his window open."

"Man, you guys sure work for your money, don't you?" the doorman said admiringly.

Carella winked slyly and stepped into the elevator. He got off at the ninth floor and walked the flight to the roof, opening the fire door and stepping out onto the asphalt. He could see the city spread out around him as he crossed the roof, the sharp, vertical rectangles of the apartment buildings slit with open windows, the water tanks atop each roof nesting like shining dark birds, the blue sky beyond and the tracery of the bridges that connected Isola to the other parts of the city, the solid heavy lines of the old bridges, and the more delicate soaring lines of the newer bridges, and far below him the sound of street traffic and the hum of a city rushing with life, kids flying kites from neighboring rooftops, a man down the street swinging his long bamboo pole at his pigeons, the pigeons fluttering into the air in a sudden explosion of gray, beating wings, the April sun covering the asphalt of the roof with yellow warmth.

He walked to the edge of the roof and glanced down the nine stories to the interior courtyard below. Gripping the ladder tightly, he swung over the tiled parapet and began working his way down to the fire escape on the ninth floor. He did not glance into the windows. He didn't want any women screaming for a cop. He kept working his way downward, not looking to the right or the left, going down the ladder hand over hand, and then marching across the fire escape, and onto the next ladder until he reached the sixth floor. He squatted outside apartment 6C and looked through the window. The apartment was empty. He tried the window.

It was locked.

"Dammit," he said, and he moved along the fire escape to the second window. He was beginning to feel like a burglar, and he wished he had a small hand drill with which to bore into the wood and a hunk of wire to slip into the hole to lift the window catch. He was beginning to feel like an ill-equipped thief until he tried the second window and lo and begorrah, the goddam window was unlocked. He looked into the apartment again, and then slowly slid the window up and climbed over the sill.

The place was silent.

He dropped onto the thick rug and hastily scanned an apartment done in expensive good taste, sleek modern furniture set low against muted wall tones. His eyes touched each piece of furniture, lighted on the Danish desk in one corner of the living room. He went to it instantly and pulled down the drop-leaf front. He hoped to find some letters or an address book or something which could give him a further lead onto the people Smith had known, and especially the identity of the deaf man. But there was nothing of value. He closed the desk and oriented himself, figuring the kitchen to be that way, off the dining room, and the bedrooms to be that way, at the other end of the living room. He walked through the living room, his shoes whispering against the thick rug, and through the open arch and into the first of three bedrooms flanking a Spartan white corridor.

There was a faint trace of perfume in the bedroom.

The bed was neatly made, a black nightgown folded at its foot. Carella picked up the gown and looked for a label. It had come from one of the most expensive stores in the city. He sniffed it, smelled the same perfume that was in the air, and then dropped it onto the bed again, wondering if the gown belonged to Lotte Constantine, wondering too if she'd been lying when she said she didn't know where John Smith had lived. He shrugged, snapped on a lamp resting on one of the night tables, and pulled open the top drawer of the table.

The first thing he saw was a series of crude drawings, either maps or floor plans, none of them labeled, all of them had several things in common. To begin with, each of the maps on floor plans, (it was difficult to tell exactly what they were supposed to represent) was marked with X's scattered onto the face of the drawing. There was no clue anywhere on any of the drawings as to just what the X's were supposed to represent. The maps had something else in common. Each of them had a name scrawled onto the right-hand corner. There were six maps in all.

The name on three of the maps was: CHUCK.

The remaining three maps had first carried one name, and that name was: JOHNNY. But the name had been crossed off all three, and another name written in its place: POP.

Johnny, Carella thought. *John Smith?*

The second thing in the drawer was a portion of a blueprint, neat and professional. He unfolded it and studied it for a moment:

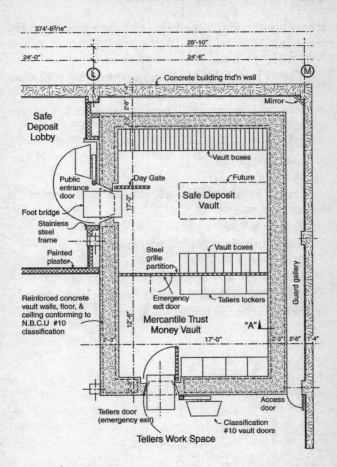

He was folding the blueprint again when the telephone rang, startling him. He hesitated a moment, debating whether or not he should answer it. He put the blueprint down on the night table, wiped his hand across his sweating upper lip, and then picked up the receiver.

"Hello," he said.

"This is Joey," the voice on the other end told him.

"Yes?"

"Joey, the doorman. The guy who took you upstairs."

"Oh, yes," Carella said.

"I see you got in."

"Yes."

"Listen, I didn't know what to do. So I figured I'd call and tell you."

"Tell me what?"

"Mr. Smith. John Smith, you know?"

"What about him?"

"He's on his way upstairs," the doorman said.

"What?" Carella said, and at that instant he heard a key being turned in the front door.

14.

CARELLA STOOD IN the bedroom with the telephone receiver in one hand, the blueprint on the night table before him, the sound of the turning lock clicking into his mind. He put down the phone at once, turned off the light and moved to the right of the door, his hand going instantly to his service revolver. He flattened himself against the wall, the gun in his right hand, waiting. He heard the front door open, and then close again.

The apartment was silent for a moment.

Then he heard the cushioned sound of footsteps against the rug.

Did I leave that living-room window open? he wondered.

The footsteps hesitated, and then stopped.

Did I leave the desk open? he wondered.

He heard the footsteps again, heard a board squeak in the flooring, and then heard the sound of another door opening. A fine sheen of sweat covered his face now, clung to his chest beneath his shirt. The .38 Police Special was slippery in his fist. He could hear his own heart leaping in his chest with the erratic rhythm of an African bongo. He heard the door closing again, a closet he imagined, and then footsteps once more, and he wondered *Does he know I'm here? Does he know? DOES HE*

KNOW? And then he heard a sound which was not familiar to him, a clicking metallic sound, as of metal grating against metal, an unfamiliar sound and yet a sound which was curiously familiar, and then the floor board squeaked again, and the cushioned footsteps came closer to the open arch at the end of the living room, and hesitated, and stopped.

Carella waited.

The footsteps retreated.

He heard another click, and then a twenty-second spell of dead silence; and then music erupted into the apartment, loud and raucous, and Carella instantly knew this man in the apartment was armed and would begin shooting within the next few moments, hoping to use the music as a cover. He did not intend to give his opponent the opportunity of being the one to start the festivities. He hefted the gun in his right hand, sucked in a deep breath, and stepped into the arch.

The man turned from the hi-fi unit alongside the wall.

In a split second, Carella saw the hearing aid in the man's right ear, and then the shotgun the man was holding, and suddenly it was too late, suddenly the shotgun exploded into sound.

Carella whirled away from the blast. He could hear the whistling pellets as they screamed across the confined space of the apartment, and then he felt them lash into his shoulder like a hundred angry wasps, and he thought only *Oh Jesus, not again!* and fired at the tall blond man who was already sprinting across the apartment. His shoulder felt suddenly numb. He tried to lift the hand with the gun and quickly found he couldn't and just as quickly shifted the gun to his left hand and triggered off another shot, high and wide, as the deaf man raised the shotgun and swung the stock at Carella's head. A single barrel, Carella thought in the split second before the stock collided with the side of his head, a single barrel, no time to reload, and a sudden flashing explosion of rocketing yellow pain, slam the stock again, suns revolving, a universe slam the stock, Oh Jesus, oh Jesus! and tears sprang into his eyes because the pain was so fierce, the pain of his shoulder and the awful pain of the heavy wooden stock of the shotgun crashing into crashing into—oh God oh mother oh God oh God

WHEN CARELLA WAS CARRIED to the hospital later that day, the doctors there knew that he was still alive, but most of them were unwilling to venture a guess as to how long he would remain that way. He had lost a lot of blood on the floor of that apartment. He had not been discovered lying there unconscious until some three hours after he'd been repeatedly clobbered with the rather unbending stock of the shotgun. It was the doorman of the building, Joey, who had discovered him at six o'clock that evening. Lieutenant Byrnes, interrogating the doorman in the presence of a police stenographer, got the following information:

BYRNES: What made you go up there, anyway?
JOEY: Well, like I told you, he'd been up there a very long time. And I had already seen Mr. Smith come downstairs again. So I—

BYRNES: Can you describe this Mr. Smith?

JOEY: Sure. He's around my height, maybe six-one, six-two, and I guess he weighs around a hun' eighty, a hun' ninety pounds. He's got blond hair and blue eyes, and he wears this hearing aid in his right ear. He's a little deaf. He come downstairs carrying something wrapped in newspaper.

BYRNES: Carrying what?

JOEY: I don't know. Something long. Maybe a fishing rod or something like that.

BYRNES: Maybe a rifle? Or a shotgun?

JOEY: Maybe. I didn't see what was under the paper.

BYRNES: What time did he come down?

JOEY: Around three, three-thirty, I guess.

BYRNES: And when did you remember that Detective Carella was still in the apartment?

JOEY: That's hard to say, exactly. I had gone over to the candy store where there's this very cute little blonde, she works behind the counter. And I was shooting the breeze with her while I had an egg cream, and then I guess I went back to the building, and I wondered if Car— What's his name?

BYRNES: Carella.

JOEY: He's Italian?

BYRNES: Yes.

JOEY: How about that? I'm Italian, too. A *paisan*, huh? How about that?

BYRNES: That's amazing.

JOEY: How about that? So I wondered if he was still

up there, and I buzzed the apartment. No answer. Then—I don't know—I guess I was just curious, I mean, Mr. Smith having come down already and all that, so I hopped in the elevator and went up to the sixth floor and knocked on the door. There was no answer and the door was locked.

BYRNES: What'd you do then?

JOEY: I remembered that Car— What's his name?

BYRNES: Carella, Carella.

JOEY: Yeah, Carella, how about that? I remembered he'd gone up on the roof, so I figured I'd go take a look up there, which I done. Then, while I was up there, I figured I might as well go down the fire escape and take a peek into 6C, which I also done. And that was when I seen him laying on the floor.

BYRNES: What'd you do?

JOEY: I opened the window, and I went into the apartment. Man, I never seen so much blood in my life. I thought he was dead. I thought the poor bast— Are you taking down *everything* I'm saying?

STENO: What?

BYRNES: Yes, he's taking down everything you say.

JOEY: Then cut out that word, huh? Bastard, I mean. That don't look nice.

BYRNES: What did you think when you found Carella?

JOEY: I thought he was dead. All that blood. Also, his head looked caved in.

BYRNES: What did you do?
       (No answer)
       I said what did you do then?
JOEY: I passed out cold.

As it turned out, not only had Joey passed out cold, but he had later revived and been sick all over the thick living-room rug, and had only then managed to pull himself to a telephone to call the police. The police had got to the apartment ten minutes after Joey had made the call. By this time, the living-room rug had sopped up a goodly amount of Carella's blood, and he looked dead. Lying there pale and unmoving, he looked dead. The first patrolman to see him almost tagged the body D.O.A. The second patrolman felt for a pulse, found a feeble one, and instantly called in for a meat wagon. The interne who admitted Carella to the Emergency Section of the Rhodes Clinic estimated that he would be dead within the hour. The other doctors refused to commit themselves in this day and age of scientific miracles. Instead, they began pumping plasma into him and treating him for multiple concussion and extreme shock. Somebody in the front office put his name on the critical list, and somebody else called his wife. Fanny Knowles took the call. She said, "Oh, sweet loving mother of Jesus!" Both she and Teddy arrived at the hospital not a half hour later. Lieutenant Byrnes was already there waiting. At 1 A.M. on April 29, Lieutenant Byrnes sent both Teddy and Fanny home. Steve Carella was still on the critical list. At 8 A.M., Lieutenant Byrnes called Frankie Hernandez at home.

"Frankie," he said, "did I wake you?"

"Huh? Wha'? Who's this?"

"This is me. Pete."

"Pete who? Oh, oh, OH! Hello, Lieutenant. Whattsa matter? Something wrong?"

"You awake?"

"Is he dead?" Hernandez asked.

"What?"

"Steve. Is he all right?"

"He's still in coma. They won't know for a while yet."

"Oh, man, I was just having a dream," Hernandez said. "I dreamt he was dead. I dreamt he was laying face down on the sidewalk in a puddle of blood, and I went over to him, crying for him, saying 'Steve, Steve, Steve' again and again, and then I rolled him over, and Pete, it wasn't Steve's face looking up at me, it was my own. Oh man, that gave me the creeps. I hope he pulls through this."

"Yeah."

Both men were silent for several seconds. Then Byrnes said, "You awake?"

"Yes. What is it?"

"I wouldn't cut in on what's supposed to be your day off, Frankie. I know you were up all last night . . ."

"What is it, Pete?"

"I want you to check out the apartment where Steve got it. I wouldn't ask you ordinarily, Frankie, but I'm in one hell of a bind here. You know, we've got these damn stores under surveillance because Meyer and Kling've got me convinced this nut's gonna hit one of them. Well,

Captain Frick let me have the patrolmen I needed, but he reserved the right to pull them if he needs them any-place else. So I had to work out some kind of a system where a team of detectives would be on the prowl ready to relieve any of these cops if something else came up. I couldn't pull Parker out of the candy store, and I couldn't get those two men back from Washington where they're taking that damn FBI course, so I had to pull two men off vacation, and I've got these two teams cruising around now, Meyer and Kling, and this other pair, ready to either relieve or assist, whichever is neces-sary. I'm practically running the squad singlehanded, Frankie. Steve's in the hospital, and I'm going out of my mind worrying about him, that guy is like a son to me, Frankie. I'd check this out myself, believe me, but I got to go down to City Hall this afternoon to make arrange-ments for that damn ball game tomorrow—of all times the Governor's got to come down to throw out the ball, and the damn ball park has to be in my precinct, so that'll mean—I don't know where I'm gonna get all the men, Frankie. I just don't know."

He paused.

There was another long silence.

"His face is all smashed in," Byrnes said at last. "Did you see him, Frankie?"

"I didn't get a chance to go over there yet, Pete. I had—"

"All smashed in," Byrnes said.

The silence came back. Byrnes sighed.

"You can see what a bind I'm in. I've got to ask you to do me the favor, Frankie."

"Whatever you say, Pete."

"Would you check that apartment? The lab's already been through it, but I want one of my own boys to go over it thoroughly. Will you?"

"Sure. What's the address?"

"Four fifty-seven Franklin Street."

"I'll just have some breakfast and get dressed, Pete. Then I'll go right over."

"Thanks. Will you phone in later?"

"I'll keep in touch."

"Okay, fine. Frankie, you know, you've been on the case with Steve, you know what his thinking on it has been, so I thought . . ."

"I don't mind at all, Pete."

"Good. Call me later."

"Right," Hernandez said, and he hung up.

Hernandez did not, in truth, mind being called on his day off. To begin with, he knew that all policemen are on duty twenty-four hours a day every day of the year, and he further knew that Lieutenant Byrnes knew this. And knowing this, Byrnes did not have to ask Hernandez for a favor, all he had to do was say, "Get in here, I need you." But he *had* asked Hernandez if he'd mind, he had put it to him as a matter of choice, and Hernandez appreciated this immensely. Too, he had never heard the lieutenant sound quite so upset in all the time he'd been working for him. He had seen Peter Byrnes on the edge of total collapse, after three days without sleep, the man's eyes shot with red, weariness in his mouth and his posture and his hands. He had heard his voice rapping out orders hoarsely, had seen his fingers trembling as he lifted a cup of coffee, had indeed known him at times when panic seemed but a hairsbreadth away. But he had never heard Byrnes the way he sounded this morning. Never.

There was something of weariness in his voice, yes, and something of panic, yes, and something of despair, but these elements did not combine to form the whole; the whole had been something else again, the whole had been something frightening which transmitted itself across the copper telephone wires and burst from the receiver on the other end with a bone-chilling sentience of its own. The whole had been as if—as if Byrnes were staring into the eyes of death, as if Byrnes were choking on the stench of death in his nostrils, as if Byrnes had a foreknowledge of what would happen to Steve Carella, a foreknowledge so strong that it leaped telephone wires and made the blood run suddenly cold.

In his tenement flat, with the sounds of the city coming alive outside his window, Frankie Hernandez suddenly felt the presence of death. He shuddered and went quickly into the bathroom to shower and shave.

JOEY, THE DOORMAN, recognized him as a policeman instantly.

"You come about my *paisan,* huh?" Joey asked.

"Who's your *paisan?*" Hernandez asked.

"Carella. The cop who got his block knocked off upstairs."

"Yes, that's who I've come about."

"Hey, you ain't Italian, are you?" Joey asked.

"No."

"What are you, Spanish or something?"

"Puerto Rican," Hernandez answered, and he was instantly ready to take offense. His eyes met Joey's, searched them quickly and thoroughly. No, there would be no insult.

"You want to go up to the apartment? Hey, I don't even know your name," Joey said.

"Detective Hernandez."

"That's a pretty common Spanish name, ain't it?"

"Pretty common," Hernandez said as they went into the building.

"The reason I know is I studied Spanish in high school," Joey said. "That was my language there. *Habla usted Español?*"

"*Sí un poquito,*" Hernandez answered, lying. He did not speak Spanish only slightly. He spoke it as well as any native of Madrid—no, that was false. In Madrid, the Spanish were pure, and a *c* or a *z* before certain vowels took a *th* sound. In Puerto Rico, the sound became an *s*. The word for "five," for example—spelled *cinco* in both Spain and Latin America—was pronounced *theen-koh* in Spain and *seen-koh* in Puerto Rico. But he spoke the language like a native when he wanted to. He did not very often want to.

"I know Spanish proverbs." Joey, said. "You know any Spanish proverbs?"

"Some," Hernandez said as they walked toward the elevator.

"Three years of high-school Spanish, and all I can

do is quote proverbs," Joey said. "What a drag, huh? Here, listen. *No hay rosas sin espinas.* How about that one? You know what that one means?"

"Yes," Hernandez said, grinning.

"Sure. There ain't no roses without thorns. Here's another one, a very famous one. *No se ganó Zamora en una hora.* Is that right?"

"That's right," Hernandez said. "Your pronunciation is very good."

"Rome was not built in a day," Joey translated. "Man, that one kills me. I'll bet I know more Spanish proverbs than half the people in Spain. Here's the elevators. So the guy who said he was John Smith wasn't John Smith, is that right?"

"That's right," Hernandez said.

"So now the only real question is which of those two guys was John Smith? The blond guy with the hearing aid? Or the old duffer who used to come to the apartment and whose picture your lieutenant showed to me. That's the question, huh?"

"The old man *was* John Smith," Hernandez said. "And whatever the blond's name is, he's wanted for criminal assault."

"Or maybe murder if my *paisan* dies, huh?"

Hernandez did not answer.

"God forbid," Joey said quickly. "Come on, I'll take you up. The door's open. There was guys here all last night taking pictures and sprinkling powder all over the joint. When they cleared out, they left the door open. You think Carella's gonna be all right?"

"I hope so."

"Me, too," Joey said, and he sighed and set the elevator in motion.

"How often was the old man here?" Hernandez asked.

"That's hard to say. You'd see him on and off, you know."

"Was he a hardy man?"

"Healthy, you mean?"

"Yes."

"Yeah, he seemed pretty healthy to me," Joey said. "Here's the sixth floor."

They stepped out into the corridor.

"But the apartment was rented by the blond one, is that right? The deaf man? He was the one who called himself John Smith?"

"Yeah, that's right."

"Why the hell would he use the old man's name unless he was hiding from something? And even then . . ." Hernandez shook his head and walked down the hall to apartment 6C.

"You gonna need me?" Joey asked.

"No, go on."

" 'Cause our elevator operator is sick, you know. So I got to run the elevator and also take care of the door. So if you don't mind . . ."

"No, go right ahead," Hernandez answered. He went into the apartment, impressed at once by the expensive modern furniture, overwhelmed at once by the total absence of sound, the silence that pervades every empty apartment like an old couple living in a back room. He walked swiftly to the arch between the living room and the bedroom corridor. The rug there was stained with dried blood. Carella's. Hernandez wet his lips and walked back into the living room. He tabulated the units in the room which would warrant a thorough search: the drop-leaf desk, the hi-fi and liquor cabinet, the bookcases, and—that was *it* for the living room.

He took off his jacket and threw it over one of the easy chairs. Then he pulled down his tie, rolled up his sleeves, crossed to the windows and opened them, and began working on the desk. He searched the desk from top to bottom and found nothing worth a second glance.

He shrugged, straightened up, and was walking toward the hi-fi unit when he noticed that something had fallen from his inside jacket pocket when he'd tossed it over the back of the chair. He walked across the room and stooped at the base of the chair, picking up the photograph encased in lucite, the photo of the dead man who had been identified as John Smith. He scooped his jacket from the back of the chair and was putting the picture into the pocket again when the front door opened suddenly.

Hernandez raised his eyes.

There, standing in the doorway, was the man whose picture he'd been looking at a moment before, the dead man named John Smith.

15.

"WHO ARE YOU?" the man in the doorway said. "What do you want here?"

He was wearing a sailor's uniform, and he took a step into the room as Hernandez's hand dropped the photograph and reached for the Police Special holstered at his side. The sailor's eyes widened.

"What?" he started, and he turned toward the door again.

"Hold it!" Hernandez snapped.

The sailor stopped. Cautiously, he turned to face the .38.

"Wh—what's the gun for?" he asked.

"Who are you?" Hernandez asked.

"John Smith," the sailor replied.

Hernandez moved closer to him. The voice had been young, and the man's body was trim and youthful in the tight-fitting Navy blues. Hernandez blinked, and then realized he was not looking at a reincarnation of the dead man they'd found in Grover Park, but he was damn well looking at a spitting image of him, some forty years younger.

"Where's my father?" Smith said.

"John Smith your father?"

"Yes. Where is he?"

Hernandez didn't want to answer that question, not just yet he didn't. "What made you think you'd find him here?" he asked.

"This is the address he gave me," the young John Smith said. "Who are *you*?"

"When did he give you the address?"

"We've been writing to each other. I was down in Guantanamo Bay on a shakedown cruise," Smith said. His eyes narrowed. "You a cop or something?"

"That's what I am."

"I knew it. I can smell fuzz a mile away. Is the old man in some trouble?"

"When did you hear from him last?"

"I don't know. Beginning of the month, I guess. What's he done?"

"He hasn't done anything."

"Then what are you doing here?"

"Your father's dead," Hernandez said flatly.

Smith backed up against the wall as if Hernandez had hit him. He simply recoiled from Hernandez's words, inching backward until he collided with the wall, and then he leaned against the wall, and he stared into the room, without seeing Hernandez, simply stared into the room blankly, and said, "How?"

"Murdered," Hernandez said.

"Who?"

"We don't know"

The room was silent.

"Who'd want to kill him?" Smith asked the silence.

"Maybe you can tell us," Hernandez said. "What was his last letter about?"

"I don't know. I don't remember," Smith said. He seemed dazed. He kept leaning against the wall, his head tilted back against the plaster, looking up at the ceiling.

"Try," Hernandez said gently. He holstered the .38 and walked to the bar unit. He poured a stiff hooker of brandy and carried it to Smith. "Here. Drink this."

"I don't drink."

"Take it."

Smith took the glass, sniffed it, and tried to hand it back. Hernandez forced it to his mouth. Smith drank, almost gagging. He coughed and pushed the glass away from him.

"I'm all right," he said.

"Sit down."

"I'm all right."

"*Sit down!*"

Smith nodded and went to one of the modern easy chairs, sinking into it. He stretched out his long legs. He did not look at Hernandez. He kept studying the tips of his highly polished shoes.

"The letter," Hernandez said. "What did it say?"

"I don't know. It was a long time ago."

"Did he mention a girl named Lotte Constantine?"

"No. Who's she?"

"Did he mention anyone called the deaf man?"

"No." Smith looked up. "The *what?*"

"Never mind. What *did* he say in the letter?"

"I don't know. I think he started off by thanking me for the shoes. Yeah, that's right."

"What shoes?"

"I got a pair of shoes for him from ship's service. I'm on a destroyer, we were just commissioned last month up in Boston. So my father sent me his shoe size and I picked up a pair for him in the ship's store. They're good shoes, and I get them for something like nine bucks, he couldn't come anywhere near that price on the outside." Smith paused. "There's nothing dishonest about that."

"Nobody said there was."

"Well, there ain't. I paid money for the shoes. It ain't as if I was cheating the government. Besides, it's all one and the same. Before he got this job, his only income came from the government, anyway. So it's six of one and half a dozen of—"

"What job?" Hernandez asked quickly.

"Huh? Oh, I don't know. In his last letter, he was telling me about some job he got."

"What kind of job?"

"As a night watchman."

Hernandez leaned closer to Smith. "Where?"

"I don't know."

"Didn't he say where?"

"No."

"He *must* have said where!"

"He didn't. He said he was working as a night watchman, but that the job would be finished on May first, and after that he could afford to retire. That's all he said."

"What did he mean?"

"I don't know. My father always had big ideas." Smith paused. "None of them ever paid off."

"Afford to retire," Hernandez said, almost to himself. "On what? On a night watchman's salary?"

"He only just got the job," Smith said. "He couldn't have meant that. It was probably something else. One of his get-rich-quick schemes."

"But he said he'd only be working until May first, is that right?"

"Yeah."

"He didn't give the name of the firm? He didn't say where he was working?"

"No, I told you." Smith paused. "Why'd anyone want to kill him? He never hurt a soul in his life."

And suddenly he began weeping.

THE COSTUME RENTAL SHOP was in downtown Isola on Detavoner Avenue. There were three dummies in the front window. One was dressed as a clown, another was dressed as a pirate, and the third and last was dressed as a World War I pilot. The window was grimy, and the dummies were dusty, and the costumes looked moth-eaten. The inside of the shop looked grimy, dusty, and moth-eaten, too. The owner of the shop was a jovial man named Douglas McDouglas who'd once wanted to be an actor and who had settled for the next best thing to it. Now, rather than creating fantasies on stage, he helped others to create fantasies by renting the costumes they needed for amateur plays, masquerade parties and the like. He was no competition for the bigger, theater rental shops nor did he wish to be. He was simply a man who was happy doing the kind of work he did.

The deaf man entered the shop, and Douglas McDouglas recognized him at once.

"Hello there, Mr. Smith," he said. "How's every little thing?"

"Just fine," the deaf man answered. "And how are things with you?"

"Couldn't be better," McDouglas answered, and he burst into contagious laughter. He was a fat man, and the layers of flesh under his vest rippled when he laughed. He put his hands on his belly as if to control the pulsating flesh, and said. "Are you here for the costumes?"

"I am," the deaf man said.

"They're ready," McDouglas said. "Nice and clean. Just got them back from the cleaners day before yesterday. What kind of a play is this one, Mr. Smith?"

"It's not a play," the deaf man said. "It's a movie."

"With ice-cream men in it, huh?"

"Yes."

"And night watchmen, too huh?"

"What do you mean?"

"The two night watchmen uniforms. The one you got 'way back, and the one you came in for near the beginning of the month. Ain't they for the movie, too?"

"Yes, I suppose so," the deaf man said.

"Will you be returning them all together?"

"Yes," he lied. He had no intention of returning any of the costumes.

"What's the movie called?" McDouglas asked.

The deaf man smiled. "The Great Bank Robbery," he answered.

McDouglas burst into laughter again. "A comedy?"

"More like a tragedy," the deaf man said.

"You filming it here in Isola?"

"Yes."

"Soon?"

"We start shooting tomorrow."

"Sounds exciting."

"I think it will be. Would you get me the costumes, please? I don't want to rush you, but . . ."

"Sure thing," McDouglas said, and he went into the back of the shop.

The Great Bank Robbery, the deaf man thought, and he grinned. I wonder what you would say, fat boy, if you really knew. I wonder what you will think when you hear the news over your radio. Will you feel like an accessory before the fact? And will you rush to the police with a description of "John Smith," the man who rented these costumes? But then, John Smith is dead, isn't he?

And you don't know that, Mr. McDouglas, do you?

You don't know that John Smith, garrulous old John Smith, was shot to death while wearing a costume hired from this very shop, now do you? Garrulous old John Smith who, we discovered, was dropping just a few hints too many about what is going to take place tomorrow. A dangerous man to have about, that John Smith. And he remained talkative even after we'd warned him, and so Goodbye, Mr. Smith, it was lovely having you in our friendly little group, but speech is silver, Mr. Smith, and silence, ahhh, silence is golden, and so we commit you to eternal silence, BAM!

The deaf man grinned.

And then, of course, it was necessary to dispose of the costume. It would not have been necessary were you not such an organized man, Mr. McDouglas. But stamped into the lining of each of your costumes is the name of your shop, and we couldn't have run the risk of the police stripping down a corpse and then coming here to ask you questions about it, now could we, Mr. McDouglas? No, no, it was far better the way we did it. Strip the uniform from the body, cart it to Grover Park, and leave it there as naked as the jay birds.

Again, the deaf man grinned.

I'm really terribly sorry to report, Mr. McDouglas, that your lovely night watchman's uniform was burned to ashes in an incinerator. But that was the only way, you see. We shall do the same thing with these costumes. The police may get to you eventually, Mr. McDouglas, but we certainly don't want them reaching you any sooner than they ordinarily might.

And when they get to you, you will of course describe me.

The deaf man grinned.

But is my hair really blond, Mr. McDouglas? Or is it bleached especially for this jolly little caper? And am I *really* hard of hearing? Or is the button in my ear a further device to confuse identification? Those are the questions the police must ask themselves, Mr. McDouglas.

I somehow feel they'll have themselves a merry little chase.

"Here we are," McDouglas said, coming from the back of the shop. "How do you like them?"

The deaf man studied the white uniforms.

"Very nice, Mr. McDouglas," he said. "How much is that?"

"Pay me when you bring them back," McDouglas said.

The deaf man smiled graciously. "Thank you."

"I've been in this business twenty-five years," McDouglas said, "and I've never been stuck with a bum check, and I've never yet had anybody steal a costume from me. And in all that time, I never once took a deposit and the people always paid for the costumes when they brought them back." McDouglas rapped his knuckles on the wooden counter. "I've never been robbed yet."

"Well," the deaf man said, grinning, "there's always a first time," and McDouglas burst out laughing. The deaf man continued watching him, grinning.

When his laughter subsided, McDouglas said. "Who's directing this movie of yours?"

"I am."

"That must be hard. Directing a movie."

"Not if you plan everything beforehand," the deaf man answered.

THAT NIGHT, they put the first part of their plan into action.

At 11:01, a moment after the night watchman at the Pick-Pak Ice Cream Company entered the elevator which would take him to the top floor of the building, Rafe ran a bony hand through his straw-blond hair, adjusted his gold-rimmed eyeglasses and, without uttering a sound, promptly picked the lock on the front gate. Chuck, burly and apelike, pushed the gate back far enough for both men to enter. He rolled it closed again and they both walked to the nearest truck. Chuck got to work on the front license plate and Rafe got to work on the rear one.

At 11:03 they looked up to the top floor of the factory and saw the night watchman's flashlight illuminating the blank windows like a flitting soul behind a dead man's eyes.

By 11:05 the transfer of plates had been effectively accomplished, Chuck opened the hood of the truck and climbed in behind the wheel. Rafe found the ignition wires and crossed them. Then he went to the gate and rolled it all the way open. Chuck backed the truck out. Rafe climbed in beside him. He did not bother to close the gate again. The time was 11:07.

It took them fifteen minutes to drive crosstown to the rented store near the new shopping center. Pop and the deaf man were waiting in the back yard when the truck pulled in. The deaf man was wearing dark-grey slacks and a gray sports jacket. His black loafers were highly polished. They glowed even in the dim light from the street lamp.

Pop was wearing the uniform of a night watchman, the second uniform rented by the deaf man in McDouglas's shop.

The time was 11:23.

"Everything go all right?" the deaf man asked.

"Fine," Chuck said.

"Then let's get the signs on. Pop, you can take up your post now."

The old man walked out to the sidewalk near the front of the shop. The other men went into the store and came out carrying a drill and a bit, an extension cord, a flashlight, two huge metal signs reading "Chelsea Pops" and a box of nuts and bolts. Chuck began drilling holes into the side of the truck. Rafe and the deaf man began fastening on the first sign as soon as Chuck was finished.

The time was 11:34.

At 11:45, the patrolman appeared. His name was Dick Genero, and he ambled along the sidewalk nonchalantly, not expecting trouble and not looking for it. He could see a light flashing behind the store rented by that ice cream company, but the truck was effectively screened from the street by the building itself. On the sidewalk, he saw a man in uniform. At first, he thought it was another cop then he realized it was only a night watchman.

"Hello," he said to the man.

"Hello," Pop replied.

"Nice night, huh?" Genero asked.

"Beautiful."

Genero glanced toward the light in the back yard. "Working back there?" he asked.

"Yeah," Pop replied. "The ice-cream people."

"That's what I figured," Genero said. "Couldn't be the shopping-center people. They're all finished with their construction, aren't they?"

"Sure," Pop said.

"You a new man?"

Pop hesitated. "How do you mean?"

"Used to be another fellow here," Genero said. "When they were first building the center."

"Oh, yeah," Pop said.

"What was his name?" Genero asked.

For a moment, Pop felt as if he'd walked into a trap. He did not know the name of the man who'd preceded him. He wondered now if this cop knew the name and was testing him, or if he was just asking a simple question to make conversation.

"Freddie, wasn't it?" Pop said.

"I forget," Genero replied. He glanced over at the center. "They sure put these things up fast, don't they?"

"They sure do," Pop answered, relieved. He did not look toward the back yard. He did not want this stupid cop to think anything unusual was happening back there.

"The supermarket opened yesterday," Genero said, "and the drugstore, too. Bank's moving in tomorrow afternoon, be ready for business on the first. It's amazing the way they work things nowadays."

"It sure is," Pop said.

"A bank is all I need on my beat," Genero said. "Another headache to worry about." He studied Pop for a moment, and then asked, "You going to be here steady?"

"No," Pop answered. "I'm just on temporary."

"Until all the stores are in, huh?"

"That's right."

"Too bad," Genero said, grinning. "You'da made my job easier."

The light behind the ice-cream store went out suddenly. Genero looked toward the back yard.

"Guess they're finished," he said.

"I wish *I* was," Pop answered. "I'll be here all night long."

Genero chuckled. "Well, keep an eye on the bank for me, will you?" he said. He clapped the old man on the shoulder. "I'll be seeing you."

Whistling, he walked up the street past the ice-cream store, turned the corner, and moved out of sight.

The time was 12:00 midnight.

The truck behind the store now belonged to Chelsea Pops, Inc.

The three men who'd fastened the new signs into place went back into the store, and down into the basement, and then into the tunnel they'd dug across the back yard.

The tunnel was no makeshift job. They had, after all, been working on it for a very long time. It was high and wide, and shored up with thick wooden beams which braced the ceiling and the walls. It had been necessary to make a sturdy tunnel because men and equipment had been working aboveground all the while the tunnel was being dug. The deaf man had been certain they were deep enough to avoid any cave-ins, but he'd made the tunnel exceptionally strong anyway.

"I don't want anyone dropping in on us," he had punned intentionally, and then grinned with the other men and got back to work.

The construction work aboveground, the legitimate work that went into the building of the shopping center, had really been an excellent cover for the daylight digging of the tunnel. With all that noise and confusion on the surface, no one even once imagined that some of the noise was coming from *below* the ground. During the night, of course, the men had to exercise a little more caution. But even then, they'd been protected by their phony night watchman.

The interesting part of the job, the deaf man thought, was that their construction of the tunnel had kept pace with the legitimate construction of the bank. The construction aboveground was open to all viewers. Painstakingly, the deaf man had watched while the vault was being built, had watched while the all-important wiring box for the alarm system had been imbedded in the concrete floor of the vault and then covered over with another three-foot layer of concrete. The alarm, he knew, would be of the very latest variety. But he also knew there wasn't an alarm system in the world which Rafe could not render useless provided he could get at the wiring box.

The men had proceeded to get at the wiring box. As the shell of the bank took form and shape around the impregnable vault, the tunnel drove relentlessly across the back yard and then under the vault itself, and finally into the concrete until the underside of the vault was exposed. A web of steel had been crisscrossed into the vault floor between layers of concrete. The steel was almost impregnable, the rods constructed of laminated layers of metal, the grain of one layer running contrary to the grain of the next. A common hack saw would have broken on those laminated steel rods in the first thirty seconds of sawing. And the crisscrossing web made the task of forcible entry even more difficult since it limited the work space. Set an inch apart from each other, crossed like a fisherman's net, each laminated rod of steel became a separate challenge defying entry. The steel mat was like an army of die-hard virgins opposing an undernourished rapist. And beyond the mat, embedded in the second layer of concrete, was the wiring box for the alarm system. Assuredly, the vault was almost impregnable.

Well, almost is not quite.

The men had a long time to work. They used acid on the steel, drop by drop, eating away each separate rod, day by day, working slowly and surely, keeping pace with the shell of the bank as it grew higher over their heads. By the twenty-sixth of April they had cut a hole with a three-foot diameter into the mat. They had then proceeded to chip away at the concrete until they reached the wiring box. Rafe had unscrewed the bottom of the box and studied the system carefully. As he'd suspected, the system was the most modern kind, a combination of the open- and closed-circuit systems.

In an open-circuit alarm system, the cheapest kind, the alarm sounds when the current is closed. The closed-circuit system operates on a different electrical principle. There is always a weak current running through the wiring and if the wires are cut, the alarm will sound when that current is broken.

The combination system works both ways. The

alarm will sound if the current is broken, and the alarm will also sound when contact is established.

Anyone with a pair of shears can knock out the open-circuit system. All he has to do is cut the wires. The closed-contact system is a little more difficult to silence because it requires a cross-contacting of the wires. Rafe knew how to knock out both systems, and he also knew how to take care of the combination system—but that would have to wait until the evening of the thirtieth. It was the deaf man's contention that the alarm system would be tested when the money was put into the new vault. And when it was tested, he wanted it to sound off loud and clear. So the cover was screwed back onto the wiring box—the box was left exactly the way it had been found—and the men ignored it for now, hacking away at the concrete floor until they were some four inches from the inside of the vault. Four inches of concrete would hold anyone standing on it, the deaf man figured. But at the same time, four inches of concrete could be eliminated in ten minutes with the use of a power drill.

The belly of the vault was open.

When the alarm was set on the day the bank opened, no one in the world would be able to tell that the vault, for all practical purposes, had already been broken into. The belly of the vault was open.

And so was its mouth. And its mouth was waiting for the more than two million dollars which would be transferred from the Mercantile Trust Company under Dave Raskin's loft to the new bank at three o'clock tomorrow afternoon.

Tonight as the men chipped away at the concrete floor, the deaf man grinned securely. Pop was outside and waiting to turn away any curious eyes. Authority loved other authority, and a night watchman, in the eyes of the police, somehow became an automatic honorary member of the force.

"Let's play some poker later," the deaf man said, almost cheerfully, secure in the knowledge that not a single living soul knew they were under the ground looking up at the ripped-out guts of an impregnable bank vault. Not a damn living soul can guess where we are at this moment, he thought, and he clapped Chuck on the shoulder in a sudden gesture of camaraderie.

He was wrong.

There *was* a living soul who could have made a pretty good guess as to where they were at that moment.

But he was lying flat on his back in a hospital room, and he was deep in coma.

His name was Steve Carella.

16.

IT WAS THURSDAY, the last day of April.

Not one cop working out of the 87th was happy to get up that morning. Not one cop would be any happier by the time night fell.

To begin with, no cop liked the idea of another cop getting shot. It was sort of hard luck, you know? Sort of hoodoo. It was something like walking under a ladder, or stepping on a crack in the sidewalk, or writing a book with thirteen chapters. Nobody liked it. They were superstitious, yes. But more than that, they were human. And, whereas during the course of the working day they were able to pretend that their profession was compounded mainly of pleasant interviews with interesting people, delightful phone conversations with lovely debutantes, fascinating puzzles which required stimulating brainwork, bracing legwork in and around the most exciting city in the world, fraternal camaraderie with some of the nicest colleagues to be found anywhere, and the knowledge that one was part of a spirited and glorious team dedicated to law enforcement and the protection of the citizens of these United States—whereas every cop fed himself this crap from time to time, there was the persistently throbbing, though constantly submerged, knowledge that this wonderful, exciting, spirited, bracing, fraternal job could get a guy killed if he didn't watch his step.

The squadroom was inordinately silent on that last Thursday in April.

Because coupled with the knowledge that Steve Carella lay in coma in a hospital bed was the somewhat guilty relief usually experienced by a combat soldier when his buddy takes a sniper's bullet. The men of the 87th were sorry as hell that Steve Carella had been shot. But they were also glad it had been he and not they. The squadroom was silent with sorrow and guilt.

THE HOSPITAL was silent, too.

A light drizzle had begun at 11 A.M., gray and persistent, moistening the streets but not washing them, staining the hospital windows, dissolving the panes of glass, covering the floors with the projection of the rain pattern, giant amoeba-like shapes that gnawed at the antiseptic corridors.

Teddy Carella sat on a bench in the corridor and watched the rain pattern oozing along the floor. She did not want the shifting, magnified globules of water to reach her husband's room. In her fantasy, the projected image of the darting raindrops was the image of death itself, stealthily crawling across the floor, stopping at the very edge of the window's shadow, just short of the door to Steve's room. She could visualize the drops spreading farther and farther across the corridor, devouring the floor, battering at the door, knocking it down, and then sliding across the room to envelop the bed, to engulf her husband in gelatinlike death, to smother him in shadow.

She shuddered the thought aside.

THERE WAS A TINY BIRD against a white sky. The bird hung motionless. There was no wind, no sound, only the bird hanging against a white sky, emptiness.

And suddenly there was the rushing sound of a great wind gathering somewhere far in the distance, far across the sky, across the huge, deserted, barren plain, gathering in volume, and suddenly the dust swarmed across the barren plain, dust lifting into the sky, and the noise of the wind grew and grew and the bird hanging motionless was swept farther upward and began to drop like a stone, falling, falling, as the wind darkened the sky, rushing, the wind heaving into the sky, overwhelming the sky until it turned to gray and then seemed to invert itself, involuting, turning to a deep black while the roar of the wind carried the bird down, down, descending yellow beak, black devouring eyes.

He stood alone on the plain, his hair whipped by the wind, his clothing flapping wildly about his body, and he raised his fists impotently to the angry descending bird, and he screamed into the wind, screamed into the wind, and his words came back into his face and he felt the beak of the bird knifing into his shoulder with fire, felt the talons ripping, tearing, felt flame lashing his body, and still he screamed into the towering rush of the black wind against his frail body, his impotent fists, screaming, screaming.

"What's he saying?" Lieutenant Byrnes asked.

"I don't know," Hernandez answered.

"Listen. He's trying to say something."

"Ubba," Carella said. He twisted his head on the pillow. "Ubba," he mumbled.

"It's nothing," Hernandez said. "He's delirious."

"Ubba," Carella said. "Ubba cruxtion."

"He's trying to say something," Byrnes insisted.

"Ubba crusha," Carella said.

And then he screamed wordlessly.

THE TWO MEN, Chuck and Pop, had started work at twelve noon. They had synchronized their watches when leaving the store, and had made plans to meet at the ferry slip at four-oh-five. A revised estimate of the time it would take to accomplish their jobs had caused them to realize they could never catch the two-fifteen boat. So, the four-oh-five it was. And, if either one of them did not appear at that time, the other was to proceed to Majesta without him.

Their jobs, actually, were not too difficult—but they were time-consuming. Each of them carried a large suitcase, and each of the suitcases carried a total of twelve bombs. Six of the bombs were explosive; six were incendiary. Pop had made all of the bombs, and he was rather proud of his handiwork. It had been a long time since he'd practiced his craft, and he was pleased to note that he hadn't lost his touch. His bombs were really quite simple and could be expected to wreak quite a bit of havoc. Naturally, neither he **nor** Chuck wanted to be anywhere around when the bombs went off, and so each of the bombs carried a time fuse. The explosive bombs made use of simple alarm clocks and batteries and a system of wiring set to detonate several sticks of dynamite. The incendiary bombs were slightly more complicated and for those Pop had to rig a chemical time fuse.

The deaf man had specified that he wanted the explosions and the fires to start sometime between 4 and 4:30 P.M. He wanted both explosions *and* fires to be violent, and he wanted Pop to make sure the fires would not be extinguished before 5:45 P.M. Pop had set each of the exploding machines for 4:15. The incendiary bombs were another thing again; a chemical time fuse could not be set with the same accuracy as an alarm clock unless a great deal of experimentation were done beforehand.

Pop had done a great deal of experimentation.

He knew that concentrated sulfuric acid when dropped into a mixture of potassium chlorate and powdered sugar would immediately start a raging fire. For the purposes of his time fuse, he needed something which would keep the sulfuric acid away from the mixture until such time as the fire was desired. This was no small task. He began experimenting with cork. And he discovered through a series of long tests, that cork would char when exposed to the acid, and that it would take four hours for the acid to eat through .025 inches of cork or, in other words, a slice of cork which was one fortieth of an inch thick.

Pop prepared his bombs.

He filled a shoe box with oil-soaked rags. Into the

center of the box, he set a small cardboard container filled with a mixture of potassium chlorate and powdered sugar, sealed so that the mixture would not spill out. Into the top surface of the small container, he cut a hole which would accommodate the neck of a small bottle. The bottle would be filled with a 70 per cent solution of sulfuric acid, sealed with a cork cap which was one fortieth of an inch thick, and then stuck into the hole in the top of the container at twelve noon, when the men left to do their work. In approximately four hours' time, the acid would have eaten through the cork and begun to drip onto the mixture in the container. A violent fire would ensue, aided and assisted by the oil-soaked rags. In other words, the fires would begin at approximately four o'clock—*approximately* because it was difficult to cut a slice of cork exactly one fortieth of an inch thick and a variation in millimeters would, because the rate of char remained constant, start the conflagration either slightly earlier or slightly later. In any case, Pop estimated, the fires would start at *about* four o'clock, give or take a few minutes either way, and the deaf man seemed more than pleased with the estimate.

At twelve noon, Chuck and Pop stuck the bottles of sulfuric acid into the holes cut in the cardboard containers, the thin slices of cork being the only thing between the acid and the mixture. Then they sealed the shoe boxes, packed their suitcases, and trotted off to disrupt a city.

BY ONE-THIRTY, when the ball game started, Chuck had set three incendiary bombs and one exploding bomb in the baseball stadium near the River Harb. He had set two of the incendiaries in the grandstand, and the third in the bleachers. The explosive had been left just inside the main entrance arch, in a trash basket there. The deaf man had figured that the game would break sometime around four-thirty. The bomb was set for four-fifteen, and he hoped its explosion would cause a bit of confusion among the departing spectators—especially since there would be three fires in the stadium by that time. To insure that the fires would still be roaring by the time the bomb exploded, he had instructed Chuck to cut the hoses of every fire extinguisher he saw anywhere in the stadium, and Chuck had done that and was now anxious to get away before anyone spotted him.

There were eight bombs left in Chuck's valise. He consulted his two remaining maps, each marked with his name in the right-hand corner, and began moving quickly toward his remaining destinations. The first of these was a motion picture theater on The Stem. He paid for a ticket at the box office, climbed instantly to the balcony, and consulted his map again. Two X's on the map indicated where he was to place the explosives, directly over the balcony's supporting columns and close to the projection booth where there was the attendant possibility of the explosion causing a fire and a stench when it hit the film. The main purpose of the blasts, of course, was to knock down the balcony, but the deaf man was not a person to turn aside residuals. In the corridor outside the balcony, Chuck glanced around hastily, and then slashed the hoses on the extinguishers. Rapidly, he left the theater. A glance at his watch told him it was two-fifteen. He would damn well have to hurry if he wanted to catch that four-oh-five boat.

He was now in possession of six remaining bombs.

The deaf man wanted three of them to be placed in Union Station: an incendiary in the baggage room, an explosive on the track of the incoming Chicago Express (due at four-ten), and another explosive on the counter of the circular information booth.

The remaining three bombs could be placed by Chuck at his discretion—provided, of course, they were all deposited at different locations on the south side of the precinct. The deaf man had suggested leaving an incendiary in a subway car, and an explosive in the open-air market on Chament Avenue, but the final decisions were being left to Chuck, dependent on time and circumstance.

"Suppose I put them where there aren't any people?" Chuck had asked.

"That would be foolish," the deaf man said.

"I mean, look, this is supposed to be a bank heist."

"Yes?"

"So why do we have to put these things where—where a lot of people'll get hurt?"

"Where would you like to put them? In an empty lot?"

"Well, no, but—"

"I've never heard of confusion in a vacuum," the deaf man had replied.

"Still—dammit, suppose we get caught? You're

fooling around with—with *murder* here, do you realize that? Murder!"

"So?"

"So look, I know there are guys who'd slit their
own grandmother's throat for a nickel, but—"

"I'm not one of them," the deaf man had answered
coldly. "There happens to be two and a half million
dollars at stake here." He had paused. "Do you want
out, Chuck?"

Chuck had not wanted out. Now, as he headed for
Union Station, the suitcase was noticeably and happily
lighter. He was itching to get the job over and done
with. He didn't want to be anywhere south of the
Mercantile Trust Company after four o'clock. If everything went according to the deaf man's plan, that part
of the precinct would be an absolute madhouse along
about then, and Chuck wanted no part of chaos.

THE OIL REFINERY was set on the River Dix, at the
southern tip of the island of Isola. Pop walked up to the
main gate and reached into his pocket for the identification badge the deaf man had given him. He flashed the
badge casually at the guard, and the guard nodded, and
Pop walked through the gate, stopped once to consult
the X's on his map, and then walked directly to the tool
shed behind the administration building. The tool shed,
besides being stocked with the usual number of saws
and hammers and screwdrivers, contained a few dozen
cans of paint, turpentine, and varnish. Pop opened the
door of the shed and put one of his explosive bombs in
a cardboard carton of trash just inside the door. Then

he closed the door and began walking toward the pay-master's shack near the first of the huge oil tanks.

By one-forty-five he had set four bombs in the refinery. He walked through the main gate, waved goodbye to the guard, hailed a cab and headed for a plant some thirty blocks distant, a plant which faced south toward the River Dix, its chimneys belching smoke to the city's sky twenty-four hours a day.

The sign across the top of that plant read EASTERN ELECTRIC. It produced electric power for 70 per cent of the homes and businesses on the south side of the 87th Precinct.

AT 3:00 P.M., they closed the doors of the old Mercantile Trust for the last time.

Mr. Wesley Gannley, manager of the bank, watched with some sadness as his employees left for the new bank in the completed shopping center. Then he went back into the vault where the guards were carrying the bank's stock—two million, three hundred fifty-three thousand, four hundred twenty dollars and seventy-four cents in American currency—to the waiting armored truck outside.

Mr. Gannley thought it was nice that so much money was being taken to the new bank. Usually, his bank had some eight hundred thousand dollars on hand, an amount which was swelled every Friday, pay-roll day, to perhaps a million and a quarter. There were a great many firms, however, which paid their employees every two weeks, and still others which had monthly bonus programs. In any case, April 30 was the end of the month, and tomorrow was a Friday, May 1, and so the bank was holding, besides its usual deposits and money on hand, an unusually large amount of payroll money, and this pleased Mr. Gannley immensely. It seemed fitting that a spanking-new bank should open shop with a great deal of cold cash.

He stepped out onto the sidewalk as the bank guards transferred that cold cash to the truck. From the grimestained window of his loft upstairs, Dave Raskin watched the transaction with mild interest, and then took a huge puff on his soggy cigar and turned back to studying the front of Margarita's smock.

By 3:30 P.M., the $2,353,420.74 was safe and snug in the new vault of the new bank in the new shopping center. Mr. Gannley's employees were busily making themselves at home in their new quarters, and all seemed right with the world.

At 4:00 P.M., the deaf man began making his phone calls.

HE MADE THE CALLS from the telephone in the icecream store behind the new bank. Rafe was waiting in the drugstore across the street from the bank, watching the bank's front door. He would report back to the deaf man as soon as everyone had left the bank. In the meantime, the deaf man had his own work to do.

The typewritten list beside the telephone had one hundred names on it. The names were those of stores, offices, movie theaters, shops, restaurants, utilities, and even private citizens on the south side of the 87th Precinct. The deaf man hoped to get through at least fifty of those names before five o'clock, figuring on the basis of a minute per call, and allowing for a percentage of no-answers. Hopefully, *all* of the persons called would in turn call the police. More realistically, perhaps half of the fifty would. Pessimistically, perhaps ten would report the calls. And, figuring a rock-bottom return of 10 per cent, at least five would contact the police.

Even five was a good return for an hour's work if it compounded the confusion and made the ride to the ferry simpler.

Of the hundred names on the list, four were really in trouble. They were really in trouble because Chuck and Pop had deposited either incendiary or explosive bombs in their places of business. These four establishments would *certainly* call the police, if not immediately upon receipt of the deaf man's call, then *positively* after the bombs went off. The point of the deaf man's calls was to provide the police with a list of clues, only four of which were valid. The trouble was, the police would not know which of the clues were valid and which were not. And once reports of mayhem began filtering in, they could not in good conscience afford to ignore *any* tip.

The deaf man pulled the phone to him and dialed the first number on his list.

A woman answered the phone. "The Culver Theater," she said. "Good afternoon."

"Good afternoon," the deaf man said pleasantly. "There is a bomb in a shoe box somewhere in the orchestra of your theater," and he hung up.

At 4:05 P.M., Chuck and Pop boarded the ferry to Majesta and spent the next ten minutes whispering together like school boys about the conspiracy they had just committed.

At 4:15 P.M., the first of the bombs exploded.

"EIGHTY-SEVENTH SQUAD, Detective Hernandez. What? What did you say?" He began scribbling on his pad. "Yes, sir. And the address, sir? When did you get this call, sir? Yes, sir, thank you. Yes, sir, right away, thank you."

Hernandez slammed the phone back onto its cradle.

"Pete!" he yelled, and Byrnes came out of his office immediately. "Another one! What do we do?"

"A bomb?"

"Yes."

"A real one, or just a threat?"

"A threat. But, Pete, that last movie theater . . ."

"Yes, yes."

"That was just a threat, too. But, dammit, two bombs really went off in the balcony. What do we do?"

"Call the Bomb Squad."

"I did on the last three calls we got."

"Call them again! And contact Murchison. Tell him we want any more of these bomb threats to be transferred directly to the Bomb Squad. Tell him—"

"Pete, if we get many more of these, the Bomb Squad'll be hamstrung. They'll dump the squeals right back into our laps, anyway."

"Maybe we won't get any more. Maybe—"

The telephone rang. Hernandez picked it up instantly.

"Eighty-seventh Squad, Hernandez. Who? Where? Holy Je— *What* did you say? Have you—yes, sir, I see. Have you—yes, sir, try to calm down, will you, sir? Have you called the fire department? All right, sir, we'll get on it right away."

He hung up. Byrnes was waiting.

"The ball park, Pete. Fires have broken out in the grandstands and bleachers. Hoses on all the extinguishers have been cut. People are running for the exits. Pete, there's gonna be a goddam riot, I can smell it."

And at that moment, just inside the entrance arch, as people rushed in panic from the fires raging through the stadium, a bomb exploded.

THE PEOPLE ON the south side of the precinct did not know what the hell was happening. Their first guess was that the Russians were coming, and that these wholesale explosions and fires were simply acts of sabotage preceding an invasion. Some of the more exotic-minded citizens speculated upon an invasion from Mars, some said it was all that strontium 90 in the air which was causing spontaneous combustion, some said it was all just coincidence, but everyone was frightened and everyone was on the edge of panic.

Not one of them realized that percentages were being manipulated or that a city's preventive forces, accustomed to dealing with the long run, were being pushed into dealing with the short run.

There were 186 patrolmen, 22 sergeants and 16 detectives attached to the 87th Precinct. A third of this force was off duty when the first of the bombs went off. In ten minutes' time, every cop who could be reached by telephone was called and ordered to report to the precinct at once. In addition, calls were made to the adjoining 88th and 89th Precincts which commanded a total of 370 patrolmen, 54 sergeants and 42 detectives and the strength of this force was added to that of the 87th's until a stream of men was pulled from every corner of the three precincts and rushed to the disaster-stricken south side. The ball park was causing the most trouble at the moment, because some forty thousand fans had erupted into a full-scale panic-ridden riot, and the attendant emergency police trucks, and the fire engines, and the patrol cars, and the mounted policemen, and the reporters and the sight-seeing spectators made control a near-impossibility.

At the same time, a Bomb Squad which was used to handling a fistful of bomb threats daily was suddenly swamped with bomb reports from forty different areas in the 87th Precinct. Every available man was called into action and rushed to the various trouble spots, but there simply weren't enough men to go around and they simply didn't know which trouble spots were going to erupt or when. To their credit, they did catch one incendiary in an office building before it burst into flame, but at the same time a bomb exploded on the fourteenth floor of that same building, an unfortunate circumstance since the bomb had been set in the laboratory of a chemical research company, and the attendant fire swept through three floors of the building even before the fire alarm was pulled.

The Fire Department had its own headaches. The first unit called into action was Engine 31 and Ladder 46, a unit in the heart of the south side, a unit which reportedly handled more damn fires daily than any other unit in the entire city. They connected to a hydrant on Chament Avenue and South Fourth in an attempt to control the blaze that was sweeping through the open-air market on Chament Avenue. Within a few minutes, the fire had leaped across Chament Avenue and was threatening a line of warehouses along the river. Acting Lieutenant Carl Junius in charge of the engine had a brief consultation with Lieutenant Bob Fancher of Ladder 46, and they radioed to Acting Deputy Chief George D'Oraglio who immediately ordered an alarm transmitted with orders to the responding units to expect counterorders at a moment's notice since he had already received word of a fire in a motion picture theater not twenty blocks from the market. Engine 81 and Ladder 33 arrived in a matter of minutes and were promptly redispatched to the motion picture theater, but by this time the hook and ladder company handling the ball park fire had called in for assistance, and Chief D'Oraglio suddenly realized he had his hands full and that he would need every available engine and hook and ladder company in the city to control was was shaping up as a major disaster.

The police emergency trucks with two-way radio numbered fifteen, and the emergency station wagons with two-way radio numbered ten, and all twenty-five of these were dispatched to the scenes of the fires and explosions which were disrupting traffic everywhere on the south side and which were causing all nine of the traffic precincts to throw extra men and equipment into the stricken area.

The north side of the precinct, the area between the new quarters of the Mercantile Trust Company and the waiting room of the Isola-Majesta ferry, was suddenly devoid of policemen.

Meyer Meyer and Bert Kling, cruising in an unmarked sedan, ready to prevent any crime which occurred against the harassed places of business on their list, received a sudden and urgent radio summons and were promptly off The Heckler Case. The radio dispatcher told them to proceed immediately to a subway station on Grady Road to investigate a bomb threat there.

By 4:30 P.M., six Civil Defense units were thrown into the melee, and the Police Commissioner made a hurried call to the Mayor in an attempt to summon the National Guard. The National Guard *would* eventually be called into action because what started as a simple plot to rob a bank would grow into a threat to the very city itself, a threat to equal the Chicago fire or the San Francisco earthquake, a threat which—when all was said and done—totaled billions of dollars in loss and almost razed to the ground one of the finest ports in the United States. But the wheels of bureaucracy grind exceedingly slow, and the National Guard units would not be called in until 5:40 P.M., by which time the Mercantile Trust Company's vault would be empty, by which time invasion reports had caused panic beyond anything imagined by the deaf man, by which time the river front to the south was a blazing wall of flame, by which time everyone involved knew they were in the center of utter chaos.

In the meantime, it was only 4:30 P.M., and the deaf man had completed twenty-two of his calls. Smiling, listening to the sound of sirens outside, he dialed the twenty-third number.

MR. WESLEY GANNLEY, manager of the Mercantile Trust Company, paced the marbled floors of his new place of business, grinning at the efficiency of his employees, pleased as punch with the new building. The IBM machines were ticking away behind the counters. Music flowed from hidden wall speakers, and a mural at the far end of the building, washed with rain-dimmed light at the moment, depicted the strength of America and the wisdom of banking. The polished glass-and-steel door of the vault was open, and Gannley could see into it to the rows of safety deposit boxes and beyond that to the barred steel door, and he felt a great sense of security, he felt it was good to be alive.

Mr. Gannley took his gold pocket watch from the pocket of his vest and looked at the time.

4:35 P.M.

In twenty-five minutes, they would close up shop for the day.

Tomorrow morning, May 1, everyone would return bright and early, and depositers would come through the bank's marble entrance arch and step up to the shining new tellers' windows, anxious to reap that three and a half per cent, and Mr. Gannley would watch from the open door of his manager's office and begin counting the ways he would spend his Christmas bonus this year.

Yes, it was good to be alive.

He walked past Miss Finchley who was bending over a stack of canceled checks, and he was seized with an uncontrollable urge to pinch her on the buttocks.

He controlled the urge.

"How do you like the new building, Miss Finchley?" he asked.

Miss Finchley turned toward him. She was wearing a white silk blouse, and the top button had come unfastened and he could see the delicate lace of her lingerie showing where the cream-white flesh ended.

"It's beautiful, Mr. Gannley," she answered. "Simply beautiful. It's a pleasure to work here."

"Yes," he said. "It certainly is."

He stood staring at her for a moment, wondering whether or not he should ask her to join him for a cocktail after closing. No, he thought, that would be too forward. But perhaps a lift to the station. Perhaps that might not be misinterpreted.

"Yes, Mr. Gannley?" she said.

He decided against it. There was plenty of time for that. In a wonderful new building like this one, with IBM machines and music flowing from hidden speakers, and a bright, colorful mural decorating the far wall, and an impervious steel vault, there was plenty of time for everything.

Recklessly, he said, "You'd better button your blouse, Miss Finchley."

Her hand fluttered up to the wayward button. "Oh, my," she said. "I'm practically naked, aren't I?" and she buttoned the blouse quickly without the faintest trace of a blush.

Plenty of time for everything, Wesley Gannley thought, smiling, plenty of time.

The tellers were beginning to wheel their mobile units into the vault. Every day at 4:45 P.M., the tellers performed this ritual. First they took the coin racks from the change machines on the counter and laced these racks into the top drawers of the units. The bottom drawers usually contained folding money. Today, both drawers and coin racks were empty because the bank had not done any business at its new location, and all the money had been transferred directly to the new vault. But nonetheless, it was 4:45 P.M., and so the units were wheeled into the vault and Mr. Gannley looked at his watch, went to his desk, and took the key which fit into the three clocks on the inside face of the vault door. The clocks were minuscule and were marked with numerals indicating hours. Mr. Gannley put his key into the first clock and set it for fifteen hours. He did the same to the other two clocks. He expected to be at work at 7:30 A.M. tomorrow morning, and he would open the vault at 7:45 A.M. It was now 4:45 P.M.—ergo, fifteen hours. If he tried to open the vault door before that time, it would not budge, even if he correctly opened the two combination locks on the front face of the door.

Mr. Gannley put the key into his vest pocket and then heaved his shoulder against the heavy vault door.

It was a little difficult to close because the carpeting on the floor was new and still thick and the door's friction against it provided an unusual hindrance. But he managed to shove the door closed, and then he turned the wheel which clicked the tumblers into place, and then he spun the dials of the two combination locks. He knew the alarm was automatically set the moment that vault door slammed shut. He knew it would sound at the nearest police precinct should anyone tamper with the door. He knew that the combination locks could not be opened if the time mechanism was not tripped. He further knew that, should the alarm go off accidentally, he was to call the police immediately to tell them a robbery was *not* truly in progress, the alarm had simply gone off by accident. And then, as an added precaution if he made such a call to the police, he was to call them back in two minutes to verify the accident. In short, should a robbery *really* be in progress and should the thief force Gannley into calling the police to say the alarm had been accidental, the police would know something was fishy if he didn't duplicate the call within the next two minutes.

For now, for the moment, there was one thing more to do. Wesley Gannley went to the telephone and dialed FRederick 7-8024.

"Eighty-seventh Precinct, Sergeant Murchison."

"This is Mr. Gannely at the new Mercantile Trust."

"What is it, Mr. Gannley? Somebody call *you* about a bomb, too?"

"I beg your pardon?"

"Never mind, never mind. What is it?"

"I'm about to test this alarm. I wanted you to know."

"Oh. Okay. When are you going to trip it?"

"As soon as I hang up."

"All right. Will you call me back?"

"I will."

"Right."

Mr. Gannley hung up, walked to one of the alarm buttons set behind the tellers' cages, and deliberately stepped on it. The alarm went off with a terrible clanging. Immediately, Mr. Gannley turned it off, and then called the police again to tell them everything was working fine. He passed the vault door and patted it lovingly. He knew the alarm was there and working, a vigilant watchdog over all that money.

He did not know that its voice was a tribute to the careful labor which had gone on below the ground for the past two months, or that it would be silenced forever within the next half-hour.

IT WAS 5:05 P.M.

In the new drugstore across the street from the bank, Rafe sat on a stool and watched the bank doors. Twelve people had left so far, the bank guard opening the door for each person who left, and then closing it again behind them. There were three people left inside the bank, including the bank guard. Come on, Rafe thought, get the hell out.

The big clock over the counter read 5:06.

Rafe sipped at his Coke and watched the bank doors.

5:07.

Come on, he thought. We have to catch a goddam ferry at five minutes after six. That gives us less than an hour. He figures we'll be able to break away that remaining concrete in ten minutes, but I figure at least fifteen. And then ten more minutes to load the money, and another ten—if we don't hit traffic—to get to the ferry slip. That's thirty-five minutes, provided everything goes all right, provided we don't get stopped for anything.

Rafe took off his gold-rimmed glasses, wiped the bridge of his nose, and then put the glasses on again.

The absolute limit, I would say, is five-forty-five. We've got to be out of that vault by five-forty-five. That gives us twenty minutes to get to the ferry slip. We should make it in twenty minutes. Provided everything goes all right.

We should make it.

Unreasonably, the bridge of Rafe's nose was soaked with sweat again. He took off his glasses, wiped away the sweat, and almost missed the bank door across the street opening. A girl in a white blouse stepped out and then shrank back from the drizzle. A portly guy in a dark suit stepped into the rain and quickly opened a big black umbrella. The girl took his arm and they went running off up the street together.

One more to go, Rafe thought.

The bridge of his nose was sweating again, but he did not take off the glasses.

Across the street, he saw the bank lights going out.

His heart lurched.

One by one, the lights behind the windows went dark. He waited. He was getting off the stool when he saw the door opening, saw the bank guard step out and slam the door behind him. The guard turned and tried the automatically locked door. The door did not yield. Even from across the street, Rafe saw the bank guard give a satisfied nod before he started off into the rain.

The clock over the drugstore counter read 5:15. Rafe started for the door quickly.

"Hey!"

He stopped short. An icy fist had clamped onto the base of his spine.

"Ain't you gonna pay for your Coke?" the soda jerk asked.

THE DEAF MAN was waiting at the far end of the tunnel, directly below the bank vault when he heard Rafe enter at the other end. The tunnel was dripping moisture from its walls and roof, and the deaf man felt clammy with perspiration. He did not like the smell of the earth. It was a suffocating, fetid stench which filled the nostrils and made a man feel as if he were being choked. He waited while Rafe approached.

"Well?" he asked.

"They're all out," Rafe said.

The deaf man nodded curtly. "There's the box," he said, and he swung his hand flash up to illuminate the box containing the wiring for the alarm system.

Rafe crawled into the gaping hole in the corroded steel bars and reached up for the exposed alarm box.

He pulled back his hands and took off his glasses. They were fogged with the tunnel's moisture. He wiped the glasses, put them back on the bridge of his nose, and then got to work.

IN THE FEVERED DELIRIUM of his black world, things seemed clearer to Steve Carella than they ever had in his life.

He sat at a nucleus of pain and confusion, and yet things were crystal clear, and the absolute clarity astonished him because it seemed his sudden perception threatened his entire concept of himself as a cop. He was staring wide-eyed at the knowledge that he and his colleagues had come up against a type of planning and execution which had rendered them virtually helpless. He had a clear and startling vision of himself and the 87th Squad as a group of half-wits stumbling around in a fog of laboratory reports, fruitless leg work, and meaningless paper work which in the end brought only partial and minuscule results.

He was certain now that John Smith had been murdered by the same deaf man who had shot and repeatedly battered Carella with the stock of a shotgun. He was reasonably certain that the same weapon had been used in both attacks. He was certain, too, that the blueprint he'd found in the Franklin Street apartment was a construction blueprint for the vault of the Mercantile Trust, and that a robbery of that vault had been planned.

Intuitively, and this was what frightened him, he knew that the murder, and his own beating, and the planned bank robbery were tied in to the case Meyer Meyer was handling, the so-called Heckler Case.

He did not question the intuition nor its clarity—but he knew damn well it scared him. Perhaps it would have frightened him less if he'd known it wasn't quite intuition. Whether he realized it or not, and despite the fact that he had never openly discussed the supposedly separate cases with Meyer, he *had* unconsciously been exposed to siftings of telephone conversations, to quick glances at reports on Meyer's desk. These never seemed to warrant a closer conversation with the other detective, but they did nonetheless form a submerged layer of knowledge which, when combined with the knowledge he now possessed, welded an undeniable and seemingly intuitive link.

But if the reasoning were correct—and it could hardly be called reasoning—if this *sense* of connection were accurate, it pointed to someone who was not gambling senselessly against the police. Instead, it presented the image of a person who was indeed leaving very little to chance, a person who was *using* the agencies of law enforcement, utilizing them as a part of his plan, making them work for him, joining them instead of fighting them, making them an integral part of a plan which had begun—how long ago?

And this is what frightened Carella.

Because he knew, detective fiction to the contrary, that the criminal mind was not a particularly brilliant one. The average thief with whom the squad dealt daily was of only average intelligence, if that, and was usually handicapped by a severe emotional disturbance

which had led him into criminal activities to begin
with. The average murderer was a man who killed on
the spur of the moment, whether for revenge, or
through instant rage, or through a combination of cir-
cumstances which led to murder as the only seemingly
logical conclusion. Oh yes, there were carefully
planned robberies, but these were few and far between.
The average job could be cased in a few days and executed in a half hour. And yes, there were carefully
planned murders, homicides figured to the most
minute detail and executed with painstaking preci-
sion—but these, too, were exceptions. And, of course,
one shouldn't forget the confidence men whose stock
in trade was guile and wile—but how many *new* con
games were there, and how many con men were practicing the same tired routines, all known to the police
for years and years?

Carella was forced to admit that the police were
dealing with a criminal element which, in a very real
sense, was amateurish. They qualified for professional
status only in that they worked—if you will excuse the
term when applied to crime—for money. And he was
forced to admit further that the police opposing this
vast criminal army were also attacking their job in a
somewhat amateurish way, largely because nothing
more demanding was called for.

Well, this deaf man whoever he was, *was* making
further demands. He was elevating crime to a professional level, and if he were not met on equally professional terms, he would succeed. The entire police
force could sit around with its collective thumb up its

collective ass, and the deaf man would run them ragged and carry home the bacon besides.

Which made Carella wonder about his own role as a cop and his own duties as an enforcer of the law. He was a man dedicated to the prevention of crime, or failing that, to the apprehension of the person or persons committing crime. If he totally succeeded in his job, there would be no more crime and no more criminals; and, carrying the thought to its logical conclusion, there would also be no more job. If there was no crime, there would be no need for the men involved in preventing it or detecting it.

And yet somehow this logic was illogical, and it led Carella to a further thought which was as frightening as the sudden clarity he was experiencing.

The thought sprang into his head full-blown: *If there is no crime, will there be society?*

The thought was shocking—at least to Carella it was. For society was predicated on a principle of law and order, of meaning as opposed to chaos. But if there were no crime, if there were in effect no lawbreakers, no one to oppose law and order, would there be a necessity for law? Without lawbreakers, *was* there a need for law? And without law, would there be lawbreakers?

MADAM, I'M ADAM.

Read it forwards or backwards and it says the same thing. A cute party gag, but what happens when you say, "Crime is symbiotic with society," and then reverse the statement so that it reads, "Society is symbiotic with crime?"

Carella lay in the blackness of his delirium, not knowing he was up against a logician and a mathematician, but intuitively reasoning in mathematical and logical terms. He knew that something more was required of him. He knew that in this vast record of day-by-day crime, this enormous never-ending account of society and the acts committed against it, something more was needed from him as a cop and as a man. He did not know what that something more was, nor indeed whether he could ever make the quantum jump from the cop and man he now was to a cop and man quite different.

Clarity suffused the darkness of his coma.

In the clarity, he knew he would live.

And he knew that someone was in the room with him, and he knew that this person must be told about the Mercantile Trust Company and the Uhrbinger Construction Company and the blueprint he had seen in the Franklin Street apartment.

And so he said, "Merc-uh-nuh," and he knew he had not formed the word correctly and he could not understand why because everything seemed so perfectly clear within the shell of his dark cocoon.

And so he tried the other word, and he said, "Ubba-nuh coston," and he knew that was wrong, and he tried again, "Ubba-nuh . . . ubba . . . Uhrbinger . . . Uhrbinger," and he was sure he had said it that time, and he leaned back into the brilliant clarity and lost consciousness once more.

The person in the room with him was Teddy Carella, his wife.

But Teddy was a deaf mute, and she watched her husband's lips carefully, and she saw the word "Uhrbinger" form on those lips, but it was not a word in her vocabulary, and so she reasoned that her husband was delirious.

She took his hand and held it in her own, and then she kissed it and put it to her cheek.

The hospital lights went out suddenly.

The bombs Pop had set at Eastern Electric were beginning to go off.

RAFE, LIKE ANY good surgeon, had checked his earlier results before making his final incision. He had run a Tong Tester over the wires in the box once more, checking the wires which carried the current, nodding as they tallied with the calculations he had made the first time he looked into the box.

"Okay," he said, apparently to the deaf man who was standing below him, but really to no one in particular, really a thinking out loud. "Those are the ones carrying the juice, all right. I cross-contact those and cut the others, and it's clear sailing."

"All right, then do it," the deaf man said impatiently.

Rafe set about doing it.

He accomplished the cross-contact with speed and efficiency. Then he thrust his hand at the deaf man. "The clippers," he said.

The deaf man handed them up to him. "What are you going to do?"

"Cut the other wires."

"Are you sure you've done this right?"

"I think so."

"Don't think!" the deaf man said sharply. "Yes or no? Is that damn alarm going to go off when you cut those wires?"

"I don't think so."

"Yes or no?"

"No," Rafe said. "It won't go off."

"All right," the deaf man said. "Cut them."

Rafe took a deep breath and moved the clippers toward the wires. With a quick, deliberate contraction of his hand, he squeezed the handles of the clippers together and cut the wires.

The alarm did not go off.

AT THE HOUSE in Majesta, Chuck paced the floor nervously while Pop studied the alarm clock sitting on the dresser.

"What time is it?" Chuck asked.

"Five-thirty."

"They should be out of the bank and on their way by now."

"Unless something went wrong," Pop said.

"Yeah," Chuck answered distractedly, and he began pacing the floor again. "Put on that radio, will you?" he said.

Pop turned it on.

" . . . raging out of control along a half-mile square of waterfront," the announcer said. "Every available piece of fire equipment in the city has been rushed to the disaster area in an effort to control the flames before they spread further. The rain is not helping conditions. Slippery streets seem to be working against the men and apparatus. The firemen and police are operating only from the lights of their trucks, an explosion at the Eastern Electric Company having effectively blinded seventy per cent of the area's streets, homes and businesses. Fortunately, there is still electric power in Union Station where an explosion on track twelve derailed the incoming Chicago train as a bomb went off simultaneously in the waiting room. The fire in the baggage room there was brought under control, but is still smoldering."

The announcer paused for breath.

"In the meantime, the Mayor and the Police Commissioner are still in secret session debating whether or not to call out the National Guard in this emergency situation, and there are several big questions that remain unanswered: *What is happening? Who is responsible for this? And why?* Those are the questions in the mind of every thinking citizen as the city struggles for its very survival."

The announcer paused again.

"Thank you, and good night," he said.

Pop turned off the radio.

He had to admit he felt a slight measure of pride.

THEY CAME OUT of the vault and through the tunnel at 5:40 P.M. They made three trips back and forth between the bank vault and the basement of the store, and then they carried the cartons stuffed with money to the truck. They opened the door to the refrigerator compartment and shoved the cartons inside. Then they closed the refrigerator door, and Rafe started the truck.

"Just a minute," the deaf man said. "Look."

Rafe followed his pointing hand. The sky was ablaze with color. The buildings to the south were blacked out, but the sky behind them was an angry swirl of red, orange and yellow. The flames consumed the entire sky, the very night itself. Police and fire sirens wailed in the distance to the south; now and then an explosion touched off by the roaring fire punctuated the keen of the sirens and the whisper of rain against the pavements.

The deaf man smiled, and Rafe put the truck in motion.

"What time is it?" Rafe asked.

"Five-fifty."

"So we missed the five-forty-five boat."

"That's right. And we've got fifteen minutes to make the six-oh-five. I don't think we'll have any trouble."

"I hope not," Rafe said.

"Do you know how much money we have in the ice box?" the deaf man asked, grinning.

"How much?"

"More than two million dollars." The deaf man paused. "That's a lot of money, Rafe, wouldn't you say so?"

"I would say so," Rafe answered, preoccupied. He was watching the road and the traffic signals. They had come eight blocks and there had been no sign of a policeman. The streets looked eerie somehow. Cops were a familiar part of the landscape, but every damn cop in the precinct was probably over on the south side. Rafe had to hand it to the deaf man. Still, he didn't want to pass any lights, and he didn't want to exceed the speed limit. And, too, the streets were slippery. He'd hate like hell to crash into a lamppost with all that money in the ice box.

"What time is it?" he asked the deaf man.

"Five-fifty-six."

Rafe kept his foot steady on the accelerator. He signaled every time they made a turn. He panicked once when he heard a siren behind them, but the squad car raced past on his left, intent on the more important matters at hand.

"They all seem to be going someplace," the deaf man said, grinning securely.

"Yeah," Rafe said. His heart was beating wildly in his chest. He would not have admitted it to anyone, but he was terrified. All that money. Suppose something went wrong? All that money.

"What time is it?" he asked, as he made the turn into the parking lot at the ferry slip.

"Six-oh-one," the deaf man said.

"Where's the boat?" Rafe asked, looking out over the river.

"It'll be here," the deaf man said. He was feeling rather good. His plan had taken into account the probability that some cops would be encountered on the drive from the bank to the ferry slip. Well, they had come within kissing distance of a squad car, and the car had gone merrily along its way, headed for the fire-stricken area. The incendiaries had worked beautifully. Perhaps he could talk the men into voting Pop a bonus. Perhaps . . .

"Where's the damn boat?" Rafe said impatiently.

"Give it time. It'll be here."

"You sure there *is* a six-oh-five?"

"I'm sure."

"Let me see that schedule," Rafe said. The deaf man reached into his pocket and handed him the folder. Rafe glanced at it quickly.

"Holy Jesus!" he said.

"What's the matter?"

"It's not running," Rafe said. "There's a little notation beside it, a letter *E,* and that letter means it only runs on May thirtieth, July fourth and—"

"You're reading it wrong," the deaf man said calmly. "That letter *E* is alongside the seven-fifteen boat. There are no symbols beside the six-oh-five. I know that schedule by heart, Rafe."

Rafe studied the schedule again. Abashed, he muttered a small, "Oh," and then looked out over the river again. "Then where the hell is it?"

"It'll be here," the deaf man assured him.

"What time is it?"

"Six-oh-four."

IN THE RENTED HOUSE in Majesta, Chuck lighted a cigarette and leaned closer to the radio.

"There's nothing on so far," he said. "They don't know what the hell's happening." He paused. "I guess they got away."

"Suppose they didn't?" Pop said.

"What do you mean?"

"What do we do? If they got picked up?"

"We'll hear about it on the radio. Everybody's just dying for an explanation. They'll flash it the minute they know. And we'll beat it."

"Suppose they tell the cops where we are?"

"They won't get caught," Chuck said.

"Suppose. And suppose they tell?"

"They wouldn't do that."

"Wouldn't they?"

"Shut up," Chuck said. He was silent for a moment. Then he said, "No, they wouldn't."

THE PATROLMAN CAME OUT of the waiting room, looked past the ice-cream truck and over the river, sucked the good drizzly air of April into his lungs, put his hands on his hips, and studied the cherry-red glow in the sky to the south. He did not realize he was an instrument of probability. He was one of those cops who, either through accident or design, had been left on his post rather than pulled southward to help in the emergency. He knew there was a big fire on the River Dix, but his beat was the thirty waterfront blocks on the River Harb, starting with the ferry waiting room and working east to the water tower on North Forty-first. He had no concept of the vastness of what was happening to the south, and he had no idea whatever that the ice-cream truck standing not ten feet away from him carried two and a half million dollars, more or less, in its ice box.

He was just a lousy patrolman who had come on duty at 3:45 P.M. and who would go off duty at 11:45 P.M., and he wasn't anticipating trouble here at the ferry slip connecting Isola to the sleepy section called Majesta. He stood with his hands on his hips for a moment longer, studying the sky. Then he casually strolled toward the ice-cream truck.

"Relax," the deaf man said.

"He's coming over!"

"Relax!"

"Hi," the patrolman said.

"Hello," the deaf man answered pleasantly.

"I'd like an ice-cream pop," the patrolman said.

THEY HAD MANAGED to control the fire at the stadium, and Lieutenant Byrnes, with the help of three traffic commands, had got the traffic unsnarled and then supervised the loading of the ambulances with the badly burned and trampled victims of the deaf man's plot. Byrnes had tried, meanwhile, to keep pace with what was happening in his precinct. The reports had filtered in slowly at first, and then had come with increasing suddenness. An incendiary bomb in a paint shop, the fire and explosion touching off a row of apartment houses. A bomb left in a bus on Culver Avenue, the bomb exploding while the bus was at an intersection, bottling traffic in both directions for miles. Scare calls, panic calls, *real* calls, and in the midst of all the confusion a goddam gang rumble in the housing project on South Tenth, just what he needed; let the little bastards kill themselves.

Now, covered with sweat and grime, threading his way through the fire hoses snaked across the street, hearing the clang of ambulance gongs and the moan of sirens, seeing the red glow in the sky over the River Dix, he crossed the street and headed for a telephone because there was one call he *had* to make, one thing he *had* to know.

Hernandez followed him silently and stood outside the phone booth while Byrnes dialed.

"Rhodes Clinic," the starched voice said.

"This is Lieutenant Byrnes. How's Carella?"

"Carella, sir?"

"Detective Carella. The policeman who was admitted with the shotgun wou—"

"Oh, yes sir. I'm sorry, sir. There's been so much confusion here. People being admitted—the fires, you know. Just a moment, sir."

Byrnes waited.

"Sir?" the woman said.

"Yes?"

"He seems to have come through the crisis. His temperature's gone down radically, and he's resting quietly. Sir, I'm sorry, the switchboard is—"

"Go ahead, take your calls," Byrnes said, and he hung up.

"How is he?" Hernandez asked.

"He'll be all right," Byrnes said. He nodded. "He'll be all right."

"I could feel the shadow," Hernandez said suddenly, but he did not explain his words.

* * *

"**ONE OF THEM SPECIALS** you got advertised on the side of the truck," the patrolman said. "With the chopped walnuts."

"We're all out of the walnut crunch," the deaf man said quickly. He was not frightened, only annoyed. He could see the ferry boat approaching the slip, could see the captain on the bridge leaning out over the windshield, peering into the rain as he maneuvered the boat.

"No walnut?" the patrolman said. "That's too bad. I had my face fixed for one."

"Yes, that's too bad," the deaf man said. The ferry nudged the dock pilings and moved in tight, wedging toward the dock. A deck hand leaped ashore and turned on the mechanism to lower the dock to meet the boat's deck.

"Okay, let me have a plain chocolate pop," the patrolman said.

"We're all out of those, too," the deaf man said.

"Well, what have you got?"

"We're empty. We were heading back for the plant."

"In Majesta?"

"Yes," the deaf man said.

"Oh." The patrolman shook his head again. "Well, okay," he said, and he started away from the truck. They were raising the gates on the ferry now, and the cars were beginning to unload. As the patrolman passed the rear of the truck, he glanced at the license plate and noticed that the plate read IS 6341, and he knew that "IS" plates were issued to drivers in Isola and that all Majesta plates began with the letters MA. And he wondered what the probability—the word "probability" never once entered his head because he was not a mathematician or a statistician or a logician, he was only a lousy patrolman—he wondered what the probability was of a company with its plant on Majesta having a truck bearing plates which were issued in Isola, and he continued walking because he figured *What the hell, it's possible.*

And then he thought of a second probability, and he wondered when he had ever seen an ice-cream truck carrying *two* men in uniform. And he thought, *Well, that's possible, they're both going back to the plant, maybe one is giving the other a lift.* In which case, where had the second guy left *his* truck?

And, knowing nothing at all about the theory of probability, he knew only that it looked wrong, it felt wrong, and so he began thinking about ice-cream trucks in general, and he seemed to recall a teletype he'd read back at the precinct before coming on duty this afternoon, something about an ice-cream truck having been—

He turned and walked back to the cab of the truck. Rafe had just started the engine again and was ready to drive the truck onto the ferry.

"Hey," the patrolman said.

A hurried glance passed between Rafe and the deaf man.

"Mind showing me the registration for this vehicle, Mac?" the patrolman said.

"It's in the glove compartment," the deaf man said

calmly. There was two and a half million dollars in the ice box of the truck, and he was not going to panic now. He could see fear all over Rafe's face. One of them had to be calm. He thumbed open the glove compartment and began riffling through the junk there. The patrolman waited, his hand hovering near the holstered .38 at his side.

"Now where the devil is it?" the deaf man asked. "What's the trouble anyway, officer? We're trying to catch that ferry."

"Yeah, well the ferry can wait, Mac," the patrolman said. He turned to Rafe. "Let me see your license."

Rafe hesitated, and the deaf man knew exactly what Rafe was thinking—he was thinking his normal operator's license was not valid for the driving of a commercial vehicle, he was thinking that and knowing that if he showed the patrolman his operator's license, the patrolman would ask further questions. And yet, there was no sense in *not* producing the license. If Rafe balked at this point, that holstered .38 would be in the policeman's hand in an instant. There was nothing to do but play the percentages and hope they could talk their way out of this before the ferry pulled out because the next ferry was not until 8:45, and they sure as hell couldn't sit around here until then, there was nothing to do but bluff the hand; the stakes were certainly high enough.

"Show him your license, Rafe," the deaf man said.

Rafe hesitated.

"Show it to him."

Nervously, Rafe reached into his back pocket for

his wallet. The deaf man glanced toward the ferry. Two sedans had boarded the boat and a few passengers had ambled aboard after them. On the bridge, the captain looked at his watch, and then reached up for the pull cord. The bellow of the foghorn split the evening air. First warning.

"Hurry up!" the deaf man said.

Rafe handed the patrolman his license. The patrolman ran his flashlight over it.

"This is an operator's license," he said. "You're driving a *truck*, Mac."

"Officer, we're trying to catch that ferry," the deaf man said.

"Yeah, well ain't that too bad?" the patrolman said, reverting to type, becoming an authoritative son of a bitch because he had them dead to rights and now he was going to play Mr. District Attorney. "Maybe I ought to take a look in your ice box, huh? How come you ain't got no ice cre—"

And the deaf man said, "Move her, Rafe!"

Rafe stepped on the gas pedal, and the foghorn erupted from the bridge of the boat at the same moment, and the deaf man saw the gates go down on the ferry, and suddenly the boat was moving away from the dock, and the patrolman shouted "Hey!" behind them, and then a shot echoed on the rain-streaked air, and the deaf man knew that the percentages had run out, and suddenly the patrolman fired again and Rafe screamed sharply and fell forward over the wheel and the truck swerved wildly out of control as the deaf man leaped from the cab.

His mind was churning with probabilities. Jump for the ferry? No, because I'm unarmed and the captain will take me into custody. Run for the street? No, because the patrolman will gun me down before I'm halfway across the dock, all that money, all that sweet money, predicted error, I *did* predict the error, dammit, I did take into account that fact that some policemen would undoubtedly be somewhere on our escape route, but an ice-cream pop, God, an ice-cream pop! the river is the only way, and he ran for the fence.

"Halt!" the patrolman shouted. "Halt, or I'll fire!"

The deaf man kept running. How long can I hold my breath under water? he wondered. How far can I swim?

The patrolman fired over his head, and then he aimed at the deaf man's legs as the deaf man scrambled over the cyclone fence separating the dock from the water.

He stood poised on the top of the fence for just a moment, as if undecided, as if uncertain that the percentages were truly with him, and then suddenly he leaped into the air and away from the fence and the dock, just as the patrolman triggered off another shot. He hung silhouetted against the gray sky, and then dropped like a stone to the water below. The patrolman rushed to the fence.

Five shots, the deaf man thought. He'll have to reload. Quickly, he surfaced, took a deep, lung-filling breath, and then ducked below the surface again.

All that money, he thought. *Well—next time.*

The patrolman's hammer clicked on an empty chamber. He reloaded rapidly and then fired another burst at the water.

The deaf man did not resurface.

There was only a widening circle of ripples to show that he had existed at all.

17.

IT WAS SURPRISING how co-operative a thief can become when he has a bullet wound in his shoulder and he knows the jig is up. Even before they carted Rafe off to the hospital, he had given them the names of his confederates waiting in the rented house. The Majesta cops picked up Chuck and Pop in five minutes flat.

It is surprising, too, how consistent thieves are. It was one thing to be facing a rap for a bank holdup. It was quite another to be facing charges like wholesale murder, arson, riot and—man, this was the clincher—possible treason. A bright boy in the D.A.'s office looked up the Penal Law and said that these birds had committed treason against the state by virtue of having levied *war* against the people of the state. Now that was a terrifying charge, even if it didn't carry a death penalty. War against the people of the state? *War?* My God!

The three thieves named Rafe, Chuck and Pop were somehow up to their necks in something more than they had bargained for. They didn't mind spending the rest of their lives in Castleview Prison upstate, but there was a certain electrically wired chair up there in which they had no particular desire to sit. And so, in concert, they recognized that a ready-made scapegoat was at hand. Or, if not quite at hand, at least somewhere below the surface of the River Harb.

And, in concert, they consistently repeated that the man in the river was responsible for all the mayhem and all the death, that he and he alone had shot John Smith and set all those bombs, that *he* had waged the war, and that their part in this little caper was confined to the robbery of the bank, did they look like the kind of men who valued human life so cheaply? Did they look like fellows who would derail trains and set fires in baseball stadiums just for a little money? No, no, the fellow in the river was responsible for all that.

And the fellow's name?

Consistently, and in concert, they identified him solely as "the deaf man." More than that, they could not, or would not say.

Their consistency was admirable, to be sure.

And, admirably, they were booked and arraigned on *each* of the charges for acting in concert, and it was the opinion of the police and the District Attorney's office that all three of them had a very good chance of frying, or at the very least, spending the rest of their natural lives behind bars at Castleview Prison upstate. The probabilities were good either way, the police felt.

On May 21, Dave Raskin came up to the squadroom. He walked directly to Meyer Meyer's desk and said, "So what do you think, Meyer?"

"I don't know," Meyer said. "What should I think?"

"I'm moving out of that loft."

"What?"

"Sure. Who needs that cockamamie loft? I tell you the truth, without the bank downstairs, I got nobody to look at out the window. Before, it was a busy place. Now, nothing."

"Well," Meyer said, and he shrugged.

"How's the cop who got shot?"

"He'll be out of the hospital in a few weeks," Meyer said.

"Good, good. I'm glad to hear that. Listen, if your wife needs some nice dresses, stop around, okay? I'll pick out some pretty ones for her, compliments of Dave Raskin."

"Thank you," Meyer said.

Raskin went back to the loft on Culver Avenue where Margarita was packing their stock preparatory to the move, flinging her unbound breasts about with renewed fervor. Raskin watched her for a few moments, pleased with what he saw. The telephone rang suddenly. Still watching Margarita's energetic acrobatics, Raskin picked up the receiver.

"Hello?" he said.

"Raskin?" the voice asked.

"Yes? Who's this?"

"Get out of that loft," the voice said. "Get out of that loft, you son of a bitch, or I'll kill you!"

"You!" Raskin said. "You again!"

And suddenly he heard chuckling on the other end of the wire.

"Who's this?" he asked.

"Meyer Meyer," the voice said, chuckling.

"You dirty bastard," Raskin said, and then he began laughing, too. "Oh, you had me going there for a minute. For a minute, I thought my heckler was back." Raskin laughed uproariously. "I got to hand it to you. You're a great comedian. Since your father died, there hasn't been such a comedian. You're just like your father! Just like him!"

Meyer Meyer, at the other end of the wire, listened, exchanged the amenities, and then hung up.

Just like my father, he thought.

Suddenly, he felt a little ill.

"What's the matter?" Miscolo said, coming in from the Clerical Office.

"I don't feel so hot," Meyer said.

"You're just upset because a patrolman cracked a case you couldn't."

"Maybe so," Meyer answered.

"Cheer up," Miscolo said. "You want some coffee?"

"Just like my father," Meyer said sadly.

"Huh?"

"Nothing. But a guy works all his life trying to . . ." Meyer shook his head. "Just like my father."

"You want the coffee or not?"

"Yeah. Yeah, I'll have the coffee. Stop heckling me!"

"Who's heckling?" Miscolo said, and he went out for the coffee.

From his desk across the squadroom, Bert Kling said, "It'll be summer soon."

"So?"

"So there'll be more kids in the streets, and more gang wars, and more petty crimes, and shorter tempers and—"

"Don't be so pessimistic," Meyer said.

"Who's pessimistic? It sounds like it'll be a lovely summer. Just lovely."

"I can hardly wait," Meyer answered.

He pulled a typewritten list closer to the phone, and then dialed the first of a group of eyewitnesses to a burglary.

Outside the squadroom, May seemed impatient for the suffocating heat of July and August.

This is the twelfth published novel of the 87th Precinct. If I may, I would like to offer my sincere gratitude at this time to Herbert Alexander, who has worked with me on this series from the time it was conceived, and whose editorial suggestions have never failed to stimulate my imagination and enlarge my original concept. Thank you, Herb.

E.McB.

AFTERWORD

WAY BACK WHEN—early in 1959, it must have been—I was still married to a woman whose maiden name was Anita Melnick. Her father's name was Harry Melnick, to whom this book is dedicated. He's dead now, but he got a big kick out of the book when it was first published. I hope my former wife enjoys it as much now. Memories don't come cheap, you know.

Harry used to own a women's dress shop on West 14th Street in New York City. All at once, most of the things that happen to Dave Raskin in these pages started happening to my father-in-law. Eventually, all the pranks stopped. Harry never found out who had targeted him for all the practical jokes. Nor was there a bank under his loft. But he had provided me with an idea—and the springboard for a new character.

Before I wrote *The Heckler*, eleven 87th Precinct novels had already been published. We were trying to establish a new series, you see. A rule of thumb for any new mystery series is that if you haven't hit the bestseller list after five tries, go hang up your sweatpants, Gertie.

I wrote the first three books of the series in 1956, and the next two in 1957. By my count, that came to five books—and still no bestseller. Maybe because they were still being published as paperback originals. I don't think there even *was* a paperback bestseller list back then. Progress, lads, progress!

The first book published in 1958 was also a paperback original. But with *Killer's Wedge* that same year, Simon and Schuster brought out the first of the books in hardcover. It startled the entire civilized world! I jest, Maude. It would take a long, long time before one of the Eight-Sevens hit the *New York Times* bestseller list. So much for rules of thumb about mystery series. And, besides, who's counting?

Anyway, there were eleven published books by the end of 1959, when I must have delivered *The Heckler* because it was first published in hardcover sometime in 1960; I'm not now sure of the month. But I can remember an evening long before then—in 1955, to be exact, while I was still writing *Cop Hater*, the first book in the series. I was riding in a car with a friend of mine on our way to meeting his wife and my then-wife (yes, Harry Melnick's daughter, Anita), whom we were taking to dinner. I was inordinately silent, and suddenly I snapped my fingers and shouted, "A deaf mute!" which was the equivalent back then of the word *Eureka!*

I had been pondering what kind of girlfriend would be right for Steve Carella, you see. Carella was merely one of the cops in the first book. I chose a deaf mute (I know, I know, the politically correct expression these days is "speech and hearing impaired," but Teddy Carella knows where she's coming from, and so do I) because I felt I could place her in desperate situations from which she had to be rescued by her stalwart police detective husband. I soon tired of these "Mr. and Mrs. North" shenanigans, however. Teddy was too strong a character to need rescuing all the time.

By the time I started concocting the villain of *The Heckler*, I knew that the person Steve Carella loved most in the entire universe was his wife, Teddy Carella, who was deaf and could not speak, but whom neither he nor she herself considered "handicapped." It occurred to me: Hey! What if the guy who's bugging Dave Raskin is *also* deaf? I had no idea at the time that the "deaf man" would become a recurring character—he's now been in five books—or that he would grow to become Steve Carella's nemesis, in much the same way that Moriarty was Sherlock Holmes's. I don't believe in the concept of good and evil. Evil is a theological term. But I knew that Teddy Carella was deaf and really *good*, and I figured if I could make this guy deaf and really *bad*, I would have a very nice contrast.

I think it's interesting, by the way, that most people don't waste too much sympathy on deaf persons. They'll risk their lives to help a blind man cross the street in heavy traffic, but the best a deaf person can hope to evoke is impatience. I hope the deaf man in these pages inspires a bit more than that. Fear perhaps? Perhaps even awe. It ain't easy being a villain.

It ain't easy writing about one, either.

There would be more than five deaf man novels were it not for the fact that's he's brilliant, and I'm not. He must forever come up with these extraordinary schemes, you see, which are foiled not by the Keystone Kops of the Eight-Seven, but instead by accident. That's hard to do. I like to think there'll be another deaf man novel down the pike. He still owes something to a woman named Gloria, I believe, who shot him and left him tied to a bed in *Mischief*. Oh dear, one mustn't do such things to someone like the deaf man, must one?

But we shall see.

Meanwhile . . .

Harry . . . thanks again.

Without you, this book wouldn't have happened.

Ed McBain
Weston, CT
June 2002

SIMON & SCHUSTER
PROUDLY PRESENTS

FAT OLLIE'S BOOK

ED McBAIN

Available in hardcover
from
Simon & Schuster

Turn the page for a preview of
Fat Ollie's Book. . . .

1

RESPONSE TIME—from the moment someone at the Martin Luther King Memorial Hall dialed 911 to the moment Car 81, in the Eight-Eight's Boy sector rolled up— was exactly four minutes and twenty-six seconds. Whoever had fired the shots was long gone by then, but a witness outside the Hall had seen someone running from the alleyway on its eastern end and he was eager to tell the police and especially the arriving TV crew all about it.

The witness was very drunk.

In this neighborhood, when you heard shots, you ran. In this neighborhood, if you saw someone running, you knew he wasn't running to catch a bus. This guy wasn't running. Instead, he was struggling to keep his balance, wobbling from one foot to the other. Nine, ten in the morning, whatever the hell it was already, and he could hardly stand up and he stunk like a distillery. He finally sat on one of the garbage cans in the alley. Behind him, rain water from a gutter dripped into a leader and flowed into an open sewer grate.

Slurring his words, the drunk immediately told the responding officers from Car 81 that he was a Vietnam vet, mistakenly believing this would guarantee him a measure of respect. The blues saw only a scabby old black drunk wearing tattered fatigue trousers, an olive-drab tank top, and scuffed black penny loafers without socks. He was having trouble not falling off the garbage can, too. Grabbing for the wall, he told them he'd been about to go into the alley here, yessir, when he saw this guy come bustin out of it . . .

"Turned left on St. Sab's," he said, "went runnin off uptown."

"Why were you going in the alley?" one of the blues asked.

"To look inna garbage cans there."

"For what?"

"Bottles," he said. "Takes 'em back for deposit, yessir."

"And you say you saw somebody running out of the alley here?" the other blue asked. He was wondering why they were wasting time with this old drunk. They'd responded in swift order, but if they wasted any more time with him, their sergeant would think they'd been laggard. Then again, the TV cameras were rolling.

"Came out the alley like a bat out of shit," the drunk said, much to the dismay of the roving reporter from Channel Four, a pretty blonde wearing a short brown mini and a tan cotton turtleneck sweater. The camera was in tight on the man's face at that moment, and the word "shit" meant they couldn't use the shot unless they bleeped it out. Her program manager didn't like to bleep out too many words because that smacked of censorship instead of fair and balanced reporting. On the other hand, the drunk was great comic relief. The Great Unwashed loved drunks. Put a drunk scene in a movie or a play, the audience still laughed themselves to death. If they only knew how many battered wives Honey had interviewed.

"What'd he look like?" the first blue asked, mindful of the TV cameras and trying to sound like an experienced investigator instead of a rookie who'd just begun patrol duty eight months ago.

"Young dude," the witness said.

"White, black, Hispanic?" the first blue asked, rapping the words out in a manner that he was sure would go over big with TV audiences, unmindful of the fact that the camera was on the witness and not himself.

"White kid," the witness said, "yessir. Wearin jeans and a whut chu call it, a ski parka, an' white sneakers an' a black cap with a big peak. Man, he was movin fast. Almost knocked me down."

"Did he have a gun?"

"I dinn see no gun."

"Gun in his hand, anything like that?"

"No gun, nosir."

"Okay, thanks," the first blue said.

"This is Honey Blair," the Channel Four reporter said, "coming to you from outside King Memorial in Diamondback." She slit her throat with the forefinger of her left hand, said, "That's it, boys," and turned to her crew chief. "Get him to sign a release, will you?" she said. "I'm heading inside." She was walking toward the glass entrance doors when the Vietnam vet, if indeed that's what he was, asked, "Is they a reward?"

Why didn't you say that on the air? Honey thought.

THIS WAS, and is, and always will be the big bad city.

That will never change, Ollie thought. Never.

And never was it badder than during the springtime. Flowers were blooming everywhere, even in the 88th Precinct, which by the way was no rose garden.

Detective/First Grade Oliver Wendell Weeks had good reason to be smiling on this bright April morning. He had just finished his book. Not finished *reading* it, mind you, but finished *writing* it. He was still rereading the last chapter, which was back at the apartment. He didn't think it would need any more work, but the last chapter was often the most important one, he had learned, and he wanted to make sure it was just right. He was now transporting the positively perfect portion of the book to a copying shop not far from the Eight-Eight.

He wondered if the sun was shining and the flowers were blooming next door in the 87th Precinct. He wondered if it was springtime in the Rockies, or in London, or in Paris or Rome, or in Istanbul, wherever that was. He wondered if flowers bloomed all over the *world* when a person finished his first work of fiction. Now that he was a bona fide writer in his own mind, Ollie could ponder such deep imponderables.

His book, which was titled *Report to the Commissioner,* was securely nestled in a dispatch case that rested on the back seat of the car Ollie drove hither and yon around this fair city, one of the perks of being a minion of the law, ah yes. The windows of the Chevy sedan were open wide to the breezes that flowed from river to river. It was 10:30 on a lovely sunlit Monday morning. Ollie had signed in at 7:50 (five minutes late, but who was counting?), had taken care of some odds-and-ends bullshit on his desk, and was now on his way to the copying shop on Culver Avenue, not four blocks from the station house. So far, the day—

"10-40, 10-40 . . ."

The dash radio.

Rapid mobilization.

"King Memorial, St. Sebastian and South Thirtieth, man with a gun. 10-40, 10-40, King Memorial . . ."

Ollie hit the hammer.

HE PARKED ILLEGALLY at the curb outside the Martin Luther King Memorial Hall, flipped down the visor on the driver's side to show the card announcing Police Department authorization, locked the car, flashed the blue-and-gold tin at a uniformed grunt who was already approaching with a scowl and an attitude, said, "Weeks, Eighty-eighth Squad," and barged right past him and the roaming television teams that were already thrusting microphones at anyone within range. He kept using his detective's shield like a real warrior's shield, holding it up to any barbarian who rose in his path, striding through the glass doors at the front of the building, and then into the marble entrance lobby, and then into the auditorium itself, where a handful of brass were already on the scene, had to be something important went down here.

"Well, well, if it isn't The Large Man," a voice said.

Once upon a time, Ollie's sister Isabelle had referred to him as "large," which he knew was a euphonium for "obese." He had not taken it kindly. In fact, he had not bought her a birthday present that year. Ollie knew that there were colleagues in this city who called him "Fat Ollie," but he took it as a measure of respect that they never called him this to his face. "Large Man" came close, though. He was ready to take serious offense when he recognized Detectives Monoghan and Monroe of the Homicide Division, already on the scene, and looking like somewhat stout penguins themselves. So someone had been aced. Big deal. Here in the Eight-Eight, it sometimes felt like someone got murdered every ten seconds. Monoghan was the one who'd called him "The Large Man." Monroe was standing beside him, grinning as if in agreement.

A pair of bookends in black—the color of death, the unofficial color of Homicide—the two jackasses were the Tweedledum and Tweedledee of law enforcement. Ollie wanted to punch them both in the mouth.

"Who got it?" he asked.

"Lester Henderson."

"You kidding me?"

"Would we kid a master detective?" Monoghan said.

"A super sleuth?" Monroe said, still grinning.

"Stick it up your ass," Ollie explained. "Anybody else from the Eight-Eight here?"

"You're the first."

"Then that puts me in charge," Ollie said.

In this city, the appearance of Homicide detectives at the scene of any murder was mandatory if not necessary. Presumably, they were here in an "advisory and supervisory capacity," which meant they only got in the way of the precinct detectives who caught the squeal. Since Ollie was the so-called First Man Up, the case was his. All he had to do was file his reports in triplicate with Homicide, and then go his merry way. He did not think he needed to remind the M&Ms that this was a fact of police life in this fair metropolis, ah yes. They knew full well that except on television, the glory days of Homicide were long gone.

The dead man lay on his back in a disorganized heap alongside a podium draped with red, white, and blue bunting. A sign above the podium read LESTER MEANS LAW. Ollie didn't know what that meant. The dead man was wearing blue jeans, brown loafers without socks, and a pink crewneck cotton sweater. The front of the sweater was blotted with blood.

"So what happened?" Ollie asked.

"He got shot from the wings," Monroe said. "They were setting up for the big rally tonight . . ."

"*Who* was setting up?"

"His people."

"All these people here?"

"All these people."

"Too *many* people," Ollie said.

"Is right."

"*What* rally?"

"Big fund raiser. Putting up lights, American flags, cameras, bunting, the whole shmear."

"So?"

"So somebody fired half a dozen shots from the wings there."

"Is that an accurate count, or are you guessing?"

"That's what his aide told us. Five, six shots, something like that."

"His aide? Who's that?"

"Guy with all those reporters over there."

"Who let *them* in?"

"They were already here when we responded," Monroe said.

"Terrific security," Ollie said. "What's the aide's name?"

"Alan Pierce."

The corpse lay in angular disarray, surrounded now by the Mobile Lab techs and the Medical Examiner, who was kneeling beside the dead man and delicately lifting his pink cotton sweater. Not fifteen feet from this concerned knot of professionals, a man wearing blue jeans similar to the dead man's, and a blue denim shirt, and black loafers with blue socks stood at the center of a moving mass of reporters wielding pencils and pads, microphones, and flash cameras. A tall, slender man, who looked as if he jogged and swam and lifted weights and watched his calories—all the things Ollie considered a waste of time—Pierce appeared pale and stunned but nonetheless in control of the situation. Like a bunch of third graders waving their hands for a bathroom pass, the reporters swarmed around him.

"Yes, Honey?" Pierce said, and a cute little blonde with a short skirt showing plenty of leg and thigh thrust a microphone in Pierce's face. Ollie recognized her as Honey Blair, the roving reporter for the Eleven O'Clock News.

"Can you tell us if it's true that Mr. Henderson had definitely decided to run for the Mayor's office?" she asked.

"I did not have a chance to discuss that with him before . . . before this happened," Pierce said. "I can say that he met with Governor Carson's people this weekend, and that was the main reason we flew upstate."

"We've heard rumors that you yourself have your eye on City Hall," Honey said. "Is that so?"

"This is the first I'm hearing of it," Pierce said.

Me, too, Ollie thought. But that's very interesting, Mr. Pierce.

Honey would not let it go.

"Well, *had* you planned on running for Deputy Mayor? Assuming Mr. Henderson ran for Mayor?"

"He and I never discussed that. Yes, David?"

A man Ollie had seen a few times here and there around City Hall shoved a microphone at Pierce.

"Sir," he said, "can you tell us where you were when Mr. Henderson . . . ?"

"That's it, thank you very much," Ollie said, and strolled into the crowd. Flashing his shield like a proud father exhibiting a photograph of his firstborn, he said, "This is all under control here, let's go home, okay?" and then signaled to one of the blues to get this mob out of here. Grumbling, the reporters allowed themselves to be herded offstage. Ollie stepped into Honey's path just as she was turning to go, and said, "Hey, what's your hurry? No hello?"

She looked at him, puzzled.

"Oliver Weeks," he said. "The Eighty-eighth Precinct. Remember the zoo? The lady getting eaten by lions? Christmastime?"

"Oh yes," Honey said without the slightest interest, and turned again to go.

"Stick around," Ollie said. "We'll have coffee later."

"Thanks, I have a deadline," she said, and followed her tits offstage.

Ollie showed Pierce his shield. "Detective Weeks," he said, "Eighty-eighth Squad. Sorry to interrupt the conference, sir, but I'd rather you told *us* what you saw and heard."

"Yes, of course," Pierce said.

"You were here when Mr. Henderson got shot, is that it?"

"I was standing right alongside him."

"Did you see the shooter?"

"No, I did not."

"You told the other detectives the shots came from the wings."

"That's what it seemed like, yes."

"Oh? Have you changed your mind about that?"

"No, no. I still think they came from the wings."

"But you didn't see the shooter."

"No, I did not."

"Guy fired five, six shots, you didn't see him."

"No."

"How come?"

"I ducked when I heard the first shot."

"I woulda done the same thing," Ollie said understandingly. "How about the second shot?"

"Lester was falling. I tried to catch him. I wasn't looking into the wings."

"And all the other shots?"

"I was kneeling over Lester. I heard someone running off, but I didn't see anything. There was a lot of confusion, you know."

"*Were* you planning to run for Deputy Mayor?"

"I wasn't asked to do so. I was only Lester's aide."

"What does that mean, anyway?" Ollie asked. "Being an aide?"

"Like his right hand man," Pierce said.

"Sort of like a secretary?"

"More like an assistant."

"So you don't have any political aspirations, is that correct?"

"I didn't say that."

"Then you do?"

"I wouldn't be in politics if I didn't have political aspirations."

"Excuse me, Alan," a voice said.

Ollie turned to see a slight and narrow, precise little man wearing a blue blazer, a red tie, a white shirt, gray slacks, gray socks, and black loafers. Ever since the terrorist bombing at Clarendon Hall, everybody in this city dressed like an American flag. Ollie figured half of them were faking it.

"We're having a conversation here," he said.

"I'm sorry, sir, but I wanted to ask . . ."

"You know this man?" Ollie asked Pierce.

"Yes, he's our press rep. Josh Coogan."

"Excuse me, Alan," Coogan said, "but I was wondering if I should get back to headquarters. I know there'll be hundreds of calls . . ."

"No, this is a crime scene," Ollie said. "Stick around."

Coogan looked flustered for a moment. He was maybe twenty-four, twenty-five years old, but he suddenly looked like a high school kid who hadn't done his assignment and had got called on while he was trying to catch a nap. Ollie didn't have much sympathy for politicians, but all at once this seemed very sad here, two guys who all at once didn't know what to do with themselves. He almost felt like taking them out for a beer. Instead, he said, "Were you here in the hall when all this happened, Mr. Coogan?"

"Yes, I was."

"Where in the hall?"

"In the balcony."

"What were you doing up there?"

"Listening to sound checks."

"While you were listening to these sound checks, did you happen to hear the sound of a gun going off?"

"Yes."

"In the balcony?"

"No."

"Then where?"

"From somewhere down below."

"Where down below?"

"The stage."

"Which side of the stage?"

"I couldn't tell."

"Right or left?"

"I really couldn't tell."

"Was anyone with you up there in the balcony?"

"No, I was alone."

"Incidentally, Mr. Pierce," Ollie said, turning to him, "did I hear you tell those reporters you went upstate with Mr. Henderson?"

"Yes, I did."

"Where upstate?"

"The capital."

"When?"

"We flew up together on Saturday morning. I'm his aide. I *was* his aide," he said, correcting himself.

"Did you fly back together, too?"

"No. I left on Sunday morning. Caught a seven A.M. plane."

"So he spent all day Sunday up there alone, is that it?"

"Yes," Pierce said. "Alone."

"You the detective in charge here?" the ME asked.

"I am," Ollie said.

"Your cause of death is gunshot wounds to the chest."

Big revelation, Ollie thought.

"You can move him out whenever you like. We may find some surprises at the morgue, but I doubt it. Good luck."

Monoghan was walking over with a man wearing a red bandana tied across his forehead, high-topped workman's shoes, and bib overalls showing naked muscular arms, the left one tattooed on the bicep with the words SEMPER FIDELIS.

"Weeks, this is Charles Mastroiani, man in charge of decorating the hall here, you might want to talk to him."

"No relation to Marcello," Mastroiani promptly told Ollie, which was a total waste since Ollie didn't know who the hell he was talking about. "My company's called Festive, Inc.," he said, exuding a sense of professional pride and enthusiasm that was all too rare in today's workplace. "We're listed in the city's yellow pages under 'Decoration Contractors.' What we do is we supply everything you need for a special occasion. I'm not talking about a wedding or a bar-mitzvah, those we leave to the caterers. Festive operates on a much larger scale. Dressing the stage here at King Memorial is a good example. We supplied the bunting, the balloons, the banners, the audio equipment, the lighting, everything. We would've supplied a band, too, if it was called for, but this wasn't that kind of affair. As it was, we dressed the hall and wired it, made it user-friendly and user-ready. All the councilman had to do was step up to the podium and speak."

All the councilman had to do, Ollie thought, was step up to the podium and get shot.

"Will you get paid, anyway?" he asked.

"What?" Mastroiani said.

"For the gig. Him getting killed and all."

"Oh sure. Well, I suppose so."

"Who contracted for the job?"

"The Committee."

"What committee?"

"The Committee for Henderson."

"It says that on the contract?"

"That's what it says."

"Who signed the contract?"

"I have no idea. It came in the mail."

"You still got it?"

"I can find it for you."

"Good. I'd like to see who hired you."

"Sure."

"All these people who were onstage with you when he got killed," Ollie said. "Were they regulars?"

"What do you mean, regulars?"

"Have you worked with them before?"

"Oh sure. All the time."

"All of them reliable?"

"Oh sure."

"None of them strangers to you, is that right? What I'm driving at, would any of these guys have come in here with a concealed . . ."

"No, no."

". . . weapon and popped Henderson, is what I'm asking."

"None of them. I can vouch for each and every one of them."

"Cause what I'll have to do, anyway, I'm gonna have to send some of my colleagues from up the Eight-Eight around to talk to them individually, just in case one of them got a bug up his ass to shoot the councilman."

"I don't think you need to worry about that."

"Yeah, well, I worry about such things. Which is why I'll need a list of all your people here on the job."

"Sure. But they're all bonded, so I'm sure you won't find anything out of the way."

"Why are they bonded?"

"Well, we sometimes do these very big affairs where there's jewelry and such laying around . . ."

"Uh-huh."

"Precious antiques, things like that, on these big estates, you know . . ."

"You're saying these men are honest individuals, is what you're saying."

"That's right."

"Wouldn't harm a fly, is what you're saying."

"Is basically what I'm saying."

"We'll have to talk to them anyway," Ollie said. "So what *I'm* saying, after you give me all their names, you might advise them not to leave the city for the next couple of days, till my people have a chance to talk to them."

"I'll be happy to do that."

"Good. So tell me, Mr. Master-yonny . . ."

"It's Mastroiani."

"Ain't that what I said?"

"No, you said . . . I don't know what you said, but it wasn't Mastroiani."

"You know, have you ever thought of changing your name?"

"No."

"To something simpler?"

"No. Like what?"

"Like Weeks, for example. Short and sweet and easy to say. And people would think you're related to an American police detective."

"I don't think I'd like to do that."

"Entirely up to you, my friend, ah yes," Ollie said.

"And I *am* American," Mastroiani said.

"Of course you are," Ollie said. "But tell me, Charles, may I call you Charles?"

"Most people call me Chuck."

"Even though most Chucks are fags?"

"I'm not."

"You're not Chuck?"

"I'm not a fag."

"Then should I call you Charles?"

"Actually, I'd prefer being called Mr. Mastroiani."

"Sure, but that don't sound American, does it? Tell me, Chuck, where were you exactly when the councilman got shot?"

"I was standing near the podium there."

"And?"

"I heard shots. And he was falling."

"Heard shots from the wings there?"

"No. From the balcony."

"Tell me what happened, Chuck. In your own words."

"Who else's words would I use?" Mastroiani asked.

"That's very funny, Chuck," Ollie said, and grinned like a dragon. "Tell me."

The way Mastroiani tells it, the councilman is this energetic little guy who gets to the Hall at about a quarter to nine, dressed for work in jeans and a crewneck cotton sweater, loafers, real casual, you know? He's all over the place, conferring with his aide and this kid he has with him looks like a college boy, giving directions to Mastroiani and his crew, arms waving all over the place like a windmill, running here, running there, going out front to check how the stage looks every time a new balloon goes up, sending the college kid up to the balcony to hear how the sound is, then going up there himself to listen while his aide talks into the mike, then coming down again and making sure the podium is draped right and the sign is just where he wants it, and checking the sound again, waving up to the kid in the balcony who gives him a thumbs-up signal, and then starting to check the lights, wanting to know where the spot would pick him up after he was introduced . . .

"That's what he was doing when he got shot. He was crossing the stage to the podium, making sure the spot was following him."

"Where were you?"

"At the podium, I told you. Looking up at the guy in the booth, waiting for the councilman to . . ."

"What guy in the booth?"

"The guy on the follow spot."

"One of your people?"

"No."

"Then who?"

"I have no idea. My guess is he works here at the Hall."

"Who would know?"

"You got me."

"I thought you supplied everything. The sound, the lighting . . ."

"The *onstage* lighting. Usually, when we do an auditorium like this one, they have their own lighting facilities and their own lighting technician or engineer, they're sometimes called, a lighting engineer."

"Did you talk to this guy in the booth? This technician or engineer or whatever he was?"

"No, I did not."

"Who talked to him?"

"Mr. Pierce was yelling up to him—Henderson's aide—and so was the councilman himself. I think the college kid was giving him instructions, too. From up in the balcony."

"Was the kid up there when the shooting started?"

"I think so."

"Well, didn't you look up there? You told me that's where the shots came from, didn't you look up there to see who was shooting?"

"Yes, but I was blinded by the spot. The spot had followed the councilman to the podium, and that was when he got shot, just as he reached the podium."

"So the guy working the spot was still up there, is that right?"

"He would've had to be up there, yes, sir."

"So let's find out who he was," Ollie said.

A uniformed inspector with braid all over him was walking over. Ollie deemed it necessary to perhaps introduce himself.

"Detective Weeks, sir," he said. "The Eight-Eight. First man up."

"Like hell you are," the inspector said, and walked off.

Visit the
Simon & Schuster Web site:
www.SimonSays.com

and sign up for our
mystery e-mail updates!

Keep up on the latest
new releases, author appearances,
news, chats, special offers, and more!
We'll deliver the information
right to your inbox — if it's new,
you'll know about it.

SIMON & SCHUSTER
A VIACOM COMPANY
www.SimonSays.com

POCKET BOOKS   POCKET STAR BOOKS

2350-01